Girl Arrested

Alexis V

ISBN- 13 978-1512207712

Dedication

To Velma (Elaine) McLean
For grace and courage through challenges.

Acknowledgements

I would like to thank my husband Peter for standing beside me always and in particular while I was writing this book. He has been my inspiration and motivation, the archetype of understanding. I wish to also recognize the work he has done on the cover illustration. He is my pillar of support.

Special thanks also go to Velma (Elaine) McLean, a true friend and great person who encouraged me to write the book. Despite battling her own personal challenge of breast cancer she was always positive and encouraging.

I owe thanks to another personal friend and former colleague, Aliea Kamara for the support given.

Thanks also to my mother-in-law, Phyllis Vincent for her encouragement.

Gratitude is also extended to the publisher who reviewed my work.

Last but in no way least, I wish to thank God for guiding and strengthening me in this writing venture.

About the Author

Alexis V

Inspired by the often exciting highly imaginative conversations, sharp witted and entertaining anecdotes of the teenage students whom she educated during a long and successful professional teaching career which included varying educational leadership posts, Alexis V turned her penmanship from marking assignments to a more electrifying pursuit, fiction writing. Alexis V writes from her study while overlooking a beautiful green tree-lined field which supports her creative thought. She lives in Suffolk, UK, is married and has two adult daughters. She enjoys cooking, reading and riding a tandem bicycle with her husband who obviously sits at the front.

Chapter One

When Charlie was sober he was the self-appointed keeper of the marina. His boat was moored more than it sailed. He went to sleep drunk early at night fall and awoke in the early hours of the morning partially sober. It was the same daily routine for the retired sea captain. As he snaked his way along in the early dawn light his eyes squinted in surveillance mode. His powdered white long hair danced about in the light wind as his crooked back stooped to his knees. His eyes and bony legs stopped at a dark trail of stains on the ground. He bent down lower and could see that the stains looked like blood. Muttering to himself with annoyance he started to follow the trail. It ended by a familiar yacht. He knew its owner.

"Hello there! Durr are you in there? Looks like something died out here, Durr? Durr?" As Charlie called out he kept walking further onto the deck. He peeped down below then quickly staggered back by the sight which caught his eyes. Charlie ran back to his boat. He picked up the phone, and frantically dialed 104 Panama City's emergency number.

"Policía! Policía!" He shouted. Charlie was bilingual and at times of agitation or fear he used both Spanish and English.

"La gente está herido y sangrando!" Charlie continued. He then repeated his plea in English. "People are hurt and bleeding!" He continued in Spanish, "Envíen una ambulancia rápidamente!" Charlie was beside himself with urgency and repeated his requests again. "Send an ambulance quickly!" He screamed.

He was urged to calm down by the emergency operator. Charlie then slowly gave the address of the incident.

"Señor, por favor quédate en tu propio barco y no volver a la escena del incidente. La policía una ambulancia está en camino." The operator replied in Spanish alone. Charlie knew that this meant, "Sir please stay on your own boat and do not return to the scene of the incident. The police and ambulance are on their way." Charlie nervously paced around and peeped outside of his boat. All he could see in his mind's eye was an awful amount of blood. Durr was lying in a pool of it. A young girl was staggering over him with a metal pole in her hand. It looked like Durr's daughter, he'd seen her before. In fact he knew the entire family.

Did they have an argument and she killed him? Charlie's brain was racing with thoughts of what could have happened. He hoped that somehow Durr was still alive but there was a tremendous amount of blood. Too much blood!

Meanwhile back on the yacht, Erica continued to stumble to her feet. She felt groggy and dazed. She was soaked. Her clothes were dripping wet. She looked at her shirt. It was red. In her hand she held a piece of metal. She finally got her footing and leaned onto the cabin post. Her head was pounding. It hurt so badly that it felt too heavy to hold upright. Still clenching the metal pole she could see that it was covered with blood!

She looked around her. The walls were blood splattered. She looked down and saw her father crunched up, lying in a pool of blood. There were gashes all over his head.

"Someone help! Help! Please help me!" Erica screamed. Still holding the piece of metal she started to wobble further on to the upper deck. She could hear sirens getting closer and closer. At last when she finally managed to stumble onto the upper deck she collapsed into the hands of a police officer.

"Help me! Help me!" Her feeble cries poured out of her shaking body. She felt cold and numb. Her head vibrated.

"What's happened here?" One police officer questioned. "Sit. The ambulance is on its way." These were firm and authoritative words.

"Where am I? What's happening?" The two police officers watched her. Then one said, "You tell me. What has happened here?" One officer used his radio and detectives were called to attend the scene.

Next the two officers watched Erica as they listened to the EMTs who confirmed that nothing could be done for the man down below. "The coroner is needed." The younger EMT said to the police as he walked over to Erica. "What is your name? Are you hurt?" The EMT asked and looked Erica over.

"Erica. My name is Erica Durr. My head hurts and I feel very sick. Is that my father down there?" She knew it was but wanted confirmation.

"Erica did you get struck on the head or did you fall?" The EMT asked her without answering her question. He took her temperature and looked in her eyes. Next he took her blood pressure and examined her hands which were heavily blood stained.

"I don't know what happened. I don't even know how I got here!" In bewilderment Erica stared at the EMT. "Why is my head hurting so badly?" She painfully cried.

"Is she ok to be questioned?" The taller of the two officers asked the EMT who continued his examination and observation of Erica.

"She has a concussion which could have resulted from a fall or a blow to the head." The EMT looked at his partner and continued. "To relieve her concussion symptoms I will apply an ice pack to her head to reduce the swelling." He then turned his next remarks to the on-looking officer.

"She has lacerations on both arms which are not serious but needle marks on her right inner arm. Otherwise she appears not to have any significant injuries. You can take over from here." The EMT said as he moved away from Erica.

Erica sat in absolute shock. Her mind was spinning how did she get here? What was happening?

"Officer, can you please tell me what has happened to my father? Please?" Erica looked in despair for an answer to the perplexing and frightening situation. She looked at herself again. Blood was everywhere on her! She seemed to be painted in blood! Thick and sticky blood! Why was all of this happening? The officers also stared at her, then one questioned.

"The driver's license on the deceased identifies him as Sidney Durr." Showing Erica the license the officer continued "Is this your father?" He asked, fixing his eyes on her face.

"Yes that is my father. What has happened to him? Let me go back down to see him." The word deceased just did not register in Erica's brain. Nothing was making any sense!

"Sorry miss but you cannot go back down there. Please may I have your full name and age?" The officer continued.

"It is Erica Durr. Erica is my name and I am seventeen years old." This all seemed like a very bad nightmare. It was all a bad dream she thought. She needed to wake up.

Soon Detectives Henriquez and Martinez arrived and took charge of the crime scene. They spoke to the two officers first on the scene. They asked them to take a statement from Charlie, to tell him not to leave his boat because Inspector Martinez would be coming to interview him. Next they turned to Erica.

"I am detective Bill Henriquez and this is my partner Carl Martinez. We will be conducting this investigation." Martinez and Henriquez surveyed the scene scanning their eyes all around. Their next gaze settled right into Erica's eyes.

"Can someone please tell me what has happened to my father?" This was a wrenching plea. She needed what she feared confirmed. The EMTs had left and they had not taken her father so she really knew that the worst had happened. Tears welled up in her eyes as she stared back at the two officers.

"I am very sorry to tell you but your father is dead. Sidney Durr is dead." Martinez said as he closely looked at her response. Erica was numb. She could not speak. Shocked and immobilized Erica's tears just flowed until she put her throbbing head into her hands and bitterly wept with loud howling sounds.

"Take these." A woman officer now arrived at the scene offered some tissues. Erica pushed them away. She wanted to drown herself in the tears. She wanted to literally sink away from this trouble. When Erica's loud crying subsided officer Henriquez and the woman officer Myles took her into the first cabin avoiding the body and the sea of blood. They all sat down while Martinez went over to the body and continued processing the scene. A police photographer and the coroner now arrived.

"Let's take it from the beginning. What happened here?" Henriquez directly asked.

"I don't know! I don't know." Erica shook her head and started crying once more. "I do not know how I got here. I seemed to have been asleep; when I awoke I was very wet. Blood was covering my clothes and hands. I was on the floor beside my father. That's all I remember!" Her shaky voice replied.

"The officers who arrived on the scene said that you were attempting to flee, running up from the lower deck with a metal chair leg in your hand. This metal leg is also covered with blood." Henriquez watched Erica and waited for her response. Erica looked at him, shook her head in denial and did not speak.

"Please stay here with officer Myles. You do not have to say anything. I need to briefly check with Martinez." Henriquez left the cabin and walked out to Martinez.

"Henriquez this looks like a very cruel attack one of great anger. Multiple blows delivered all to the head. The likely weapon is that metal chair leg." Martinez was surmising. "A girl's anger at her father but what's the motive? What would drive her to such a vicious attack?" He asked

"Martinez a young pretty girl and her father alone on a yacht? We have seen it before." Henriquez said and raised his eyebrows.

"We need to caution this girl. Read her, her rights. Take her in for a full examination, finger prints and drugs tests." Detective Henriquez concluded and Martinez concurred. They both returned to the cabin where the distraught Erica and officer Myles were waiting. Detective Martinez had the task of placing Erica under arrest. In a firm voice he spoke to Erica.

"I am placing you under arrest for the suspected murder of Sidney Durr. You have the right to remain silent when questioned; you have the right to an attorney…" Martinez continued his caution but Erica's brain cells had shut down they had died. She wasn't listening.

"Are you willing to answer my questions without an attorney present?" Henriquez asked her. Erica's head was whirling. Nothing that the detective had just said made any sense! It was all a blur. The only words which stood out were *'I am placing you under arrest for the murder of Sidney Durr!'*

"Wait a minute! I did not kill my father! I did not!" While Erica protested she was gently handcuffed by officer Myles and walked to the police vehicle. She was gently pushed into the police car. Myles and Henriquez transported Erica to the station while Martinez remained behind at the murder scene.

Still dazed head hurting and heart pounding, Erica Durr was under arrest for murder! Her mind a melee of thoughts. She couldn't remember anything not one single thing of the night. Could she have really killed her father? She asked herself. Could she?

Tears ran down her cheeks as the car jolted along and on reaching the police station she was processed. Fingerprinted, urine and blood samples taken and nails scraped. Her blood soaked clothes were exchanged for a clean orange prison jumpsuit. All her actions seemed to be robotically performed.

In time she was given a hot drink and asked if she wanted something to eat. That was kind but food was very far from her mind. She didn't know what took precedence in her thoughts. Was it her father's death? Or was it her plight as an accused murderer? Which would she pick? She opted for sitting and wailing. She had never felt so helpless in her entire life. She was arrested for murder!

Chapter Two

Back at the marina Charlie was cashing in on this tragedy. While waiting for Inspector Martinez to come over to question him. He had called the newspapers and a TV reporter. He had ensured that he would be paid for this *'hot news.'* They had taken their time in coming though and the girl had been taken away but none the less it was news. Charlie thought. As Martinez made his way to Charlie's he was swamped by the TV and newspaper reporters.

"How the devil did all of you get here so quickly?" Martinez pushed them aside and continued walking to Charlie's. The reporters were relentless and followed him.

"Officer, can you confirm that a man has been murdered here? Can you tell us who he is and if you have a suspect?" The reporters pressed Martinez.

"Yes I can confirm that a man lost his life. However, we have to first verify his identity and inform his next of kin. Now please excuse me." Martinez was annoyed by the presence of the press.

"Can you tell us if you have arrested anyone for this crime?" One reporter prodded.

"No further comment at this time." Martinez climbed on to the deck of Charlie's boat and disappeared below.

"Charlie you won't be responsible for that press gathering out there would you?" Martinez annoyingly asked.

"You big, ass-cat! I saw it all! The girl did it!"Charlie declared. "And as I told the other officer I went to sleep very early and had not heard or seen anything prior to what I saw on my early morning rising. Caught her red handed!" Charlie finished off. Martinez questioned him more then had him sign the statement. He was about to leave when Charlie queried.

"Was that not Durr's daughter? He used to have another young pretty one with long dark hair. A flirt he was. Shame his wife seemed very nice." On asking Charlie about the other lady he could not give more details. Martinez however noted this down.

"Thank you Charlie for taking the time to give the statement. We will be in touch with you if we need any further information. If you also remember anything else no matter how small or insignificant, do not hesitate to call me. Here's my card." Martinez said.

As Martinez left Charlie's and went back to Durr's yacht the reporters were still milling around filming and taking pictures. He ensured that the officers present secured the crime scene. The coroner had completed his task and the body was now released to be taken away.

With the body removed Martinez continued his search of the yacht. He also kept in mind the blood stains outside on the deck and berth. Durr's name also kept ringing a bell and he called in to the station to run a check on Sidney Durr. His feeling that the name was significant was confirmed. Sidney Durr had been reported as missing but the report was quickly cancelled by his wife.

Sidney's wife had just migrated but she had taken his children their housekeeper had said. So how was it that his daughter was back in Panama City? Putting this to one side he now quickly remembered that he needed to inform Sidney's wife of his death and soon. Before the press broke all rules and released the news which he was sure Charlie had provided.

"Hello Henriquez." Martinez said as he answered his now buzzing phone. "I was just about to call you." He said to his partner.

"Did you realize that the victim was reported as missing and then the report was withdrawn by his wife?" Henriquez asked Martinez.

"Yes I was about to ask you that but first the press has been here and they don't play by the rules. So please contact Mrs. Durr before she gets wind of it from the media."

Martinez was irritated by the media and he paused before he continued.

"You will have to inform her by phone I am afraid. Ask her to get a friend to come over. When the friend is present tell her to call you back. Break the news to her as gently as possible. She has a dead husband and a daughter now in custody." Martinez stated.

"But why is her daughter here in Panama City? Did they all not travel together?" Henriquez asked surprised.

"I am as puzzled as you are. But we will investigate to get to the bottom of this." Martinez hung up and continued his search of the yacht. From the looks of things there was definitely a terrible fight.

Meanwhile in the station Erica was asked if she wanted to call anyone. She was still rather confused. She couldn't focus; she had nothing on her, not even her mobile phone. She could not even recall her friend Sofia Grant's mobile phone number neither her house number.

The Grants, she suddenly thought! What will they think? What will her mother think? These thoughts were unbearable, worse than her awful headache. It was now 8 am and she was led from the interrogation room back to her cell.

"Do you want to call an attorney or speak to your mother?" Henriquez firmly asked over again.

"I haven't done anything and this will be all cleared up. You will have to let me go. I have not killed my father!" Erica shakily emphasized.

Inwardly she thought that with this declaration of innocence that things would work out. She'd be back at the Grants and the police would find the real killer. Erica's swollen eyes pop out at Henriquez, a deluge of tears flowed. Henriquez and Myles walked away.

The four walls of the confined space of the cell looked extremely bleak. Memories of her life within the not too distant past suddenly came flooding into her thoughts but yet she found it incredible to even remember a single event about last night. She was in fits of tears and her mind was spinning.

Erica's frantically circled the cell. Soon she stopped, muttered and went into self-interrogation. Her legs wobbled; she squeezed her temples! Her frantic lips trembled and questions tumbled out.

"Could I have really killed my father? Could I? Think! Think! Remember!" She loudly spoke to herself. As she wildly stumbled about she slipped, fell onto the small grimy bed and her head forcefully struck the side wall. Her face creased with pain as she momentarily lost consciousness.

Chapter Three

The past of many previous weeks and months now sailed by starting out from the time when Erica and her younger sister Emma peered out of the window of a plane at the pale blue sky. It seemed like an eternity since they had left Tocumen International and boarded a plane to what Erica deemed the journey to nowhere. Sitting in a plane gave her an unwelcomed opportunity to wrestle with her thoughts. There was nothing she could do to stop her mind from thinking. She had resigned herself to a life of despair when her parents got the final decree of their divorce.

Her mother was determined to start a new life as far away as possible from the old, taking her two daughters with her. In Erica's head a voice was screaming,

'What about us? We are leaving friends and our home behind? A place we had grown up in and for all the bad times we stilled loved it.' Erica knew that these questions would revolve in her head throughout this journey. The friends didn't matter to Emma. She didn't ever manage to keep any but leaving the familiar was something especially difficult for her.

Erica couldn't help but focus on one very special friend. Tears swelled up in her eyes. Her relationship with Gerardo was growing a relationship which she had kept a secret from her parents. Gerardo had said that he was ten years older than her. This would be frowned on by her mother and father. They didn't mind her having male friends but they had to be boys of a similar age. They felt that she needed protecting from any older members of the opposite sex who would be a corrupting influence, a distraction from her education. They had argued. She had already started school one year late and so needed to be focused. As Erica looked out at the fluffy white clouds mixed in with the blue streaming sky, she remembered Gerardo and how they had shared such great times, laughs, walks in the meadow, kisses and caresses all too taboo but all too heavenly. On these meetings it was blissful ecstasy to feel herself in the arms of a strong man, a man not a boy. A man who taught her how to forget the turmoil that raged within her home life.

When she was with him she only knew how to be fulfilled all anxiety and fear left her body. He was like a purge, a soul cleanser. She did not even get a chance to say goodbye to her rock, her support. It seemed that she was whisked away to what appeared to be a certain soul destroying death. Her mother had signed up to a two year work contract on an island that time had forgotten.

To onlookers Erica's family was the typical happy unit but it was far from this simple description. Her mother Karis Palmer married her father Sidney Durr the first man who probably told her that he loved her when she was twenty one. She had met Erica's father immediately after leaving university and starting her first job as an accountant.

She had often told Erica that she was drawn to his strong personality and he to her charming smile and grace. Karis often made reference several times to the fact that when Erica's father started up his own shipping business that he wanted her to leave the company she worked for and work for him. She never did. She remained independent of her husband's business helping him out in the early days when he needed audits done. She always said that she did not think that it was a wise thing to work solely for his company in case it folded. If it did then there would still be another stable income to depend on.

Her husband saw this differently he felt that she had no trust in his ability to be successful. That as his wife and as the Catholic she was, then she should also be following the desire to fully support her husband. He said that she was selfish and only thinking of her own career advancement. Karis often thought that his statements seemed more symbolic of a man trapped in the past or in the basement of his own controlling mind.

Erica felt that her mother had a kind heart and a generous way about her. She was the champion for the underdog, running clubs; she sought to help those young people 'who had lost their way in the world.' She always dressed smartly and looked the essence of elegance in whatever she wore.

It was such a shame that her mother's sweet nature was turning to bitter resentment for a husband who forgot his wife's birthday and their wedding anniversary almost every year. He had become a distant husband; an infrequent house guest and an insignificant father.

Erica tried not to take sides but it was inevitable that she would be caught up in what seemed like rancorous constant feuds between her mother and father each time he was at home or each time he called on the phone. This made her mother extremely sad, not just for herself but for her and Emma.

The damage that this shattering marriage was causing was evident since Emma's behaviour was presenting social difficulties. She was finding it challenging to settle down in her first year of high school. For Erica Gerardo was her solace. She forgot all the issues she was faced with at home and threw herself into Gerardo's arms. His arms always felt like a protective bubble encasing her from the worries of the world; sweet bliss and pleasure she experienced.

Erica often thought her mother must have felt like this when she first met her dad but how did it get this terrible? To shouting, name calling and even divorce? Surely you just don't fall out of blissful love? Erica couldn't imagine not being in love with Gerardo. The thought sent an eerie chill up the back of her neck.

Chapter Four

On the other hand Sidney Durr was not Catholic in fact Karis had said that he did not believe in anything or anyone but himself apart from when he used religion to try to control or coerce her. Erica believed that her mother was somewhat afraid of her husband who was not only strong of mind but of build with a temper to match.

Despite retaining her financial independence there was still a measure of apprehension which Karis had of him. He was the director of his own Shipping Company. A business which started out small but soon grew and became very successful but success does come often with a high price. Part of that high cost often involves being ruthless which can permeate slowly into family life, as it had done to Sidney's.

During several family arguments Erica and Emma would hear their mother accusing their father of his ongoing long stays at the office and his prolonged business trips to Canada and Guyana. She also questioned his deep involvement with the family of his business partner Hanif Osman. Hanif was the eldest brother of five but he had an older sister Elaina. Hanif was in his sixties but was still not satisfied with life it seemed and always wanted more.

Erica could not remember her father playing any significant part in her younger years. He seemed to practice absentee parenting. Somebody else was to fill in for him. This meant that the responsibility rested on their mother. Erica found herself referring to him as Sidney Durr and not dad

Sidney was tall with lots of hair for his age since most men of fifty plus years are balding or have receding hair lines. He didn't. He had a cleft in his chin very broad shoulders and a paunch. Poor eating habits, long working hours and being a stranger to the gym had taken its toll on him. He was now obese. His road to success had impacted on him physically and to some degree psychologically.

He was ever certain that her mother was cheating on him. To him his suspicions were made tangible in the fact that she changed her hair style or lipstick; answered the phone on the first ring; wore a sleeveless dress on a very hot day. Went to lunch with a group of coworkers and one of them happened to be a male so she was definitely having an affair. He therefore became even more controlling and accusing.

His imagination about Karis' supposedly infidelity could have been housed in a zoo since it was so extremely wild and varied. He had lots of confidence as a business man but as a husband insecurities surfaced a dime a dozen. These led to increased friction between him and Karis and ultimately this amongst other things sealed the fate of the now doomed marriage.

Chapter Five

Throughout the constant family feuding Erica had still managed to achieve her brown belt in Karate. She was so very proud of herself and truly elated with heaps of joy but very disappointed that her father had not been there to see her perform. Despite having disdain for him, deep down inside she wished that he could have seen her accomplishment. Somehow she still wanted his seal of approval.

She had worked really hard to reach this point in her Karate training. Brown belt qualification she knew showed her undoubted commitment to martial arts. This was something that she wanted to achieve which to her represented real maturity. Most of all she wanted Gerardo to see that she was all grown up, no longer a teenager.

She had text him to let him know of her achievement and to share her joy. She had invited him to sit anonymously in the audience but he had said that he did not want to least her mother should make the connection between them. He stayed away. This was hard but Erica accepted his wisdom.

Her Karate trainer reminded her that she however still had a long way to go before gaining the ultimate respect of the experienced Karate masters in achieving her black belt. She was determined to.

"Erica I am so very proud of you!" Karis had exclaimed as she hugged and kissed her. Karis could not help herself for adding, "Your father, where is he, another one of his no shows?" Erica could have done without that reminder. She however squeezed her mother tightly.

Emma too was doing well at Karate. She had achieved her yellow belt. Erica knew that the traditional yellow belt was designed as a symbol of the emerging sun. Brilliant hope, something Emma truly needed to get her through her difficult periods. For Emma progression to this stage meant that she would be able take part in gentle sparring sessions. This level of achievement was significant in aiding her development which was in question at this time. Karis was so very proud of her too but Emma had to telephone their dad and leave a voice mail message about her success. Erica just didn't bother to text him.

Their father later replied in a text to Emma and said that he was in a meeting but was happy that she now had her yellow belt. Emma read out the text to Karis and Erica with a saddened look on her face. She was disappointed because her dad had not seen her greatest achievement.

Emma had not been in school very much that term. She was not getting on very well with her classmates and teachers. This had led to several suspensions which placed more anxiety about returning to school on her and she was now refusing to attend. It seemed to be a downhill spiral for Emma. Now her most significant achievement had not been seen by her dad.

Chapter Six

The flight continued and there was no steward service on this private six seater plane. By now Erica had listened to music; watched an onboard movie and ate too many snacks in vain attempts to pass the time without crying. Memories now were bitter. Exactly what kind of place were they flying to? She asked herself while looking back at her mother.

Erica desperately hoped that her mother had done lots of back ground research on this place they were moving to since she wanted to continue with her martial arts training. Her mother's acceptance of this new job seemed very rushed. It was only a matter of just under two weeks in this entire process of moving to another country.

She wanted to dispel her angry feelings and she allowed her mind to flash back to her former home which was forty minutes outside Panama City but nestled in a beautiful suburb. To calm herself she thought of its exuberant displays of flowers in the well-manicured gardens. The beautiful magenta bougainvillea; pink and orange panama queens; purple verbena and orchids of every shape and size that burst out of the moist soil, were all fantastic! She loved that garden.

Within that magnificent picture was remembrance of one of the many stormy occasions when her father was at the breakfast table set within this beautiful garden. He always served himself up with too much butter and marmalade on his toast. An over-abundance of sugar in his coffee, not giving a single thought to his poor diet and the effects it was having on his waist line.

He would bite into his toast and seemed to savour each morsel as though he was a condemned man and it was his last meal. Her father had a love affair going, not with his wife but it was with food. Somehow she felt that her dad thought that he was invincible and nothing could touch him. She guessed that secretly her mother was thinking that fate would be kind to her and give him a reality shock of a physical catastrophe. One that would make him re-evaluate his life. In some ways Erica felt respect for him; for his business achievements but she was angry confused and disillusioned with him as a father and husband.

At these times of rare occasional family togetherness Emma and her usually waited and counted to ten before a subtle conversation between their father and mother turned into a melting pot of accusations. Kindled by their father's jealousy and distrust and stoked by the fire of their mother's ridicule of him. Karis would hurl endless insults at him. During this slinging match their father would retort every now and then between bites of toast, to remind their mother of a few of his life held beliefs.

"The material things in life do not come from staying at home and cuddling the kids and you. Cuddles are not legal tender; they are not accepted in shops!" Sidney would shout back. Then suddenly his raging eyes would spin to Erica.

"Erica! Where were you last night?" Her father heatedly asked. Erica's trembling hand held a glass of fresh orange juice; it became suspended in mid-air. She glanced downward at Emma whose shoes were on, left on right. Emma looked up and pouted while their father glowered at Erica.

"Mum knows where I was last night." Erica answered.

"Erica stayed over at Sofia's, Sidney that is where she usually is." Karis stated.

"I didn't ask your mother. I asked you! You are becoming feral! Your mother is too busy not being a mother!" Her father stated and took up his third piece of toast. Erica held her head down. Her mother glared at him. His sharp suspicious eyes reciprocated. Emma's intense, penetrating stares hit Erica as they accused her for this fiery argument. Erica looked away and softly responded.

"Dad I spend lots of time over at Sofia's as Mum just said." Erica fearfully explained.

Her father gorged on ever increasing slices of toast, gulped more sugary coffee while his eyes darted from Karis to Erica. "I am sure that your mother has absolutely no idea where you really are. She's just covering for you to protect herself." Her father retorted.

Emma shifted about and her nervous legs kicked the table. Karis' blazing eyes heated her angry stare. Her husband's distrusting looks burned back. Erica and Emma cringed as Karis' hot-tongued outburst of ridicule now flew out at Sidney.

"You are a pathetic example of a parent doing an abysmal job; if you weren't so inept things would be better!"

In turn Sidney then launched his attack on blaming their mother for Emma's difficulties at school. He would remind Karis that his understanding of her religion meant that a woman's place was in the home raising her children. This would be the fuse to ignite the explosives in their mother's brain and engage her lips to spew forth wrath.

There would be verbal exchanges between Sidney and Karis which no underage child should hear. They would weave a tapestry of obscenities which stretched across the length and breadth of the Panama Canal! Then they would both quickly come to their senses and close the orifices through which all the venom spewed.

Their father would then rise from his seat, storm out, trampling on any flower or plant which dared over hang his path. Leaving his unfinished breakfast, which wasn't a bad thing after all, going away from his morning's feast; evading the lurking heart attack or stroke; in all, he would live another day for another battle. As he marched off, Emma shouted out to him. "Dad you have crumbs on your shirt!"

Now facing this relocation reality this flight seemed to last forever and it did not help Erica to continue looking at her watch. She was certainly not looking forward to the landing neither the future. Karis sat one seat behind her and Emma;

and every now and then she asked how they were. Emma didn't answer and Erica wondered what she was thinking.

Emma wasn't good at expressing her feelings and she kept playing the game on her handheld console. "We are ok." Erica lied. What else could she say or do at thousands of miles up in the sky, she sullenly thought. Throw a tantrum? She had grown past that. Screaming out that she loved Gerardo and wanted to go back to him would not work. Hers was a secret love affair. She gave the bravest response she could drag from where the broken pieces of her heart were, on the soles of her shoes and said, "I am just fine."

Her thoughts were centered on her hopes and dreams not on anything else. All these now seemed years away. It was at this time of the day, school breaks, that she would text Gerardo and arrange for meeting him later. She so enjoyed his company. She felt delighted, thrilled to the depth of her very being to be in love with a man who could teach her about being in love.

Gerardo was tall and slim with great body tone. Blackish-brown neatly cut hair and hazel eyes which seem to draw her closer with every glance. His eyes seemed to reach down and encircle her even when his arms weren't touching her. He just had that magic effect of making her feel loved and wanted.

She wore makeup and did all of the things she thought a mature 'woman' would do to show the love of her life she cared. She saved up her allowance and bought Gerardo the best cologne and after shave. She liked the feel of his short beard as she nestled her head against his chin. Erica reveled in the smell of his body. She thought it oozed of stamina, strength and dependability. He was always on time to meet her and never missed a meeting.

Those meetings she recalled with a chuckle. She would tell her parents that she had extra music lessons or that she needed to study with her best friend Sofia Grant who would cover for her. On one occasion Gerardo chanced to take her to a theatre performance. He had mentioned that he was going and she begged him to come along. She had persuaded him and he finally agreed.

He had told her that she had to come in disguise so no one would know that she was a teenager. Erica remembered saying to him, "I am eighteen in a matter of months for God's sake, already at the age of consent!" Gerardo was worried she guessed not just because he was so very much older but if her dad found out he would literally tear Gerardo apart limb by limb.

Erica immediately bought a beautiful but rather mature and revealing dress along with the ticket for the performance. It was the musical Chicago. Deep down Erica felt that this performance was more apt for her mother. It featured women who literally did away with men, murdered them! Something she was sure possibly passed through her mother's mind. Erica was certain that if she could have read her mother's thoughts that the pages would have had inscribed on them, 'fifty ways of how to become a widow.'

With the ticket tucked away in her bag she telephoned her mother to say that she would be spending the night at Sofia's. It was Friday she thought so hopefully her mother won't object. Karis quickly agreed and said that she was busy trying to calm Emma down since she was not having a very good evening. Emma's medication had been changed and it seemed to be affecting her mood more. Erica was overjoyed at not having to weave a further web of lies as to why the short notice about staying over at Sofia Grant's home.

Sofia was a great friend and could keep secrets at no end. Erica knew that she was never a blabber mouth and wasn't in anyway a threat or challenge if she met any friend's boyfriend. Sofia wore ordinary every day clothes which did a marvelous job at hiding her gorgeous figure.

She didn't at all lack self-confidence, she just didn't care at this time of her life about all the other 'girly' stuff that drove and steered the female mind. She was immune to criticism of her looks by the popular opinion of the cliques around school. Sofia didn't march to the beat of anyone's drum. In fact she had her very own orchestra playing her own sweet symphony.

Erica liked her and trusted her with her clandestine activities with Gerardo. In fact Sofia helped her to build her nocturnal persona to attend the theatre performance with him. When Erica reached Sofia's house, Sofia was surprised but happy to see her.

"I did text you to say that I was on my way." Erica jokingly said.

"Erica my phone is switched off, charging so I did not get your text." Sofia swiftly replied.

"Hello Erica." Sofia's mum called from the kitchen. "Are you staying for the weekend? And are you still on that liquid diet? Which means that you will be spending all your time in Sofia's room and not joining us for meals?" Mrs. Grant asked all in one long monologue.

The diet fad was all part of the grand scheme so that when Erica sneaked out to meet Gerardo, Sofia's parents would think that she was upstairs taking a liquid meal and avoiding the sight of food. Erica hated this deception especially because the Grants were a great family and lovely parents. However her hormones appeared to be the master of her destiny and all that Erica could focus on was her burning desire and love for Gerardo. Being with him at all costs was all that mattered. With a very quick hello to Mrs. Grant, Erica rushed off to Sofia's bedroom.

Twenty minutes later she looked in the mirror after Sofia had finished her makeup artistry and could hardly recognize herself. "Wow!" was Erica's only response. Even the wig that Sofia had sneaked out of her mother's collection looked fantastic on Erica. She was transformed into a voluptuous woman, through the clinging light blue gown with a plunging cleavage and spaghetti straps. She felt as though she was no longer seventeen but twenty-seven.

Gerardo would be amazed she thought but quickly came back to the present.

"Sofia, how will I climb out of your bedroom window wearing this gown? Any ideas please, as to how I will get outside to meet the taxi down the street?" Erica's worriedly questioned.

"Don't worry my parents are going out to their usual club, they will leave soon and then you can walk boldly out of the front door." Sofia cheerily answered.

"That's great! Don't want to ruin my outfit." Erica remarked with a broad satisfied smile covering her delicate face.

Chapter Seven

Gerardo was waiting in his car as Erica's taxi pulled up. He did not move as she walked up to the car. Clearly he hadn't recognized her. She tapped on the window and he was startled. "Jesus Erica! Is that really you?" Before she could answer he said, "My Lord! You look smashing what a transformation!" Gerardo exclaimed.

His eyes however quickly turned away from her and scanned the queue of people which was winging its way slowly to the entrance. Erica tugged on his arm and spoke.

"Who are you looking for?" He didn't answer but kept his eyes in stealth mode and continued looking around.

"If you are looking for my mother she is at home with Emma. My father has a mistress, she is his work so you won't see him either and all my friends, I am sure would much prefer the Lion King. Remember my age?" She joked and smiled.

"You don't need to remind me, let's join the queue." Gerardo said somewhat edgy.

As they inched their way towards the entrance Erica felt elated that she was with her precious Gerardo. All that mattered was sitting close to him adoring his handsome features and enjoying his company. She wasn't deeply interested in the musical but any chance that she could get to be near to him she had to take.

He had never said that he loved her and she hoped to hear those words worth more than gold ring in her ears tonight. Maybe this would be the night. She had shown him that she was mature enough to appreciate this musical in wanting to be here and that her taste was refining. Surely he could see that she was a woman, in not only body but in mind. They finally got to their seats and the musical started. Erica was actually enjoying it. This must mean she shyly thought, that she was definitely developing, acquiring an adult taste and appreciation; something she wanted to do so very much for Gerardo. In the subdued light she looked at Gerardo he still seemed uneasy and she whispered in his ears.

"Relax my darling we are together nothing can go wrong." He held her hand and she squeezed his with undiluted pleasure thinking of how they would spend the night after the performance. She imagined being invited back to Gerardo's place. She had never been there before during this year long secret romance. Possibly he would take her there and fulfill her wildest dreams.

The fifteen minute break however found Erica and Gerardo still sitting in their seats. Gerardo firmly held on to the fear that they would somehow be discovered if they went to the restroom. Erica took this opportunity to ask him what his plans were after the musical.

"We can grab something to eat from a takeaway, park up, eat and I'll drop you off at Sofia's before dawn." This was a bit of a letdown but Erica still got the chance to be with him and that was all that mattered.

The break was almost over when everyone who was fortunate enough to actually make it to the restroom or to the bar started the exodus back to their seats. The usual pleasantries of excuse me, sorry were being quickly exchanged. As people sought to avoid stepping on others' toes or hooking jackets to seats as they crawled over each other to get seated before the lights dimmed completely.

Then suddenly in the slowly dimming light Erica heard a distinct deep throaty, "Excuse me please, excuse me," which made her blood curdled so much so that she felt no warmth in her body. It was definitely her father's voice. He was making his way back to his seat one row below them.

From blood curdling fear to abject terror even worst yet her eyes became riveted on the dark haired young, very young woman who was holding her father's hand as he guided her back to their seats. Erica squeezed Gerardo's arm so hard that it hurt her and startled him into looking at what panic had gripped hold of her.

It seemed as though Erica's piercing gaze made her father look upwards and his focus came directly on her eyes she thought but it was actually the slowly dimming light that he looked up at but also misfortune made him catch her gaze. There and then she knew her fate was sealed. He stopped trying to find his seat. Stood erect and stared into her eyes with disbelief. Then he slowly moved on breaking the stare but still watching her all the while as he manoeuvred his way back to his seat.

Maybe he didn't recognize her, just maybe he will doubt what he saw, she anxiously thought. Gerardo didn't instantly know that it was her so just maybe her dad doesn't know either. Erica whispered her thoughts to Gerardo and then said,

"If there is a God please let my father think that his eyes are deceiving him, please?" Sidney Durr and his lady friend finally got back to their seats. Gerardo whispered back with icy cold determination, "We have to go, right now!" He firmly stated as he gripped her arm and pulled her up from her seat. He pulled her along the row of people. Her feet twisted, ankles jerked.

They hurriedly exited the theatre and raced to the car. Gerardo got in and they sped away. There was stony silence during this drive. This was not at all how Erica had wanted the night to end. In a few minutes he pulled into a layby. Instantly Gerardo was beside himself with questions not directed at Erica but to himself.

"How did I allow this to happen? My sense has been lost in juvenile ways. You shouldn't have come." He went on and on. Then finally he allowed some semblance of rationality to creep in. In a cynical tone he spoke.

"That woman, that woman with your father, she was not your mother, was she?" This was more a statement rather than a question. Then before Erica could respond he continued his rant. "Your father is a bloody cheat!" Loud laughter erupted from Gerardo and then he abruptly stopped. Very angrily he now shouted.

"That sanctimonious piece of shit! Working hard, long hours! You told me he said this when your mother complained about him coming home late. Yeah! I bet he was very busy, out with that bomb shell!" Gerardo angrily roared.

Erica timidly reminded Gerardo of the situation at hand. She was frightened. "Gerardo that maybe very true but he is still my father and he did see me out with you. You, a man some ten years older than me! How am I going to go home? He will rip you to pieces and I shudder to think of what will become of me." Erica nervously continued speaking.

"He will blame my mother for all this and it will cause an enormous slinging match to determine who the worst parent is. Not to mention that my mother will be very disappointed in me since she thinks that my only indiscretions are coming home late after staying too long watching movies at Sofia's or at the cinema with the 'crowd' from school." Erica's pronouncement seemed dire.

"My mother could never imagine this! What am I going to do now?" Looking at Gerardo for an answer but getting none, Erica continued.

"Maybe he really didn't recognize me. Do you think?" She asked a very silent Gerardo. Gerardo's eyes then turned to slits and a frowning glare spread across his face.

"I'll tell you what you are going to do right now. Get out your mobile phone. Get it out now!" Gerardo angrily shouted.

"Why?" Erica asked beginning to get alarmed.

"Don't ask questions just follow my instructions. You are going to text this message to your father. Start now." Gerardo ordered. Gerardo started his dictation to a trembling Erica. Her fingers could barely grip her phone far less press the buttons to write the text which Gerardo called out.

"Dad I saw you with a woman tonight, mum is thinking of divorcing you and you really don't want another woman in the divorce picture and if mum finds out she will take you for everything you have rather than a nice decent little settlement. So if you keep my secret, I'll keep yours." Gerardo stopped.

Erica managed to type this long text as dictated. A death sentence she thought. She kept her finger away from the send button. She needed time to let it all sink in. She read it over three times with Gerardo shouting angrily in her ears.

"What the hell are you waiting for?" She had never seen this side of him before but she had no choice but to hit send. What she thought was going to be her night of mature pleasure, absorbing a musical she could not careless for but being with the man she loved, now turned into such a sour and frightening experience. She was now an 'emotional blackmailer.'

Erica fell deep into thought wondering what her father would think when he saw that text. It was not dad can I use the credit card? It was not dad, just to remind you my Karate show is on 3rd March. It was not dad, are you coming to parents' evening? She thought, as fear gripped her. She was now blackmailing Sidney Durr! What response would she get? She trembled, just thinking of it all! Gerardo's voice now interrupted her thoughts.

"Babe you have done it. He won't dare challenge you about tonight. You've got him now. Maybe we should have also asked for money. I bet he won't say a word to your mother, so relax." Gerardo's now carefree summation of things was not shared by Erica but she felt powerless to protest. He did not have to face Sidney Durr at least not in the morning, she worriedly thought.

Erica leaned on Gerardo, she sniffled. His arms remained still. She tried to put her head on his chest but he reined back and pointed at his chest. She looked at him wondering what the matter was, he frowned and then spoke.

"Makeup! My shirt!" Gerardo cautioned as he turned away and looked out the window into the blackness of the night.

Erica sat up and watched him. She had assumed that after the musical that they would have ended up back at his place even though he did mention parking up. However she was curious to see where he lived and imagined that it had to be just as fabulous as his expensive car but they were just seated parked up in this shaded layby.

"Thought we could've gone to your place." Erica said while waiting for an answer but none came so she spoke once more. "My dad will kill me! For tonight and for that text!" Erica anxiously stated as her eyes flooded with tears.

Gerardo breathed out as he looked at her. He then put his arms around her and kissed her. Her heart now battled a mixture of fear of her father and love for Gerardo.

Chapter Eight

After a short while Gerardo started the ignition and drove to a drive-through, bought a meal and sped away to another layby not too far away from Sofia's house. Erica was not hungry her appetite and all her emotions had been shot dead. She was devoid of feelings. As she sat in the car while Gerardo ate she recalled how she had met him. She was helping her father move office. She was carrying files from his office to new premises he had bought and had refurbished just across the street from his old office when she stumbled into Gerardo.

He helped her retrieve the fallen mass of manila folders. She thanked him and apologized for her father's archaic compulsion for retaining computer and also paper files. He introduced himself as Gerardo Abram and had been extremely polite in helping her to carry the files while striking up a light but yet intense conversation and all the while surveying her with his eyes.

It was evident that Gerardo was a 'ladies' man' and Erica was flattered to think that such a dashing older man could find her interesting enough to ask for her mobile number. She quickly gave it to him. From that moment onwards each time her phone rang or she received a text her heart would leap in anticipation that it was Gerardo.

Three days later it was. He asked if she would like to meet up and just go for a walk and chat. 'Get to know each other.' He had said. That was the first of so many rendezvous in secluded woods or the meadows both of which oozed with wild exuberance and was quite symbolic of Erica's growing feelings for him. Tonight however was not Erica's dream of wild passion but so long as she was close to him nothing else mattered. She always let herself sink into his strong caresses as he pulled her close and tonight was no exception but she was feeling afraid.

With the takeaway all consumed and his hands and mouth cleaned, he stripped off his shirt and she gave into the demands of his burning kisses. He could however sense the tension in her so he stopped put back on his shirt and started up the engine to drive around the back road to Sofia's to drop her off.

As the car got closer to Sofia's back garden Erica texted her to say that she was on her way back. Erica's phone rang instead of a response text from Sofia.

"Erica." Sofia whispered and continued, "You are back early! My parents are awake!" Erica could not get in a word and Sofia rattled on. "You will have to climb in through the window." Before Erica could object Sofia hung up.

They had not worked out a plan for Erica getting back into the house wearing her theatre dress and stilettoes. A dress which was so tight that it restricted even blood flow! Climbing through a window dressed like that was impossible.

"What's wrong?" Gerardo brusquely asked.

"I have to climb through Sofia's bedroom window. Her parents are back home and are awake!"

Frantic with the thought of contemplating such a manoeuvre dressed like that did not help her already pounding heart. Erica's heart was throbbing, not from love but from fear of being caught by Mr. and Mrs. Grant. Worst yet she felt that falling from Sofia's bedroom window which was an attic conversion and very high up from the ground, would be the final nail in her coffin tonight.

Mrs. Grant would be mortified to also see her wearing one of her wigs. This had been a difficult year for Sofia and her parents. Mrs. Grant had been diagnosed with cancer and had undergone chemotherapy. She had lost all of her hair and had a variety of wigs which she wore.

This would be an absolute insult to her if she found Erica wearing one of them. Even though Erica knew that Sofia had the benefit of parents who saw the lighter side of life. They both would probably laugh it all off. They would no doubt however frown on deception. Erica would probably get Sofia grounded for the rest of her natural life.

"Ok babe, here we are." Gerardo was at the side road which was adjacent to the Grants' beautiful home set in mature gardens and bordered by tall palms. Erica would have to sneak around through the trees as Gerardo did not dare approach from the front of the house. Luckily the Grants did not have a security system. They felt that too much security told would-be burglars that you have something to steal. They did not take too favorably to dogs either and did not own a firearm. She was indeed fortunate on not being easily detected. Ripped to pieces by a dog or shot on sight as an intruder. Her dilemma however still remained. Her brain was being electrically charged and she queried Gerardo.

"How on earth am I going to climb through an attic window wearing this?" This was indeed a question to Gerardo but he did not respond he just kept slowly driving. The car finally stopped and Gerardo muttered.

"Shame I was cheated by not seeing the musical to the end. Call me tomorrow babe." He kissed her goodbye and waited for her to get out of the car. Erica got out and went into 'Ninja mode.' Crouching low and slinking briskly around the back of Sofia's house.

Sofia's breathing was clouding up the glass of her bedroom window as she pressed her face onto the window pane. Her eyes scanned the garden looking for Erica. She had the most incredulous look on her face as she stared down from the glass window. She saw Erica below standing in just her strapless bra and undies! Her shoes bag and dress all now hidden in the bushes. This was the only way Erica could master climbing all the way up to an attic window. She had to do so virtually naked!

When the Grants remodeled the house Sofia chose the attic space for her bedroom, this was who Sofia was, the unconventional girl. Erica made it into the warmth of the bedroom and refused the snacks Sofia had hidden away for her. She wasn't hungry. She was afraid! That was the only emotion of willful choice opened right now to her. Fear!

"How did it all go with Prince Mysterious?" Sofia eagerly asked with a drool implying that this was probably more than a theatre outing. Prince Mysterious was the alias Sofia had given Gerardo since none of them really knew who he was. Erica couldn't hold back her feelings which by this time were moving through a myriad of states. From love to hate, to anger, to disgust, disbelief, hurt and pain! In her head these emotions were shared out to her father, mother, herself and also to Gerardo.

She started to sob uncontrollably. Sofia looked shocked. "Don't tell me he's dumped you?" Sofia asked. Erica kept weeping with Sofia trying to keep her quiet in fear of her parents hearing the crying. "Shush, shush." Sofia whispered and put her arms around Erica. "Well don't tell me that you are pregnant? Are you?" Sofia pressed her friend.

"Oh Sofia it's worse than that!" Sofia now had the most astonished look on her face and said, "So tell me what can be worse than teenage pregnancy?"

"My father saw me at the theatre with Gerardo." Erica blurted it all out in what seemed like one long word and not a sentence and kept weeping. "Erica for heaven's sake please stop crying and repeat what you just said." Sofia asked.

"Sidney Durr saw us! He saw us!" Looking even more astounded with her eyes bursting out of her head and firmly fixed on Erica's face, Sofia whispered, "Your father saw you and Gerardo? You know what this means don't you? Do you know what this all really means?" Sofia was asking questions which she wasn't really expecting answers for.

Between choking on her tears and the gurgling sounds which emanated from her parched throat, Erica managed a feeble, "Yes Sofia, I know what this means." That was an automatic response since Erica didn't really know what it all meant. It was just a superficial answer coming from a teenage brain that felt up to this point of time, that she was a mature woman.

Despite Sofia being an excellent confidante, Erica somehow could not bring herself to tell Sofia the entire truth. She just couldn't tell her about her father's unfaithfulness and the blackmailer she had become. What if her father called up the Grants, Sofia too would be in trouble. They silently looked at each other in utter despair.

Chapter Nine

Dark rain clouds summoned in the morning probably symbolic of Erica's mood which was down and in the dumps. "You're back early from Sofia's, didn't expect to see you until this evening. How's Susan now? I heard the good news that the cancer is in remission."

Erica did not answer any of the questions her mother was asking but just pretended to be engrossed in practicing her Karate moves but desperately wanted to find out where her father was and said, "I didn't see dad's car when I came in, is he away?"

"Said he had a business meeting early this morning so he decided to spend the night at the town house since he also had to work late last night." Her mother's reply was an unconcerned one.

"Yeah, right." Erica's cynical response was typical of her dislike for her father but now more enlightened about his working late excuses. She went on, "Isn't it funny how dad can almost never make it home in the evenings?"

"Now when did you care about your father being at home? You are almost never here. You never want to help out with Emma and she really wants to be with you." Erica felt that she didn't need this right now from her mother. She just didn't need a kick in the teeth at this time.

Karis stared at Erica since she felt that often she was in a war zone. In a battle with Sidney, refereeing between Emma and Erica; arguing with Emma's school about how she was being managed and fending off unscrupulous dissatisfied clients, who wanted her to fix the books so that they could evade taxes.

Karis continued in her one-sided conversation with Erica. "Anyway I am taking Emma to the speech therapist at 12 o'clock and then shopping. You are welcome to come along and we can all have a 'girly day' out." Karis was trying in a last ditch attempt to get Erica involved but this gesture only got back a polite refusal from Erica.

"Thanks for the offer mum but I want to practice my Karate moves. I really want to get my black belt." Part of her answer was true, she did want to move on from her brown belt but she also wanted to be at home to face her father. She needed to get it over and done with. She still however did not want to face her father alone but at the same time she also did not want her mother to be at home when she finally did see him. To confront him and for him to confront her, was an ugly and extremely alarming thought.

She kept looking at her phone to see if her dad had responded to her text. He hadn't. Maybe he had not seen it. Too taken up with his young beauty she thought. "Who was that young woman?" Erica said to herself out aloud. She had never seen her before but still she wasn't sure. There was something about her which stood out and made her feel that she had seen her before. She seemed far too familiar.

Her thoughts quickly turned to her mother who thought that all that occupied her father was his work. How shocked she would be if she knew of this woman. Erica knew that she needed to plan her defensive and offensive attack of words when her father finally came home. What would it all be? She silently asked herself.

It was Saturday and it was Teresa's day off. Teresa was their 'girl Friday.' She was their cook, housekeeper and special 'age-old friend.' Teresa had worked for her parents since she knew herself and Erica wished now that she was there. Erica did not want to be all alone in this empty house. Empty in the sense that very little family togetherness existed and now she shuddered in thought at facing Sidney Durr in it.

Gerardo had not yet returned any of her numerous text messages asking what to do and say when her father came home. Where was Gerardo? She felt like running through the house and screaming his name coupled with, help, help! She came to her senses knowing full well that, that would be childish. Wasn't she the mature woman last night who commenced a blackmailing plan on her father? What folly. What a mess she had got herself into.

It seemed like an eternity but the hours had passed and Erica had fallen off to sleep from the exhaustion of rehearsing her speech to her father and from lack of sleep the night before. She was now suddenly awakened by footsteps on the parquet floor of the sitting room. Her adrenaline was overflowing and her brain was poised to use her mouth as a lethal weapon against her father.

As the door slowly opened her heart it seemed froze and she felt cold with fright. Motionlessly she waited for Sidney Durr to appear. As the door was slowly pushed opened she heard from behind it, "Erica, are you asleep on the sofa again?" Before she could regain her composure or even answer her mother walked in and continued her questioning.

"Why are you standing in the middle of the room looking so frightened?" Karis asked surprised and went on lecturing. "Sleeping in the daytime causes bad dreams. I thought you were practicing your Karate moves."

Emma then quickly burst into the room joining Erica and Karis. This gave the startled Erica a chance to catch herself. An opportunity to thank her lucky stars it was not her father. No need now to answer her mum's questions. Emma filled her in on all that she had missed in not going shopping with them. Karis however took this as her opportunity to let Erica know a few of her significant observations.

"You are becoming more and more like your father in isolating yourself. You are focusing solely on your own interests and not sharing in family activities." Erica stared at Karis without answering. She thought that if her mother only knew how right she was about her and her father. Two deceptive souls they were, she thought.

They had an early dinner which Karis made a point of cooking since she did not have the time during the week to prepare evening meals. Teresa did the week days' cooking and Karis the weekend ones. Karis was an excellent cook. She made dishes which just the smell of, made her children hungry for, even after not heeding her warning and stuffing themselves with chocolate or other snacks before the meal. They still had big appetites for her food.

Today's special was one of their favourites. Karis' very own pan fried sweet potato wedges. Served with what the girls called brick chicken. Pieces of thinly cut chicken soaked in herbs, spices, sesame seeds and lemon juice and fried in a shallow pan with sesame seed oil, until crispy.

As the girls all settled down to dig into this mouthwatering feast they heard the door unlock and in walked their father.

"I can't believe you guys were going to start without me." He said.

"We never know if or when to expect you." Karis replied looking at him sourly. "I'll set a place for you." She disappeared into the kitchen leaving Erica with the stony gaze of her father! Her heart started to pound. A meal which was generally a pleasure to eat and enjoy now became her revulsion.

When Karis returned with cutlery and a plate for Sidney, Erica asked to be excused under the pretext that a sudden attack of PMS cramps had only just seized her. With her face wrenching in imaginary pain and holding her stomach, Erica whispered in her manufactured agony, "Please mum, may I be excused?"

"Oh dear Erica you mustn't forget to take the Primrose oil before you get an attack, it does help." Karis replied sympathetically. Her father glared at her with eyes that looked like toughen glass.

She escaped to her room and then sent a text to Gerardo again. She seriously needed help. All the rehearsing of what she would say when her father came home seemed lost in fright. Her hand trembled as she locked the door to her room and sank under her pillows. Room temperature was ambient but she was cold and hot all at the same time. With her brain sprinting and wondering why there was no answer from Gerardo, she closed her eyes and waited for her father's knock on her door to come but thankfully she fell asleep.

Chapter Ten

Weeks passed and Erica was still waiting for her father to approach her about the night at the theatre. She felt as though she was walking on eggs not knowing at what moment one would break. When would her father confront her? The usual sparring matches intensified between her mother and father but not once did he ever enter into any discussion about his infidelity or her relationship with Gerardo.

Each time their paths crossed when he was in the house, she just got a steely-eyed glare. She had quickly forgiven Gerardo for ignoring her in the previous weeks when she felt sure that her father was going to 'get her.' He had not returned any of her anxious texts.

Erica thought that she had shown mature thinking and agreed to resume meeting him in their usual 'hot spots,' surely this would impress and convince him that she was more than a fickle-minded teenager. Sofia however had said, that it showed that she was gullible and that Gerardo was a predator and that she was his prey. Sofia firmly stated to Erica, "A man must be there for you through all types of weather. When you are afraid and anxious is a good starting point."

Erica thought that Sofia was too damned sensible and that that was why she did not have a boyfriend. More precisely a man that was strong and handsome like Gerardo. During this visit to Sofia's, Erica looked at her friend smiled and then spoke.

"Sofia, what you really need is a good man." Erica jokingly stated.

She then climbed out of Sofia's bedroom window and went on yet another one of her secret meetings with Gerardo.

Chapter Eleven

Her blackmailing text to her father seemed to have worked well. He had not once confronted her at any time and this she thought was due to dating an older man who would know how to control her father. A younger man would never have been bold or experience enough to think of something like it even though she wondered how Gerardo guessed that her mother was contemplating divorce. Anyway Gerardo was brilliant, she thought and a broad smile came across her face.

This Sunday morning however found Erica with a forlorn face but she kept up practicing her Karate moves. Thoughts crept into her mind of the face of that young woman at the theatre with her dad. For some reason instead of diminishing with time, the woman's face grew more familiar.

Exhausted, she finally stopped her training and went to her room. As the rain drops streamed down the window pane they seemed like bars trapping her inside a life she seemed not in control of. Despite the presumed control she now had over her father with him not lecturing to her anymore, she still felt trapped. She was in love and was not able to publicly declare it. Also holding a secret about her father's unfaithfulness made her feel as though she was under siege, under arrest by circumstances.

She watched from her bedroom window as her father's vehicle pulled away. He had loaded it with three suitcases. Unusual she thought but this must be an extended business trip or one of pleasure with his 'unknown lady friend.'

It had been a quiet morning, surprisingly no fights between her father and mother, not even a shout from Emma. Just uncannily quiet. The silence was broken by Teresa's appearance at Erica's bedroom door. She was surprised to see Teresa since she did not work on Saturdays or Sundays.

"Erica your mother wants you and Emma to come to the family room," she said. "Why? And how come you are here today? Isn't it your day off?" Erica asked Teresa.

They had a specially carpeted room with no chairs just lots of soft cushions. As small children they would romp with their mother and occasionally with their father. These days Emma used it most since often she needed to go there to calm down from her panic attacks and shouting and screaming at everyone. With no answers to her questions, Erica followed Teresa and joined by Emma, to the family room.

They all sat down on the lush carpet including Teresa and looked at Karis. There was a mixture of anger and deep sadness in her eyes. Then she said in a brave tone, one too high pitched so they all knew she was holding back tears.

"For some time now you all know that we have not been a happy family and I am as much to blame for this unhappiness as your father is." She paused, looked at Erica, Emma and then on to Teresa and then continued. "Sidney and I have decided that it is best that we separate and see if absence will make our hearts grow fonder or further. Today he has moved out and will be temporarily living at the town house. Girls he said that he will be back during the week to talk to you both." Karis said all this in a calm flurry of words, finished her statements and wiped away a tear.

Typical Sidney Durr Erica thought. When it came to family life he never faces up to difficult situations he always leaves it to mum. Emma started to cry. Teresa looked sad. Karis looked shattered but in some ways relieved. Erica seemed emotionless. She could not find any significant feelings and just sat there staring at the blue wall. After a few minutes, she then mustered some strength and reciprocated the hugs from her mother, Emma and Teresa.

Without being asked Erica whispered "I am fine. I'm ok. Is everybody else ok?" Erica felt that to be honest she was fine to some extent. This was now an even more broken family.

She clearly knew that no matter how bad something is, when it is gone there is still pain. However there would be peace at the breakfast table for one thing and her knowledge of her father's unfaithfulness would now be null and void. What about his knowledge about her and Gerardo? How would he now use this? She thought annoyingly. She needed to speak urgently to Gerardo. She rang his mobile but there was no answer.

Chapter Twelve

Gerardo could see the caller on his mobile was Erica but he was in conversation on the landline telephone and could not take Erica's call. No names were to be used on these calls which came through from Guyana. The person he was speaking to on the other end asked in a sharp voice, "Who's calling on your mobile? Why don't you answer it?"

"It's just Jim Gagnon letting me know that he and Lee will be arriving later." Gerardo lied and with a dismissive voice said, "Speak to you later." He hung up the phone and ended the conversation. Lately he had started to feel that he was being tugged like a puppet on a string but he was determined not to let anything interfere with the 'plan.' He knew that his every move was under question.

Erica on the other hand he thought was like a cool breeze. No accusations. He smiled as he remembered how Erica was impressed with the expensive black sedan he drove. She had even at times filled the car with petrol as he drove her around in the countryside in *black beauty*. That was the affectionate name Erica had given the car. No matter what, he knew that Erica loved him and would do anything for him.

Just then he was jolted into action and shouted out loud, "Lee and Jim! Christ, I need to shift my ass and clean up this place quick!"

Lee and Jim Gagnon were two wealthy Canadian brothers. He knew they would be ringing the doorbell soon and he needed to ensure that the house and cars were in tip top shape.

Lee more so than Jim, was very particular about the property and did not like things to be out of place. Often Gerardo thought that Lee had OCD. He was also a tight ass miser and never wanted to part with any money, if Lee could recycled loo roll, he would have.

The Gagnons were reticent about their lives and they never talked about their business affairs. Gerardo did not even know what type of business they were into some kind of lawyers but they seemed to be also involved in business in Guyana. Mail went to a post box which they rented and he sometimes drove them there to collect it. Panama City was their supposedly holiday residence during the Canadian winter or whenever they felt like a break. The only information he ever gleaned was when they had dinner parties. He would listen in on conversations in passing.

Gerardo now went to work like an ant on a chain gang until everywhere was spotless and everything in its place.

Chapter Thirteen

Dismissing from her memory her unanswered call to Gerardo back then, brought Erica directly back to the four hour flight she was still on. Four hours to a teenager can seem like a lifetime and Erica continued recounting the not too distant past. She recalled that the prospect of her father's repatriation back to their home to resume the marriage never actualized. Absence did make their hearts grow further. The Durrs went on to a very swift and acrimonious divorce. In fact Sidney Durr never kept his promise to return to talk to Emma and her about the separation.

Instead he became more and more distant and they hardly saw him. Despite him and Karis having been granted joint custody of Emma, he never fulfilled his parental duty to have her spend time with him. Erica knew that he hated her for having found him out. Emma got the occasional text from him but she got nothing. Karis reverted back to her maiden name of Palmer.

The day the decree absolute came through and their mother told them that the divorce was now final; Erica whispered to herself, 'I have kept his secret and he has kept mine.' In Erica's mind Gerardo and she could be an even 'bigger item' now. Regrettably as time went on Gerardo seemed to want the secrecy to remain.

Her mother appeared to be recovering emotionally from the divorce war zone through burying herself in her work.

Strangely enough Gerardo never asked her if she had divulged her father's secret to her mother but would constantly ask her about her father. On one occasion Erica was bold enough to ask, "Gerardo do you want to try dating Sidney? How many times must I tell you that I do not know what my father is doing now?" Not only the constant questioning bothered Erica but mentioning her father opened old wounds.

"Ok, Ok, don't get your bra straps in a twist." Gerardo said to Erica. "I won't ask again." Back then, that put an end to reminders of her father.

She now glanced over her shoulder and caught her mother looking ahead in the plane at her and Emma. Karis fought back a tear. Had she done the right thing in relocating them? She felt that Erica would bounce back from the change but could Emma even cope with it?

Emma had recently been diagnosed with Asperger Syndrome Disorder. This now explained her difficult behaviour but the diagnosis also gave hope of how to deal with its challenges. Karis was aware that Erica was convinced that ASD was a new name for plain and simple bad behaviour. Erica believed that it was an excuse for Emma to persuade others to allow her to do what she wants.

However the tranquility of a remote island Karis thought, would offer her younger daughter some respite from the intimidation she had faced at school. She would get her a one to one teacher and maintain her Karate training which she enjoyed. She hoped somehow that Sidney would find time for his children and they could travel back and spend school holidays with him. Karis knew that this was wishful thinking on her part.

To be honest if she admitted it to herself, the swift pace of change, the quick divorce and settlement had indeed taken its toll on her. The divorce although it seemed that it was the right thing to do, now seem very emotionally scarring. The wounds were not healing as well as she thought that they would. She seemed to want to forget about Sidney and her marriage to him faster than the time that was passing would allow.

Friends had seemed determined to keep her up to date with his social life, something she did not want to know or talk about. Then he seemed to disappear. No texts from him to

Emma had come through on her phone for quite a while now, he had it seemed blanked his family completely.

Before the relocation announcement, Erica could see her mother doing internet searches for jobs abroad but Erica would drop subtle hints designed to keep them right where they were. Hints about Emma's difficulty with change and her unsettled mood becoming worse if they went away to relocate.

Then Erica would also throw in, "This is the end of my high school and the start of my college I really want to go to college with all my friends." Her mother would look up and give an answer meant to reassure.

"Don't worry Erica all will be well." In her mind Erica would think, just the type of parent response I need. Also lurking very much in the fore front of her mind was Gerardo Abram, her soulmate.

Then that fateful day came, a day that Erica will never forget. They were all gathered in the family room to hear the most devastating news any parent could hope to deliver to a teenager. Erica couldn't believe that she was now about to be uncoupled from the reins of love. The words which unhinged Erica's heart were bound together in one sentence from her mother. "I've just been offered a fabulous job contract with a company which handles offshore accounts on an idyllic island."

Karis was beaming with joy and somehow expected to see the same on her children's faces since she was convinced that getting away from the past would do them good.

Teresa, Emma and Erica all looked stunned. Karis continued on. "You'll all love it. It's like a paradise, un-spoilt and untouched." She had said with a too bubbly voice which was masking her real feelings.

"Why do we have to leave here?" Erica asked. "What's wrong with here?" Erica thought that she just could not understand the adult mind.

Her father was gone, war-filled days over but it all seemed not forgotten. Now they were losing their home.

"Here, this place is filled with memories, good but too many bad ones." Her mother replied. "We need to move on, a fresh start for us all." Her mother declared.

Erica really did not want to rebel. She did not want to turn this into an adversarial relationship with her mother. Lord knows her mother had had enough fighting with her father and battling Emma's mood swings but what would become of her? How would or could she survive living without her Gerardo? How?

"Thanks for understanding and being in on this with me guys. We leave in two weeks." Her mother interrupted her panic filled thoughts with these statements which made it all worse.

"Teresa-?" Emma started to ask and Karis finished, "The house will be rented and Teresa will stay on to ensure that it is kept in good shape." They were also now losing Teresa too! Erica just could not comprehend it all but said nothing. Karis beamed excitedly supplying more information about the relocation. "All the arrangements for our travel are being made by the company so all you guys need to do is to decide what you want to take with you and the rest can easily be replaced on one of our 'girly shopping days' when we get there. All other items which you leave behind will be placed in storage."

The words 'girly shopping days' and 'replaced' struck some very uncomfortable chords in the melancholy blankness Erica now found herself being immersed in. She was no longer a girl, as her mother believed but a woman in love and stripped to the bone of all emotion by the thought of the separation from her precious Gerardo. Nothing or no one could replace him.

Her mind now returned to the flight. They had made a short stop in Miami and were now on board again. Flying time was still passing slowly. To calm herself from the internal fury raging within her from being apart from her Gerardo, she looked up some information on the island they were headed to on her IPad. She gained some useless, at least to her it was or what could be deemed interesting information, depending on how you looked at it and turning to look at her mother she read it aloud.

"The islands have many underwater cave systems. One called Cottage Pond and another one called the Boiling Hole. We could go in the Cottage Pond one when we get there mum." Erica declared and carried on, "Here's another tip, Horatio Nelson of Trafalgar Square fame was stationed on the mainland and he suffered one of his few defeats trying to retake the island from the French. They also have the third largest barrier reef system in the world and boast of being a great dive site." Erica concluded sharing her research.

"There you go mum some useful information to save us from the boredom when we are living there. Imagine that, we can explore a cave!"

Erica was being sarcastic but also cleverly concealing her pain since she could only think of Gerardo. This divergent research provided no refuge or comfort from the despondency of her bleeding heart. She then vainly attempted to console herself by listening to music. My Chemical Romance was playing but it wasn't one of her favourites. It was old.

Just then the Skymaster lurched and jolted her back to the real situation at hand which was this despairing journey that was soon to come to an end. This turbulence in the air that the plane was going through distinctly represented the feelings she was experiencing right now.

Chapter Fourteen

L ooking at Emma, Erica could see that her gaze was now fixed on the window of the plane as though her eyes were glued and transfixed and unable to move even though she seemed as though she wanted to look away. What was it that held her gaze? Erica wondered but dare not ask her. It was best to leave Emma alone when she was at peace. The plane was making its descent and Erica too joined Emma and looked out of the window and could see nothing but barren land, a few shrubs, open fields with brown burnt grass.

No skyline with city sky scrapers and bustling traffic signifying vibrancy and life. Even though she knew that these would be missing from this island but if this was the country side then where were the lovely green meadows, fields and animals? If this was the tranquil paradise then it was sorely overrated! Where were the fields of growing crops, farm animals and farm vehicles?

Nothing could convince Erica that they weren't being taken to some secluded place to become sex slaves to satisfy the wild fantasies of some eccentric mean old recluse! This was a private flight. The plane was owned by the company her mother was contracted to work for. They were alone on it, with only the pilot and co-pilot.

Erica thought that even her mother who was always the epitome of self-control and confidence looked decidedly worried but she seemed to be concealing it all in her question to them. "Girls are you excited about this adventure of a new start to things? I am really looking forward to it all and hope that you are too." Erica's brain was screaming a loud empathic no but for her sister's sake she could only mumble a very weak and feeble, "Yes." Emma gave no response.

Anxiety seized her but she had to be strong for Emma who was five years younger and having ASD did not help in a situation like this for her older sister to behave worried. She had to restrain her wild imagination even though being very much afraid by the unknown that awaited them.

More than ever she was terrified of not fitting in and making friends but most of all not ever again feeling Gerardo's solid arms around her body and the touch of his lips, creating a vibrant heat within the depths of her being. How did life deal her such a cruel hand? She questioned herself inwardly.

She had just completed high school and finally was free at last to make decisions or so she thought. To become the all-encompassing envy of every girl who chased after Gerardo. She quickly recalled the many times he told her how lucky she was to be his number one girl. Once she even remembered jokingly asking him, "Number one of how many Gerardo?" He didn't answer, he just smiled but she knew that she was his one and only!

All that really mattered to Erica and all that her existence was based on were to be able to one day walk proudly beside Gerardo and wait for the proposal. She was not interested in merely moving on to college and forget wishing for an engagement ring! She knew she was capable of being a wife and student simultaneously. She was convinced that she was meant to be his wife.

All the lilies in the meadow back home screamed out their names. Gerardo and Erica! Time after time when they met in their hidden bushy alcove and had passionate encounters.

Sadness now engulfed and covered her like a thick shroud since Gerardo did not meet her to say goodbye. He had said that he was no good at goodbyes. 'What we have is special.' He had said, 'It will survive time and distance until we meet again.' Those promises Erica had written in her heart and had kept his text on her phone reading it repeatedly.

Emma now tugged on her arm bringing her mind back and shouted, "What place Erica? Nothing down there thought this would be pretty. It's not! Looks all dry, very brown no rain water, no plants grow?" Emma was twelve intelligent but in some ways limited by having ASD. She sometimes found it difficult to moderate her speech and when anxious she did not make complete sentences. This was one of those times.

Often Emma's speech was also either abnormally loud or very quiet. This time Erica wished that she had chosen exceptionally quiet since the co-pilot looked back at them somewhat surprised at Emma's questioning description of the place which Erica believed to be his home land.

Erica too shared Emma's view but judging from the co-pilot's expression she thought that she needed to keep that opinion to herself. He almost glared at them and firmly stated in a quaint accent, "We are proud to say we have a very beautiful tropical paradise and no one who comes to it wants to leave. In fact most stay."

Erica's brain raced and to herself she muttered, "Stay? He said stay?" Stay was the worst word that could ever be printed in a dictionary or uttered when a teenager is removed from the love of her life and dragged to live elsewhere. Erica frantically hoped that her mother's hearing had become defective and impaired by the turbulence and that she had not heard the offer to become a permanent resident of what looked like a bad representation of a Jurassic world!

She struggled with every bit of her maturing sensibilities and pulled them by the boot straps of her teenage emotions directly to her brain and responded to Emma in a diplomatic and sensible way which would satiate her and gratify the co-pilot.

"Emma this is only the landing strip there is a lot more to come." Who was she convincing? Only the co-pilot she believed, to land them safely.

Erica was fighting back tears. Emma was asking question after question and Karis was trying to answer her and also focus her mind on this relocation decision which she had made. She had been given a great job offer but had she done enough research on this island? What had she done in her hasty efforts to put the past behind?

She had been promised rent free accommodation. Free schooling for Emma or the one to one teacher she had asked about. Erica's college she was told would be facilitated but this was not clearly explained. She would get a company vehicle and all utilities would be paid. She would be responsible for paying her telephone service. Medical bills would be covered by the company's insurance for her and her family.

She would get a paid holiday each year for her and two children and a husband if she had one. At the end of the contract she would receive a forty percent gratuity. She had the option of renewing her contract if her service was rated good. Her contract also stated that she would be paid in US dollars.

These details of her job offer sounded superb and were written in the contract she had signed which her attorney had first looked over and sanctioned. Everything seemed in order but doubts were quickly swarming over Karis now. "Have I done the right thing?" She muttered quietly to herself. Maybe I have been as selfish as Sidney in dragging my girls out here, she thought. "Have I been thinking only of how I feel and my desire to forget the past?"

Karis' mind ticked over with more questions. Am I being a rational parent and truly looking out for my girls? Or am I causing them more instability? She went on and on doubting her decision and her motives. Finally stopping the self-interrogation, she now looked forward in the plane at Erica and Emma and tears came. She quickly held them back and started to think of the new life ahead and how she can rebuild her relationship with her daughters.

Karis needed desperately to be strong. She knew that she needed to be enthusiastic and cheerfully optimistic about this move. There was no place for being skeptical and depressed. Her mood would help to set the tone for the girls' own confidence in this their new life. She needed to be positive.

They all would be away from the trauma of the bitter divorce and former family bickering. She was hoping that this change would also bring the two girls closer together. That Emma's Asperger would be subdued.

There was desperation in Karis for her life to be renewed. She was seeking respite after years of a failing marriage and shattered emotions. She wanted her personal feelings to match her professional ones. She needed to feel like a successful woman in a personal way. This move was to be her panacea.

The plane had almost landed and Karis switched her phone back on. She glanced at it and right across the screen there was a text message from Teresa. It read, 'As soon as possible please call home the police have been here about Mr. Sidney.'

Chapter Fifteen

They had landed safely in Providenciales and all their luggage was now removed from the plane. Erica had to leave too many of her 'creature comforts' behind but still she had the most suitcases. Relocating to this place was hard. Extremely difficult since only what was needed and essential could they bring. Even most of her great feelings and emotions had to be left behind.

First impressions of this place did not inspire confidence in being able to replace all her needed stuff. She certainly could not replace Gerardo. The plane was on what looked like a landing strip for heaven's sake, she quickly observed. Immigration and Customs was one and the same person all in one area.

Karis was speaking to the pilot who told her that the company was sending someone to meet them to take them to a hotel for the night. After that he went on to say that they would get another plane to the island which she would be based on. Emma was listening and all this was too confusing for her. She started to pace back and forth becoming more and more agitated. Erica remained quiet and sullen.

Karis was juggling all this information along with the thought that she needed to call Teresa and this all made her anxious too. "Erica!" Karis called out and continued, "Please can you help Emma? Take her to the ladies and let her put some fresh water on her face."

"Sorry madam but I need to complete the immigration process before your daughters can go off to the toilet." The officer stated.

Well that saved Erica from Emma's protesting of not wanting to go with her but it put Erica right back into her apathetic trance.

After being processed by Customs and Immigration they were met by John Humphrey. He was one of the company's managers, a balding tall man in his forties with a cheery smile. He warmly greeted them and spoke to Emma about his daughter whom he said was two years younger, surprisingly Emma listened. Although Emma found social situations somewhat difficult she found it easier to socialize with people that are older or younger rather than peers of her own age. She did quietly respond to John with a few nods.

John had a lovely large red people-carrier and the drive would have been superb if it was being driven on paved roads. The road surface was uneven and the view from the plane's window was even more flattering than the reality that now faced them. There were a few buildings, none were two-storey. So far the tallest structure was a dis-used windmill.

Karis engaged in work related conversation with John probably to hide the apprehension of bringing her daughters to a desolate place which seemed to lack stimulation for teenage development, Erica thought. A place devoid of shopping malls and cinemas!

John was not a native but an expatriate who had lived there for over ten years, he told them.

"What a masochist!" Erica whispered to Emma who just stared back at her without responding.

John happily told Karis that he had continued to extend his work contract repeatedly and probably would stay. Karis missed several bits of what John was saying to her and gave him the random, "Oh yes, yes, yes." She was heavily in thought over Teresa's message and couldn't wait to be checked into the hotel to find out what Teresa had to say about Sidney and the police. She irritably thought that Sidney Durr was still having an overriding influence on her life and peace of mind.

John checked them into the hotel which seemed more like a bed and breakfast. It was a new establishment that did not seem to fit into the surrounding environment of a 'lost world.' Erica concluded to herself.

The Durr girls had one room adjoining their mother's. Erica went into her protesting mode.

"Mum can you please tell me why I have to share a room with Emma?" Before Karis could reply, Erica moaned on, "Why can't Emma share with you?" Emma was not to be left out of this fray and quickly butt in with a loud, "I don't want to be in there with Erica. She hates me!" Karis held her head in her hands in an attempt to show that this verbal battle of wills was not needed.

When the two girls were finally silent Karis said, "We need to put squabbling behind and cooperate with each other. The company has paid for two rooms, we could have had one. Would you both prefer that we share one room? I can ask for one with a double bed and a single bed." Karis warned. Her mind was now on contacting Teresa and she wanted to put a quick end to this feuding. Without a response, Erica and Emma crept back to their room.

Karis knew that Teresa would be anxiously waiting for her to call and so she immediately called her. When the phone rang Teresa picked it up quickly on the very first ring. In a flurry of words she said, "Miss Karis I am so glad to hear you. The police came to the house this morning y dijo que el Sr. Sidney está perdido." Teresa in her haste had thrown in some Spanish and then she continued in English. "They said that in order to begin an investigation they need to verify this missing person's report with the family first. His secretary is the person who reported him missing."

Karis could not understand it all. Teresa was speaking so swiftly and with fear in her voice, that at times she was speaking in Spanish, giving her the explanation of why the police were looking for Sidney.

"Teresa! Teresa!" Karis softly exclaimed and then said firmly, "Slow down. Please tell me again why the police are looking for Sidney." Teresa repeated it again but all in English this time. Very slowly and deliberately she spoke. "Mr. Sidney is missing."

Teresa then said that two police officers had called at the house earlier that day. They had asked for Karis and when they were told that she had only just left that morning they enquired about where she had gone and wanted to contact her. Teresa had told them that she would ask Karis to ring them since she did not want to give out Karis' number without her permission.

"Ok Teresa, please give me the number for the police. I will call them from here. Thank you Teresa and don't worry." Karis hung up the phone.

"My Lord!" Karis exclaimed loudly. This made Erica and Emma run into the room. "What's wrong mum?" They asked in unison. "Your father is missing." Karis said it with shivers running down her spine. "Sidney is missing!" The two girls stared with wide-eyed shock. Karis could not contain herself. She started to cry followed by Erica and Emma.

Karis eventually composed herself and first rang Vanessa, Sidney's secretary. "Vanessa sorry to call you at home but I understand that you have reported Sidney as missing. Is that correct?" Karis enquired.

"Hello Karis, Sidney has not been in the office for over three weeks. Neither has he returned any of my calls." Vanessa informed her.

"I contacted his partner Hanif Osman who also said that he has not heard from him either. Have you or the girls heard from him lately?"

Karis gave a direct, "No." Sidney was an only child and his parents had died several years ago. His mother was Canadian and his father was German. With the exception of his children that was the extent to his family. Karis assured Vanessa that she would contact the police to verify that they too had not heard from him.

With her mind racing Karis tried to remember if she had packed her old address and telephone number book. Before she called the police she wanted to speak to Hanif Osman Sidney's partner. Following the divorce she had removed 'old contacts' from her mobile. Wiped the slate clean, she had thought at the time.

Hanif Osman was not one of the people she had wanted to remember. He had his hands in several business pies and some she believed to be really messy. He was affiliated with gold mining in Guyana along with the shipping business he and Sidney ran. He had made a subtle pass at her earlier on when he had first linked up with Sidney's business and her horrified outright refusal was something he did not easily forget since each time they met, he never really spoke to her.

She needed to muster up enough strength to call Hanif. Surely Sidney must be having another midlife crisis and is off somewhere exotic having a blast. In her mind the Sidney she knew cared only about work and making money but lately since the divorce from reports of their friends he seemed to be living it up with the young ladies. She kept getting news about him and a very young dark haired woman.

It would however have been great if Sidney Durr remembered his daughters. Erica and Emma she thought, they were innocent in all this but sadly the causalities of a failed marriage. He still had a duty to be a father. No. It was more a bond to his children. He had the task of building a legacy of love between him and them no matter how he felt about her his now ex-wife. He really shouldn't continue to let the girls down. She felt some anger as these thoughts ran through her mind.

Karis was jolted back to reality by the sound of a car's horn as it passed the hotel. She opened her suitcase and rummaged through her clothing but could not find any signs of an old address book with Hanif's number. She rang Sidney's secretary again.

"Apologies Vanessa but can you please give me Hanif Osman's telephone number?"

"I am so very sorry Karis but I do not know it off hand." Vanessa said regrettably and went on explaining. "I do not have a company mobile only my own personal phone. When I get to work tomorrow do you want me to tell Hanif to contact you?" Vanessa asked.

Karis noted that Vanessa did not say that she would give her Hanif's number tomorrow but rather that she would tell Hanif to contact her. "Thanks very much Vanessa but that won't be necessary. I will deal with things, please do not ask Hanif to call." Karis said cautiously. "Have a good evening and sorry to have disturbed you. Bye." Karis ended the call.

One thing Karis knew she did not want Hanif to know her number. She did not even want him to know where she was. Karis also recalled that Vanessa did have a company mobile. Why was she lying? Karis asked herself. Was it fear of losing her job if she gave out Hanif's number or was there more to it all?

Crying had at last taken its toll on the two girls. Erica and Emma were exhausted from the flight and from shedding tears over the news of their father being missing. They were now lying on their beds when Karis came and said, "Girls take a shower and go to sleep. There is nothing any of us can do until we hear further from the police." She kissed her daughters and closed the adjoining door to her room. Karis then contacted the police to say that she too had not heard from Sidney.

The police officer spoke kindly to Karis and listened as she explained that she was divorced from Sidney. He said that despite her divorce from Sidney that she and Sidney shared joint custody of Emma and as such Emma was regarded as Sidney's next of kin.

"Has Sidney contacted his daughters?" The officer asked.

"Not in a while." Karis replied.

"How long ago would that be Mrs. Durr?" Somehow Karis could not bring herself to say that she was no longer a 'Durr' but said to the officer, "Three months now."

Karis thought that Sidney did not even know that they had left Panama City and were relocating. She had not wanted to tell him in fear of his objection to her taking the children away. Despite not visiting them he would still want that measure of control of dictating their activities.

"We will need you to fill in a missing person's report but we understand from your housekeeper that you are away." The officer next asked, "Can you please give us a fax number so we can get it to you ASAP? You then need to fill it in, sign it and fax it back to us?" The officer directed.

"I will have to get back to you tomorrow since we only just arrived." Fax number? Karis thought angrily, they had only just landed and Sidney was making life complicated. She did not want a fax coming through on the hotel line and she certainly did not want to tell John Humphrey of her domestic troubles. All that she could think to do was to go to sleep. Sleep if it came would be a welcomed cure for this dilemma.

In the adjoining room Erica peeped at Emma and saw that she was asleep. She was glad that Emma could find some peace. Sidney Durr was still her father and no matter what she thought of him, she still felt a measure of sadness at this latest turn of events. She went into the bathroom and turned the shower on at its highest level. She then rang Gerardo.

His mobile went to voice mail. "Darn it." Erica said. She then left a message. "Gerardo we have arrived. I miss you and love you madly! The police have said that my dad is missing." Erica said all in what seemed like one breath and continued, "Do you know of anything?" Erica queried and ended with, "Love you very much text me please."

Putting away her mobile Erica finally took a hot shower which misted up the bathroom so much so that she could hardly see. This mist seemed to exemplify how she was feeling. Everything was unclear. No visible signs of happiness. She dried herself, sank into the bed and finally fell asleep but only after a series of ugly thoughts of what may have happened to her father.

Chapter Sixteen

Gerardo was busy with the arrival of the Gagnon brothers. The brothers had an excellent countryside estate in El Valle de Anton, Cocle Province. One of Panama's most exclusive areas and their property had magnificent features. In particular its landscaped grounds kept in immaculate condition by Gerardo. It had a main house and two guesthouses. The main house had six bedrooms and four bathrooms. All these areas were well utilized when the Gagnons entertained.

Gerardo welcomed Lee and Jim. He took their luggage to their rooms and then retired for the night in the guest house where his quarters were. He knew that later ladies always joined the Gagnons brought by taxi and he wasn't needed on those occasions.

He looked at his mobile and saw a missed call and a voice mail message alert. He listened to Erica's voice from the voice mail and actually thought that he really did miss her. He however was somewhat annoyed at the message about her father being missing. He scrolled through the call log on his phone and made a call to Guyana. Again no names were to be used during these calls.

"What's happening" Gerardo asked eagerly. "Fill me in on progress." He urged but asked another question before he got an answer stating, "A problem maybe up."

"What kind of problem?" A sharp voice asked from the other end of the line. "Sidney Durr has been reported as missing." Gerardo hastily added.

"Who reported him missing and how do you know this?" This quick and sharp but distrusting question was now levelled at Gerardo. He had to think quickly on his feet as to how he would respond to this last question. "The Gagnons are here, remember. They were talking to each other about it and I over-heard them." Whew! That was a brilliant cover lie.

Gerardo thought to himself, hoping that he wouldn't be asked how the Gagnons knew Sidney Durr.

He wasn't dealing with an impetuous young Erica. Cunning, skillful sharpness was what he had to work with. "Ok. Thanks for letting me know." Came the voice on the other end and the call was ended.

Gerardo was tempted to call back and ask for more information on how everything was going. He resisted because he feared opening up a can of worms about the lie he had just told. He was tired from all the cleaning up he had to do for the Gagnon's arrival and just did not want an argument.

Before crawling into bed he peeped through the guest house window and looked out at the main house. The brothers were well known for their lavish 'private' parties, for bringing young ladies over to spend the night. They were not married and accountable to anyone. In the morning he would have to clean up the mess of the previous night. He lay awake thinking that soon he would be able to give up this miserable job and have enough money to rest easy. It all depended on the plan working out.

Over in the main house the Gagnon's were enjoying the night. They reveled and partied like teenagers despite being in their early sixties. Their indulgence in the profane fueled their penchant for the company of young ladies. These girls it seemed were provided on demand. Whatever the rich brothers wanted their source could supply without question.

As Lee sipped yet another drink of many for the night, his favourite cocktail Last Word, a drink which he learnt arose in Detroit during Prohibition and fell dormant for decades, until revived by Murray Stenson in Seattle. Last Word a multifaceted herbaceous drink and like the French 75 it's one that would make a gin lover of anyone, Lee thought and it certainly did for him. Its name was synonymous with Lee's personality. He liked to have the last word within any conversation.

After another glorious sip, Lee briefly thought of their business prospects and the trust their service providers had in them. He and Jim had the gift of persuasion. Lee now jokingly said to Jim, "You certainly know how to wheel the deal. You always say the right things to the young ladies."

"What?" Jim asked being slow to catch on to Lee's inference. Slowly he caught on and laughingly joked, "Oh I know what you mean." Jim then walked away and in a serious voice he said, "My dear our job offer is an opportunity of a life time..." This offer the brothers made countless times to each young lady and all eagerly accepted.

Lee Gagnon thought that this was far better than the poverty the girls had been removed from in their home land. Jim Gagnon shared this view also. He had said over and again, "Lee we are providing these girls with a far more superior life style than they would have had in their native land. We should get an honour from their government for reducing poverty." Jim smugly stated.

Despite his callous views Jim still had more of a conscience than Lee. Underneath it all he felt that corruption in high places did little to help the ordinary citizen and compounded the poor man or woman's life chances. Jim knew also that he and Lee had shares and a significant interest in the gold mining industry in Guyana. He also knew very clearly that corruption in the mining industry was not simply restricted to the country's borders.

Up front Jim and Lee Gagnon were known as immigration lawyers and only a selected few knew of their investment portfolio in Guyana. All these other financial pots they stirred were hidden from public scrutiny.

The Gagnons had a source in Guyana. Mr. Big they called him. He was trusted and reliable. He ensured from his end that he selected only the best prospective employees. He took care of all the arrangements for getting them over to Panama City. The Gagnons then finalized all the preparations for the last stages of delivery to their clients abroad.

Tonight they had three young ladies but Mr. Big had fouled up. One of the girls was very ill. Lee immediately got on the phone to Mr. Big.

"One girl is causing trouble. She's having several asthma attacks." He irritably said.

"She's got a clean medical certificate from the doctor-." Mr. Big calmly started to respond but was cut off by Lee.

"This is a liability." Lee interjected.

"So what the hell do you want me to do?" Mr. Big snapped back. Lee lowered his voice, "We can't send her back she may talk to the wrong people." Le warned.

"Well again what do you want me to do?" Mr. Big repeated and carried on impatiently, "Handle it Lee!" Mr. Big shouted and hung up the phone.

"Bloody bastard!" Lee shouted as he paced the floor.

"You didn't get the last word Lee." Jim said smirking.

Lee and Jim now had a problem on their hands. They had to be swiftly decisive. They reasoned to separate the two girls from the ill one.

In the morning the plan was to let their clerk take the other two girls into the US embassy in the city, as was the normal procedure and put in the visa applications. This was still the plan but with one less visa application.

Chapter Seventeen

John Humphrey sat patiently in the reception area of the hotel. He seemed to know all of the employees and engaged in light conversation with them. Karis and the girls appeared from their rooms. "How are all of you today?" John asked. Erica wished he hadn't asked. Karis managed a cheerful, "We are fine John and how are you?"

"I am swell thanks." John cheerfully said. Erica's teenage brain could not resist thinking that John's weight even though not overly obese did indicate his feelings. Today she thought was to be a mean day. A day of being just horrible even if only in her mind!

With pleasantries exchanged between them and John, they had breakfast. Then John loaded their luggage into his vehicle for yet another journey to what their mother believed to be the 'promised land;' the place that would help them to recover and move on. Erica thought that so far nothing had indicated that this dream would come through.

She and Emma were filled in on the latest news surrounding their father's disappearance which was not much apart from their mother suspecting Vanessa of being up to no good with Hanif or their father. Erica considered telling her mother about the dark haired woman she saw with her dad but again she thought it best not to do so at this time. It would only bring more hurt and pain for Karis and also reveal her own deception.

Different pilots were present now for this short twenty minute flight on to the island John referred to as North C. This time John Humphrey accompanied them. The co-pilot was introduced as Avery Miller's son Ethan. Erica thought that he looked like her age. Avery Miller was the owner and director of the company her mother was to work for.

Ethan had a very cool carefree expression and his smile was charming. He was very tall and browned skin. He however was not as mature as 'her Gerardo.' She was determined to be hostile. She gave Ethan a very cold glare without speaking. Karis whispered, "Don't be rude dear," as she nudged Erica into giving a subtle greeting.

"Hello." Erica snapped while under looking Ethan.

Erica looked at her phone hoping to see a missed call or a text from Gerardo. There were no texts or calls. Disappointment seemed to be courting her. It was quickly becoming her best friend.

Emma looked through the plane's window as she did on their first flight and the expression on her face said it all. The scenery was the same as before but this time Emma closed her eyes and drifted off to sleep. Karis looked at her daughter and felt that Emma's new medication was causing her lethargy but was it really the medication or was it what she was looking down at?

Karis wanted to quickly get settled so that she could contact the police. Sidney was now occupying space in her mind again. It felt like an intrusion. For Erica she wanted to get to wherever this new place was and get on with feeling miserable at missing Gerardo. She knew that coupled with missing Gerardo was the fact that her father had not been heard from. This disturbed her; after all he was still her dad.

When the plane landed thankfully there was no immigration or customs to go through again. This was classed as a domestic flight. As she helped John with their luggage, Erica heard her mother thanking the pilot and the co-pilot that Evan boy or was it Ethan? Whatever his name was, she didn't care, but her mother was looking for her to say thank you also. She grudgingly did.

After another bumpy drive on yet another unpaved road, they finally were dropped off at a house which surprisingly was rather nice.

"Karis if this is not to your liking and you feel that it is unsuitable, then please let me know and we can move you." John told her mother.

"We will look around and let you know." Karis replied. One thing Erica knew was that her mother did not hastily commit herself apart from accepting this job. Erica supposed that in some ways she had to if she was to take the plunge and leave the past behind.

"Where are the shops and stores?" Erica asked John.

"Oh yes, where are the stores?" Karis joined in. She wanted to get a fax machine. John explained that there were only two small shops on this island, others were on the island they had just left but the main shopping was brought in from Miami.

"Oh these are the keys to the car. It's a company vehicle and now leased to you." John stated and carried on, "The insurance papers are in the glove box-." Before John could say another word Karis interrupted him, "Is there an active telephone line in the house?"

"The line is here but it will need to be activated by you since you will be responsible for the bills." Karis' heart sank. Karis politely thanked John and said that they would be fine. They weren't fine at all. She wanted to use a phone immediately. She wanted to receive the fax. The missing person's form and quickly! She wanted action now. She wanted her ex-husband to be found and to be off her mind!

Ironically enough Karis thought of when she was married to Sidney Durr, how many times she wished that he did go missing. "How many times," she whispered but now she wanted him to be alive, to be accounted for. This was all a very confusing quandary and worrying situation.

Erica looked at her mother and said, "Let's see if the police can e-mail the form to you. You can download it and sign it electronically and then send it back to them." Erica inwardly felt that Gerardo would be pleased at her mature suggestion. Karis smiled and hugged Erica. She then immediately telephoned the police and barely got a signal with just enough time to say to e-mail her the form before the call was lost.

Erica now changed her mind about being hostile and mean. Her emotions were flitting between immaturity and rationality. She now asked Emma if she would like to go explore outside of the house which backed on to a beach. Emma was still withdrawn and declined the offer. Going outside gave Erica some space and time to be alone with Gerardo's last text to her. She placed the message on her screen. The words stared up at her. 'What we have is special. It will survive time and distance until we meet again.'

Chapter Eighteen

On North Caicos Erica quickly discovered that a signal for a mobile phone was very temperamental. She had to go upstairs in the bathroom and hold her phone outside the window to send yet another text and voice call to Gerardo. Next she tried Sofia and was surprised to hear Sofia's voice. "I never thought that I would be so glad to hear you!" Erica exclaimed to her friend.

"Oh Sofia, this is like a very bad dream. No! A nightmare!" Erica blurted out. "Make up your mind Erica dream or nightmare which is it?" Sofia asked and carried on. "Now you see there is a distinct difference between the two. One can be very terrifying while the other can be a wonderful fantasy." Sofia expounded in her usual whimsical way.

"Bloody hell Sofia, will you restrain your IQ from trapping and bombarding me with educated explanations!" Erica shouted. "It's a fucking nightmare if you want to know!" Erica bellowed into the phone.

"Now, now, resorting to swear words shows a lack of mature intellect." Sofia jokingly chided. "Ok Erica what's the problem now?" Sofia seriously asked.

"First, I hate this place! It's horrible! It's barren more like an Amish paradise! The house is nice but seems like a prison enclosing me!" Before Sofia could say anything Erica launched on, "Have you seen Gerardo around? Or have you seen my father? He is missing!"

"Well Erica I think I maybe saw Gerardo-." Sofia was saying but was sharply interrupted by Erica. "Sofia these are not multiple choice questions. "Did you or did you not see either of them?" Erica hurriedly probed.

"Well no. Did you say that your father was missing?" Sofia asked and was now worried. "Well unless you are becoming hearing impaired, yes I said that he was missing!"

Sofia went silent with some measure of disbelief. "Sofia I need your help." Erica pleaded.

"Heard that line many times before." Sofia jokingly said. "What do you want me to do now, hope it's legal?"

"Will you stop joking about it? This is serious! Ring up my father's office and ask to speak to him." Erica continued to instruct Sofia. "Listen carefully to what Vanessa says to you about where Sidney is if she says anything at all. Then call back a bit later, disguise your voice and ask to speak to Hanif Osman." Erica instructed.

"What if they both take the call?" Sofia asked. "Then hang up." Erica commanded.

"I am sure that you know why you are making me ask for this man Hanif Osman because I sure as hell do not!" Sofia said. Erica wanted to find out if Hanif was in her father's office since he rarely came there and this maybe significant for establishing what has happened to her father. Erica remembered that her mother didn't trust Hanif. Sofia said that she would get right on to the calls.

Chapter Nineteen

Most people would agree that Erica by contrast had a high quality of life even in relocating to the island which she hated. Valentina on the other hand, who grew up virtually on the streets of Guyana lived in a rundown part of Georgetown. Poverty surrounded and was consuming her. All this somehow had made Valentina a tough and determined woman.

The economic situation in her home country Guyana had wide disparities between the 'haves and the have nots.' Unfortunately she was one of the latter but things would soon change she thought. She now however sat in the even more decrepit place she called home but with thoughts of a new life. She looked at the photos of what would soon be her new house. Soon she would be unlocking the door to enjoy some of its luxury.

Valentina had been given up at birth and was placed in an orphanage run by nuns. She did not know who her real parents were and this often made her feel dejected and angry. She was taken from the orphanage and then was passed from pillar to post, being raised by several different people who had their own interest at heart. She would quickly discover that her innocence would be used and abused.

Her vulnerability as a child would be exploited time and time again. There were no real child protection bodies. Not even the authorities truly actively represented young children. Child protection laws were absent or ineffective back then and even now she thought.

Valentina remembered that her school education was virtually non-existent and what education she did have back as a child was acquired in practical terms from working around the mining communities at a time when she should have been in school. Her education was mainly developed in the 'school of hard knocks.'

Later in her struggle to survive, she was at last taken in by a kind couple who treated her with respect and raised her just as if she was their own daughter. They encouraged her to get an education and paid for her and one of their sons to complete distance learning degree courses. At last she had an education but still no job prospects materialized. Life was still hard.

When she thought that her life was somewhat settled her foster parents were exploited out of their land and mine by overseas investors. These were people who hid their identity behind a company. Her parents' land was acquired for far under its real value. An inconsequential amount and mined for its gold. Her foster parents, Clarence and Millie Hawkins did not have the financial backing to support large scale mining on their own.

They did not have the necessary economic support to fight the acquisition either since it was backed by the authorities in a claim that a public road had to be built to provide necessary links for the local mining workers. Strangely enough when the land was acquired no road works ever commenced. This Valentina learnt was yet another 'sell out' to overseas investors. The Hawkins' long fight for justice never materialized. This meant that they lost everything.

Clarence Hawkins became ill, suffered two strokes and passed away. Millie battled angina and depression. Her depression had begun when she and her husband fought the acquisition of their land. Losing the battle made her depressive state worst. A few months after Clarence passed away, Millie took her own life, an overdose. Valentina was devastated. On that fateful day when Millie took her own life Valentia was filled with rage and anger more so than grief but she knew that 'revenge is a dish best served cold.'

Her mind now switched back to the present. Her life of poverty would soon come to an end. Things were climaxing for a nice change. The house was the first step. Funds were being carefully transferred into bank accounts. She wished that she could get more.

Her thoughts were interrupted by her ringing mobile phone. She answered it quickly, "Hello," she cautiously said but knew this call would only come if there was trouble.

"The last thing which you have asked to be done has been refused." This statement was filled with irritation. "Exactly what do you mean by that?" Valentina snapped.

"The calls which you have asked to have done are just not happening!" The defeated reply was resolutely said.

"Well make them happen!" Valentina's voice ordered loudly into the phone.

"I'm telling you there's down right refusal along with grogginess. What do you want me to do next?" Exasperation filled this question.

"I will take it from here. Just make sure that you keep a very close eye on things and before you leave be sure to lock up tightly. You are doing a brilliant job and don't forget the major reason." She hung up the phone.

Chapter Twenty

Back on the island ears of remorse flooded Karis' eyes as she looked around her new home on the island while also remembering the 'old' home she had just left behind. She looked at the email on her phone and had not yet seen a reply from the police. As she started to reminisce again about leaving Panama City in ran Emma.

"Dad has text me! It's a text from Dad! Look mum see it is dad!" Emma was bursting with excitement and carried on without letting Karis speak. "You see he is not missing after all!" She declared.

Erica had returned and heard Emma's voice and ran to see what the commotion was about. "What's happening? What's this all about?" Erica swiftly asked.

"It is dad! He is alright. He has just text me!" Emma said with joy. Karis looked at Emma without speaking. Erica took the phone from Emma's hand and read the message out loud. 'I'm fine. Just need some space away from things and work. Lots of love Dad.' She looked from Emma to her mum.

"Well that explains it." I will let the police know. Karis said, wanting to put an end to Sidney's disappearance and settle down to concentrating on her new home and life.

"Explains what mum?" Erica asked and without waiting she went on speaking. "Exactly what does this explain? Could you tell me? And what is it that you will let the police know?" Erica was questioning her mother's haste to put this away.

"That Sidney is not missing and that he has made contact with his daughter Emma." Karis said.

"Oh I see, a text message takes him off the missing person's list. When you called him on your mobile and then several times using Emma's and the calls all went to voice mail. He never returned any of them. Do you not remember? Teresa also called him and got the same." Erica pressed her mother with these analyzing questions and statements.

"Erica how long have you become Nancy Drew?" Karis sarcastically asked.

"Mum look at the text. Take a good look at that text message." Without waiting for her mother's response, Erica turned to Emma. "Emma, when did dad ever end a text message to you with lots of love Dad?" Erica asked while looking Emma squarely in the eye.

Emma threw her hands in the air and walked away leaving Erica and Karis. "For God's sake Erica, Sidney is not missing this text proves it." Karis reasoned but Erica was relentless and kept on questioning its validity.

"Even though it has been sent from his work mobile and not his personal mobile, you still believe it is genuinely from dad?" Erica kept up her attack on the authenticity of the text message.

"Mum it's the work mobile, he never texts us on his work mobile." Erica firmly stated. Karis stared at her daughter.

"I am calling the police and letting them know that there is no need for them to e-mail me that form. Sidney is not missing and that's the end of this detective business Erica! The end!" Karis said with firm determination and at the same time with annoyance.

Erica stormed back to her room and listened as her mother called up the police. She just had a bad feeling about all of this. Worse yet her mother's phone got a signal! Erica felt her mother was wrong to stop the police from starting an investigation but what could she do?

She was waiting for Sofia to call her back to see if she had been told anything from Vanessa. This was hardly likely to produce anything of significance but she would wait. Gerardo was still in her thoughts and she was hurting from missing him. Some of her pain was now being replaced by thinking about her father. Strangely enough, she thought she wouldn't care but she did care about what may have happened to him.

She had been outside to the back of the house and now she decided that she would walk down the road. She pushed her head into Emma's room and asked, "Would you like to go for a walk down the road to see what is out there?"

"No I don't want to see anything! Go away Erica!" Emma's agitated reply was forceful.

"Well Emma mum can't say I didn't try to be nice to you." Emma threw a shoe at Erica and got up and slammed her bedroom door shut. Erica just couldn't understand ASD. Erica knew that she could be mean by choice and by time and occasion but ASD made Emma mean all the time.

"I'm off to explore this delightful place." Erica mockingly said to her mother. She was convinced that the first steps toward insanity were walking around aimlessly. Stepping through the door now, would be her first! She was frantic in thought and felt powerless and would go mad if nothing positive happened soon.

"Please don't go too far." Karis warned. "What's the worst that could happen to me? Get bruised and cut to pieces by the thorn bushes? See you later mum." Erica closed the door behind her and walked off.

She wasn't far down the road which seemed to stretch down the middle of the island when a lovely little sports car went past her and then reversed.

"Hello there." A voice from behind the wheel greeted her. She looked at the driver and saw that it was Ethan Avery. Or was it Evan?

"You seem to get around." Erica replied.

"A nice hello back would be better." Ethan said.

"Well hello and is it Ethan or Evan?" She said grudgingly. Without answering her question he went on speaking as he slowly drove along.

"Thought you would be unpacking, didn't expect to see you strolling around." Ethan said.

Erica fumed inside and thought, who the hell does he think he is to be dictating her actions?

"Is this not a free island, where I can do as I please? Or is it owned by you?" There was hostility in her reply.

"Just trying to be friendly but I can see that you want to be left alone so bye for now." He drove away and Erica thought good riddance!

She walked a fair distance until she saw what resembled a shop. She went inside to look around.

"You must be the new accountant's daughter." The woman behind the cash register stated. Before Erica could answer she carried on, "I'm Belinda." The woman smiled and next said, "You have just arrived so go down to the beach and have a good soak in the sea water. It will relieve jet lag."

"I'm Erica. Thanks for that advice." Erica said as she looked around.

"Do you want anything in particular?" Belinda inquired.

"No, just looking around." To be honest Erica felt that there was not much in the shop. A few groceries some can goods and a few toiletries. No real creature comforts and no fax machine either! As she stepped outside her phone rang.

She answered quickly. "Sofia! What did Vanessa say?" Erica shrieked impatiently. "A nice hello Sofia and how are you Sofia, would be great." Sofia said teasingly.

"Hello Sofia." How are you Sofia?" Erica said in a whinny voice.

"Now, now, no need for mocking behaviour." Sofia scolded.

"Sofia I am dying to hear what Vanessa had to say. Please end my misery and tell me!" Erica pleaded.

"Well for one thing Hanif Osman answered the phone."

"What?" Erica interjected.

"Do you want me to finish or will you keep interrupting?" Sofia asked.

"Ok, I will keep quiet." Erica promised.

"As I was saying, when I called the person on the other end was not Vanessa but a male and he said, 'Durr shipping may I help you?' I was surprised and thought that it was your dad. So I said, is this Mr. Durr? The man said, 'I'm afraid he is not in. May I help you?' Sofia explained. "Next I said, may I ask to whom am I speaking?" He said, 'Hanif Osman.'

"Finally I said, no I'll call again and I hung up the phone."

"Where in the hell is Vanessa? Why is Hanif Osman in Panama City?" Erica said all at once.

"Erica you should first start by saying, thank you Sofia for making the call." Sofia chided.

"Hoped you withheld your number?" Erica asked Sofia.

"Give me some credit for being smart. Now tell me what is significant about Hanif Osman being in Panama City?" Sofia queried.

Erica clarified to Sofia that Hanif rarely came to her father's office but rather her father always went to see Hanif Osman in Guyana. Erica also filled Sofia in about the text message from her father to Emma and about her suspicions about her father as still being missing. And now why was Hanif in her father's office? This Erica had no answer for, only suspicions.

Sofia also told Erica that she had started asking questions about Gerardo and was waiting to hear if anyone she asked came back with anything of interest. Sofia promised to call her as soon as she got any news. Even if she found out nothing, she would call her tomorrow. Sofia promised.

Erica walked back home with her brain working overtime. Between dodging some very large iguana lizards, which there seemed to be an overabundance of and listening to the extremely loud cawing of overhead crows and ravens, she was having fits of bad feelings.

There was sadness about leaving Gerardo. He must be angry too at her departure and this probably is why she had not heard from him. She remembered he had made a promise that nothing could separate them. She held on to this since this was all that she now had.

The road she walked represented all the unexplained disparities in life. Somewhat of a shamble of a place, no proper paved roads but yet expensive American left hand driven vehicles passed her as she walked. This was a British Overseas territory. The laws here observed driving on the left hand side of the road. Therefore these left hand driven vehicles made no sense to her at all. It was all symbolic of her life now. It was making no sense at all!

Her thoughts were unexpectedly jarred by a high pitched voice which came from behind a rather tall fence.

"Hello, I'm Jessica. You must be Miss Palmer's daughter Erica." Everyone on this island seems to know everyone and everything! Erica thought but responded with an artificial warm, "Hi, yes I'm Erica."

"You'll like it here. It's quiet and peaceful and the beach is lovely." Jessica added. Do I look as though I am lacking for peace? Erica thought and went on thinking that training for beach bum accreditation is probably done on this island since it seemed to be the only pastime. Everyone was recommending it. Erica mused inwardly but said, "Yes, I will just love it here." Erica watched as Jessica looked her up and down. Next Jessica came out from behind her high fence and started to walk alongside her.

"This is my home and my mother is one of the primary school teachers." Did I not guess that that was where she lived? Did I need a tour guide? Erica thought irritability. This was the last thing she wanted at this time, a chatty, self-adhesive, self-imposed friend!

"Do you like playing squash?" Before Erica could answer Jessica rattled on, "I am the under 18 champion, no one has been able to beat me." Jessica beamed. "Probably because no one ever physically tried." Erica muttered under her breath but a bit too loudly.

"What was that? You want to try?" Jessica asked, looking at Erica in an alarmed way.

"Sorry I am not a Squash player. I am into Karate." Erica firmly stated.

"That's a mean archaic sport. I don't like fighting." Jessica said.

"Well different strokes for different folks." Erica replied and secretly thought that she really didn't want conversation of a personal nature so she changed the subject and asked, "Are there really only two shops on this island?"

Jessica proudly replied, "Yes. Just two but you can go over to Providenciales or into Miami. Next time I am going to Miami shopping you can come along."

Judging from the one shop she had seen so far, Erica knew that not Providenciales but definitely Miami would be where she would be going to shop. "How are flights scheduled for flying to Miami?" Erica asked the island self-appointed information rep.

"You get one from here straight there if you know the pilot." Jessica said with a coy smile. "Or there is one from here to Providenciales then another to Miami. You could also go over by boat and then fly to Miami. It's fab! You get a fun day to spend, spend, spend, and spend!" Jessica said excitedly.

"Sounds like an adventure just to go to shop." Erica said sardonically. "Well it all depends on how you look at it. Flying gives me a chance to get close to the man of every girl's dream, here on North C." Jessica said this with a swoon in her eyes as though she would faint.

"Ethan! Ethan Avery!" She drooled on, as though she was about to salivate. "Ethan has his pilot's license and he flies. He can also skipper a boat to Miami." She informed Erica.

As they passed a recess of rundown houses Jessica pointed to one and proudly said, "My Haitian lives there."

"Your Haitian? What exactly do you mean by your Haitian?" Erica asked alarmed.

"She is the woman who cleans and washes for us. She is our servant. There are many Haitians running over here now, the place is getting filled with them!" Jessica said.

Was this place revealing its true identity very quickly through the mouth of this child? Erica could not believe that at this point of time that the perceived well-off could think of others in such an unflattering light and possibly treat them in the same way. The more this girl talked the more her words seemed to condemn her as a person to be avoided.

"Guess you will be coming to the high school with me or are you eighteen yet?" Could this jabber mouth not see that she was a full-fledged woman? Erica angrily thought.

"Sorry Jessica but I am past high school. It's college for me now."

"I'll still see you because the high school and the college are one and the same." Jessica smartly enlightened Erica.

"What do you mean?" Erica asked with unease.

"Not enough of us children here for a separate college, only twelve so you get college tuition in the high school alongside everyone else." Jessica said with a tinge of glee in her voice.

"Just what I need." Erica let her thoughts slip out too loudly in this mournful statement which Jessica heard.

"Well are you too high and mighty to mix?" Jessica asked in an upset way. Actually yes, Erica wanted to say yes. Yes. I am past the childish ways of high school. I was moving on nicely into adulthood with the man of my dreams, when I was chopped down. However putting restraint on her lips, Erica looked at Jessica said nothing and continued walking.

Jessica gave Erica an entire run down on almost everyone on the island. Erica learned that Avery Miller owned a Cay, an entire island for himself! Jessica said that he lived in an expensive property. He also owned four small island hopping planes, Jessica called them, two yachts and a barge. Jessica said that he was generous to the school and donated books and equipment. His wife had died and he never remarried. His only son Ethan was his only family here but he had many more relatives in England.

John Humphrey Jessica said was a weasel who told Avery Miller everything that went on with the workers in the company. She said that he stayed on there since he could not work anywhere else. Her father Jessica emphasized had said this. He and John never got on since her father was cheated out of a managerial position by John. John, like all the other expats was applying to become a 'belonger' since his residence permit will soon expire. Jessica said scornfully. No doubt what caliber affection she held for John Humphrey and there was definitely some bad blood there between her father and John.

Erica had learned a new term today amongst other things as she was not familiar with the word 'belonger.' It somehow had a bad connotation to it and she hoped that her mother's two year contract would be just that and no more! Shorter if at all possible!

"Oh, my Lord! You've kept me talking so much that I did not realize that I have walked you almost to your door! Now I will have to walk all that way back to mine!" Jessica exclaimed to Erica with blame and surprise.

"I kept you talking?" Erica felt that there was nothing in the world that could ever keep this girl's mouth closed.

"Yes, you wanted to know so much. Anyway see you at school." Jessica said as she turned back and walked briskly away. Erica felt that if she never saw that girl again it would be too soon! "Bye." Erica replied.

As Erica neared her new home thoughts of Sidney Durr returned to her head and she could not get him out. She doubted that, that text was from her dad. He was never sentimental with them. His usual texts more so to Emma than to her, never were 'mushy, lots of love,' as this new one ended, "Never!" Erica said aloud. That text Erica concluded was not written by her father and she was determined more than ever now to find out what was happening even if her mother had given up.

Erica opened the door and called, "Emma please can I see your phone?" The usual protest came. "What for?" Emma queried.

"I want to read that text from dad." Erica firmly replied.

"Why?" Emma asked in objection.

"Just give me the damn phone!" Erica said annoyed. She had had enough for the day. Surprised by Erica's use of language, Emma passively handed over the phone. Erica read the text again, twice over.

"Emma did you text him back?"

"No Signal." Emma replied. Erica took the phone to her room with Emma following. Erica typed a new message which said, 'Dad are you ok? Call us and let us know where you are, call please, don't text.'

Erica held the phone through the window and hit send.

"Why are you putting the phone through the window?" Emma asked, with wide eyed amazement.

"To get a signal" Erica said. "Here you go, take back your phone and thanks. If he calls you let me or mum know immediately."

"I want dad to come home." Emma said with a tinge of sadness in her voice. "I just want him home." Erica also wanted to say 'me too' but she just couldn't, despite the turmoil she was feeling. She felt restrained by all that was happening. Her emotions were all under arrest.

A sense of hopelessness crept over Erica. She looked around their new home which thankfully was furnished tastefully. A radio was on a table in the hallway. She turned it on. She needed a distraction. Like the phone there was no signal. She could not pick up a station but did this island have a radio station? She wondered.

"Mum is there a radio station in this place?"

"I guess so do a search." Karis said.

"What do you think I have been doing?" Erica snapped.

"Don't be rude it just probably needs an aerial." Karis tried to reassure.

With a sigh Erica gave up. She switched the radio off and retreated to the back of the house to the highly over-rated beach. She could see in the distance barges and boats sailing by. As she walked on, suddenly she heard a voice say, "Hi again neighbour." The voice came from between the palm trees. Erica paused and saw that it was that Evan boy!

This time there was no harm to speak since she was tired and exhausted from being angry and horrible, therefore she said, "Evan you seem to get around and change roles quickly, pilot, sports car driver and now beach bum. What is your main role?"

"I am very versatile but not with my name. I am actually Ethan." He replied with a smile.

"Sorry I have to try to remember all the new people and new names." Erica apologized but she really wanted to forget Ethan. Her focus and center of life was left behind. It all rested back home with Gerardo. She felt that she couldn't care less if he was Evan or Ethan. He wasn't Gerardo!

"Settling in as yet? Unpacking started?" Ethan went on cheerily. Why these people can't leave me alone in my gloom, Erica inwardly thought. How will she answer him? Leave me alone. Go away or should she give a social response and pray that he goes. She chose the latter.

"I really should be getting back since I do have a lot of unpacking to do as you said."

"Ok see you around." Ethan said, as he slipped back into the palm trees and walked away. That worked. It worked! Erica rejoiced. Just then her phone rang. "Hello mum."

"Where are you Erica?" I am behind the house along on the beach."

"Your dad just text Emma that he is ok," her mother said. Before Erica could speak, Karis went on, "Hope you are satisfied now. He is fine and not missing." With no chance of Erica getting in a word, Karis proceeded to give her daughter more direct instructions.

"I want you to please come home and start unpacking. Try to get yourself settled here in our new home." Karis hung up. Erica felt that she had just been given a prison sentence.

Chapter Twenty-One

Vanessa had spoken to Hanif about Karis' call. Hanif Osman had been in business with Sidney Durr for several years. His investment supported the company to grow into an extremely lucrative and viable shipping line. He however was now troubled by the developing situation. He had told Vanessa that he was closing the office for a couple of days in order to have an audit conducted. He had given her those days off as part of her paid holiday.

She was loyal and trusted but neither he nor Sidney made her party to the 'finer details' of their business affairs. She had information on a need to know basis. He had done more for Vanessa than he had for most of the other girls along the way. She was different from most. She was intelligent, tall and graceful and had lots of promise. He liked her and had matched her up with his youngest brother Omar Newman.

Omar and Vanessa had moved to Panama City at Hanif's request. Omar did some related shipping work but not a lot. To keep business in the family Hanif had told him. Many people however were unaware of the family link. Hanif also knew that Omar was somewhat indolent so demands were kept at a minimal. Sidney himself although not a blood relation was as close as family could be but his wife Karis was a 'thorn in the flesh.' She did not conform.

Hanif remembers why he had teamed up as a behind the scenes business partner with Sidney. He needed connections with a shipping line. Sidney needed financial backing to make his company sustainable. They shared a symbiotic business relationship. It was working well for several years but now trouble seemed to be looming. Hanif did not like the unpredictable. Like Sidney, he always loved to be in control.

Hanif now made a quick call to his brother.

"Omar I have not heard from Sidney and there are things here which need to be arranged." Hanif spoke sharply into the phone.

"I got a text from Sidney saying he needed time to clear his head from the divorce. He damn well knows that I don't like this text message business. I tried calling him and all I bloody-well get is his voice mail!"

"Bloody fool!" Omar said and carried on, "He has been divorced for years only the written paper has now made it official. Especially when he's in Guyana, who could have been more a single man than Sidney? So who's he trying to fool with all this sentimental rubbish?"

Omar was not one for sparing words and it was clear that he did not favour Sidney Durr. Jealousy lurked since he felt that Sidney was too close to Hanif his older brother.

"Get your ass down here now! Your skillful forging is needed ASAP." Hanif gave Omar these orders and hung up the phone. Hanif had an underlying motive for getting Vanessa to report Sidney as missing. While Sidney was losing himself in his so called depression of his divorce, Hanif felt that he could go for the jugular, to attack fiercely in order to have no doubt about winning.

Hanif had been planning with the help of Omar to take full control of Sidney's business. He could now put this takeover bid into motion. Omar on the other hand was unsure as to whether Hanif did not truly know where Sidney Durr was and what had happened to him. Omar had his doubts.

However Omar was happy to help Hanif take over. He longed to be running the business since lately Sidney did not want to 'play by their rules'.

Chapter Twenty-Two

Doubts were surfacing everywhere even over in Guyana. In Morgan Hawkins' mind there were many misgivings about what was being done and he candidly voiced them. "What if we get caught?" Morgan cautiously asked Jake.

"Relax, enjoy the morning. Isn't it going to be great to have a 'real house' to live in? Won't it be really super having a swimming pool, sauna and the works?" Jake's reply was both jubilant and casual while he looked at pictures of the new house shrugging off Morgan's worrying questions.

Morgan was the thinker. He was not rash but level headed. He was an Environmental Health Officer. He worked very closely with McLloyd Mining and he was only too aware of all the rules which were broken within the gold mining industry. In his country the blind eye approach was often used within the mining community.

Sitting with Jake made him remember how very lucky he was to have gotten the post which meant having to inspect mining companies to ensure that people's living and working surroundings were safe, healthy and hygienic. At McLloyd Mining he did more than inspect. He went very deep whenever he could to get more information.

He had the right training for the job. He had good spoken and written skills and excellent expertise for dealing with people from all backgrounds. His degree and training also gave him a good level of scientific understanding to be able to recognize risks and work with the mining community to promote safety. However in reality very little of this happened.

In this regard he had a very tough job on his hands since following safety guidelines meant care for workers and involves a cost for the right equipment and following set procedures which many investors were not prepared to spend money on. McLloyd was one of them. They did not want to spend. They ignored or broke all of the rules but he got paid. He also had his own agenda. His mind quickly now shifted back to the situation at hand.

"Does it not worry you that all is not going as it should?" Morgan asked this next perturbing question which seemed to appear irrelevant to Jake.

"Morgan you think too much it will all work out. You'll be basking in Florida soon, not to mention the cash sums some of which have already been put into your off shore bank account." There was excitement in this reply. No fear or worry was being shown by Jake.

Morgan's inside knowledge of McLloyd Mining gave him leverage. He now wiped his doubting aside and concurred that Jake was right. They were getting what they had set out to achieve. It was only a matter of time before it all came together fully.

"We both need to get moving." As Jake said this he stood up from sitting on the old tattered sofa and reached for his car keys. He could not stay any longer talking. He had to return to his post at the old mining plot. "Are you handling things properly out there?" Morgan worryingly asked Jake.

"Yes I am." Jake said calmly.

Jake had taken time off from work to 'handle things' since he was paid as a casual worker. Wages were dependent on the hours he worked. He was a heavy duty operator and he handled the machinery with skill but wages were very low to the point of being insulting. Exploitation was seriously at work within his country. The authorities seemed to be doing very little to stop it so Jake knew that he had to fight to survive. This was clearly what he was doing right now.

However before he returned to the old mining plot he had to make a stop. He drove to a side street where anything could be had for the right price. He bought a supply of several not very legal sedatives, drugs and alcohol. This mix was ideal. It promoted absolute blankness and accelerated submission. This cocktail never failed to work. He could always depend on it to deliver. He knew that this time would be no exception. The potent mix delivered with perfection would do the trick. They were worth the money paid.

Jake was clearly mindful that he still had to exercise caution since it was easy to overdose and that just won't do at this time. Some measure of alertness was required for the tasks which remained unfinished. It was so evident that when taken ecstasy was apparent but the dosing and timing had to be precise. This euphoria could all well also turn to deadly aggression. It had to be managed and controlled.

He was fully aware that Morgan's level of education above his gave Morgan the authority to be 'the thinker' but Jake knew that his own real education was just as potent. His had been acquired in practical terms, from being on the street. He had been to the 'University of Life.'

He knew that he was capable of handling the things assigned to him. He had seen how the cocktail of drugs and sex impaired reasoning and allowed coercion to work. He was in 'this' no matter what. They just needed one last big score before they could end it all. Just the one last score but it was not dependent on his timing and brawn. It was not his call. He had to wait for the orders. To be told when.

Chapter Twenty-Three

Back in Panama City the Gagnon brothers as usual were successful in getting the visa applications granted for the two girls. Their clerk took care of everything at the embassy. The girls happily went off to commence work with a promise of new opportunities.

"Jim we never fail to pull it all off, do we?" Lee said over breakfast. Before Jim could respond Lee hurriedly said, "Jim I noticed that before they left the two girls were asking you about the other girl. What did you tell them?"

"For Christ sake Lee why are you interrogating me?" Jim retorted crossly.

"Well my learned colleague we need to have our stories right!" Lee firmly stated. "So answer my question."

"Ok I told them that she had to be taken to the hospital during the night. After she was treated I dropped her off at the airport B & B because she had decided that she wanted to return to Guyana and that's that!" Jim answered crossly.

"Thank you." Lee said in a cynical voice.

As Gerardo slowly walked over to the main house thoughts of what was happening back in Guyana crowded his mind. How things were progressing was important. He wanted to get out of this menial job. He was destined for better than this he thought.

Today he knew that he had to face a day of cleaning. He never looked forward to mornings when the brothers were at the property after a night of entertaining ladies. As he walked his phone was vibrating and he noticed the numerous missed calls and texts from Erica. He would humour her today he thought. He would send her a text message. He believed that that should keep her 'pleased' for a few days, he reasoned. He'll tell her that he has buried himself in his work since she has left. That actually won't be a lie since the Gagnon brothers did create a greater demand on his time. He would text her later.

He had now reached the main house. "What the hell?" Gerardo almost shouted as he entered the house. A trail of muddy foot prints went right through the house. He muttered again to himself, "What the hell have those two been up to?"

"Good morning Gerardo." Lee Gagnon said walking into the room. Without a word of apology or explanation for the filthy floor Lee went on to say, "Can you get on to this immediately?" Looking at Gerardo and pointing at the dirty floor.

"We're out to the city now and then lunch. We will also need you to get the shopping for tonight's dinner party. Josephine will be in to do the cooking. Come on Jim. Let's get a move on." Lee called out as he took the keys to the Jaguar and walked out the door.

Gerardo watched as they left wondering what they had been up to, to make such a muddy mess. They were a strange lot. Probably out burying money to avoid taxes, no doubt he thought. Gerardo cleaned up the place and took the shopping list and went off to do Lee's bidding.

He did his usual 'flash around town' to flaunt his handsome physique and impress the girls as he drove *black beauty*. He parked the car and just then he remembered Erica's numerous messages and calls. He went into the quiet café where he used to meet her outside of and wrote the simple text message as from before to Erica. It said, 'You will always be in love with me. We were made for each other. Remember that babe.' Gerardo hit the send button. He then deleted all of the messages to and from Erica while his eyes did a survey of the café.

Just then he got up and deliberately bumped into a young girl carrying some packages.

"Oh dear, I'm very sorry, please let me get those." This was Gerardo's statement to the unassuming girl, who dressed somewhat like a tom boy. "Its fine, I've got it." The girl quickly responded and vehemently resisted. "No, please don't." She strongly said. Gerardo was not deterred. He needed an amusement, a distraction. A replacement for Erica would 'fit the bill.'

"Come on what's your name? I've been watching you drink your latte and those lips just look so exquisite. Come on at least tell me your name." He didn't use his usual line, 'Have I seen you somewhere before?' In reality he did distinctly feel that he had, as he stared at her.

"So what's the pretty name? I would really like to get to know you better." Gerardo sly said.

"The name's Sofia." Filled with disgust Sofia hurriedly turned and walked out of the café. She got on to the first bus which stopped. Her head was spinning. She could not believe the arrogance of that Gerardo!

She had waited in that very same café with Erica when he picked Erica up from outside, for one of their 'romantic encounters.' It was inconceivable how Erica could love this jerk! Sofia remembered that she had told Erica that Gerardo was a predator. She was guessing back then but her assumptions were now confirmed!

In her anger and surprise she did not realize that one of the waitresses from the café had got on the bus after her. The young girl now seated behind her leaned over and said, "I can see that, that creep just upset you." Sofia turned her head to listen and agree.

"That's his ruse to any young girl he takes a fancy to so don't worry. I'm Marrianna." She scribbled on a piece of paper and said, "Getting off at the next stop. Here take my number, call me. My mother works for the same people Gerardo works for." Sofia took the paper and said, "Thanks." What should she do with this information? Could Erica handle hearing it?

Chapter Twenty-Four

Josephine was an excellent cook. She always prepared exquisite dinners for Jim and Lee Gagnon. She had worked for them for several years and could serve up any of the African, Spanish and Native American dishes which made up Panamanian cuisine. The Gagnon brothers loved her cooking. This night was to be outdoor dining and the brothers had invited four prominent socialites.

The brothers were direct and to the point with staff and Josephine didn't mind since she got on with what she was paid to do. She knew that she was being underpaid but this was her third job which helped to pay the bills. She knew where she stood with the Gagnons but their caretaker Gerardo was a worry. His several insistent advances made her threaten to report him to the Gagnons but still he was as sly as a fox.

Pedro had worked with Gerardo and had prepared the gazebo on the far side of the grounds for this outdoor dinner. It looked spectacular with the candle lights and the starry sky above. At these times for an outside dinner, Pedro was brought in by Lee Gagnon to help clean up the grounds before and after the party.

Pedro was in his early twenties and already had numerous children from different women. Like Josephine he held down numerous odd jobs to make ends meet. Pedro once said that being a ladies man was very costly. Gerardo felt that he was very irresponsible for having so many children. Gerardo didn't think too much of Pedro. Josephine however knew that both Pedro and Gerardo were typical men of their cultures, womanisers. Josephine felt that Pedro and Gerardo's ambition in life was to live to one hundred and then be shot by a woman's husband.

These Gagnon dinner parties were loathed by Gerardo. He had to help Josephine serve. That meant dressing in a butler's uniform. He despised the uniform. He felt like a servant but knew that he was far better than this. He looked forward to the time when he could soon burn the filthy uniform! That time was in sight.

Lee and Jim looked resplendent in their evening suits. The suits however masked their true personal identity. They surveyed the dishes which Josephine had prepared. They delighted in their choice of foods. The starter would be *Empanadas*, pastry filled with vegetables and shrimp. Followed by the main course of *Corvina Con Salsa de Maracuja y coco;* sea bass with passion fruit and coconut sauce. Topped off with the desert of *Pastel de tres leches,* a fruit cake soaked in cream.

This was to be the night where deals were made. They had a few of their accounts held at the bank of the manager who was a frequent dinner guest. Their parliamentary representative and two potential shareholders husband and wife Timothy and Susan Grant were also invited. The Grants were looking to build a portfolio in the gold mining industry which the Gagnons held sizeable shares in back in Guyana.

"Lee if we pull this off and the Grants buy in we get forty percent this time for the introduction and ten percent per year on yields. Not bad at all, more than the cost of a night's dinner." Jim Gagnon remarked to Lee with a broad smile.

"We must tread cautiously. Has anyone done a background check on the Grants? Who we let in is important." Lee warned.

"Mr Big as you well know is responsible for all checks and he has given the Grants the green light." Jim stated emphatically.

"Mr Big is slipping up if we go by that sick girl we just got. We don't need liabilities and certainly no more trouble." Lee stressed. Jim looked at him and thought that Lee's cynical comments were souring the mood so he changed the subject to the weather and put on some classical music.

Gerardo was responsible for ushering the guests in and taking them to the outside Gazebo. He welcomed the investment banker first and thought that one day soon he would have his very own butler and roles would be reversed. He would be sipping cocktails and somebody else would be serving him. He waited in the kitchen for the arrival of the other guests.

Pedro waited there also for the time to commence the clearing away. His face looked very unhappy. He was telling Josephine that he had received a court summons for non-payment of child support. Gerardo listened but was bent on ignoring him. Pedro had borrowed money from him and had not yet repaid it. He therefore interrupted Pedro's conversation with Josephine.

"How's life treating you Josephine? Is that daughter of yours still living at home? Saw her today." Gerardo tried to make light conversation but Josephine it seemed had not forgiven him from when he made indiscrete advances towards her.

"Let's keep to our work and let's not talk about me. There's the doorbell, get to it Gerardo." Josephine ordered. Gerardo looked at Josephine contemptuously and walked on.

"Good evening. Welcome to the Gagnon's residence." Gerardo said, with a false happy smile.

"We are Tim and Susan Grant." The Grants said cheerily.

As Gerardo led them to the others he could not help but feel that he had met Susan Grant before even though he was certain he hadn't. There was something about her. Her large black eyes and high cheek bones, all seemed too familiar. Leaving them with Lee, he quickly returned to answer the door for the final guest.

The night progressed and Josephine's superb dishes were enjoyed by all. The guests wandered around and remarked on the beautiful grounds surrounding the Gagnon's estate. Jim was in his element. He was a good orator and should have been a politician. His charisma ensured that he sealed deals and got what he wanted.

In Jim's mind the Grants were buying in hook line and sinker. He was sealing the deal and ensuring that he and Lee's retirement fund was healthy. Investment in gold mining was lucrative but all the side perks which came along as bonuses were great. The Grants especially Tim however seemed a bit too interested in labour costs, the workers and environmental work safety.

"Cheap labour means more profits for you the investors. We do operate within safety guidelines and are inspected regularly by Environmental Health." Jim stated.

Jim tried to reassure the Grants that the gold mining company which they were affiliated with was above board. Silently Jim thought that possibly they should stay clear of the Grants. They seemed like too much of champions for the rights of the underdog and environmental activists.

"Hope that you are not thinking that Tim is interrogating you. Pay no attention to him. In the sixties he was a 'peace and love hippie.' He still has visions and flashbacks of saving the world." Susan Grant said glibly. They all started laughing. Susan hoped that Jim's apparent fears of 'letting them in' had been alleviated by her remarks. It was important that they gained the Gagnon's trust.

"Sir shall I serve coffee and or tea now?" Josephine asked Jim.

"Not yet. Everyone is enjoying the wander round the grounds."

"This is a lovely property with such mature gardens. You must value the workers that look after it all." Susan complimented Jim and Lee.

"Yes, Gerardo does an excellent job of it all." Jim boasted.

"You on your own keep these massive grounds in such good shape?" Tim Grant asked while looking at Gerardo, who stood close by waiting on the Gagnons beck and call.

"Indeed I do." Gerardo really wanted to say, 'I do it all for very little thanks and pay but what the heck it'll soon be over!' Tim Grant was looking at Gerardo as Gerardo was staring at Susan. Gerardo therefore broke his gaze on Susan Grant but could not help but feel that he had met her somewhere before.

All had seemed to be going well and the night was drawing in. Lee started to usher the guests from the leisurely stroll back towards the main house. Pedro commenced his duties of clearing away.

"What's that wonderful smell that garnishes the air? It's so heavenly." Susan asked, taking in deep breaths of the fragrant air.

"I'll show you the divine aroma which is being emitted in the night air." Jim said proudly with a smile. He recommended that they end the walk by heading around the back of the green house where there was an abundance of the Brunfelsia Gigantean plants, more commonly referred to as Lady of the Night. Jim loved this highly fragrant South American shrub with its creamy-white two inch flowers. It emitted an intoxicating fragrance that intensified at night.

Pointing to rows and rows of the Lady of the Night Jim Gagnon proudly said, "This is the heady fragrance which fills the night air. Isn't it just lovely?"

Just then breaking the solemnity of enjoying the fragrant air, the ring tone of a mobile could be loudly heard. Who could be lurking in the not too distant foliage? Gerardo thought.

"Gerardo, would you please check on who maybe behind those bushes?" Jim asked.

"No I'll check." Lee quickly interjected and commenced walking. Pedro also started walking off in the direction of the ringing but was swiftly ushered back to his tasks by Lee.

"It's probably just teenagers playing pranks." Lee assured the group as the phone continued its ringing. As Lee walked off everyone remarked on how odd it seemed. The phone kept ringing and then abruptly stopped.

Lee returned looking very flustered and said, "Didn't see a soul, they probably ran off." Lee tried to explain.

Inwardly Lee was thinking that sometimes Jim had shit for brains. Why the hell did he have to walk the guests past the green house and why the hell didn't Mr Big do his job properly this time? No girls were allowed mobile phones!

Chapter Twenty-Five

In the silence of the morning Sofia was awakened by her parents knocking on her bedroom door to remind her that she had a dentist appointment at 9 O'clock. She had over slept. She had had a very restless night and did not finally get to sleep until well after 2 am. As she showered she remembered what rather who had kept her awake, thoughts of Gerardo and Erica.

Sofia loved days when her only problem was deciding on wearing baggy jeans or trousers. She thought affectionately about Erica. How Erica would say that 'the very heart of romance was uncertainty,' when they would talk about not knowing much about Gerardo and where Erica's romance with him would lead. Now Sofia did not know what to do about her knowledge of Gerardo.

Marrianna the waitress from the café had filled Sofia in on some of the 'gaps' on Gerardo. There were more than gaps. These were deep chasms! How could she tell Erica that he was not a well-groomed rich and dashing handsome 'prince?' That he did not own *black beauty*, the car Erica admired but that Gerardo was paid to 'groom her.' Seriously she thought, how could she tell Erica that he is just the chauffeur and caretaker for the rich? What about coming on to her? Erica would never believe that Gerardo would even give her a glance!

Sofia knew in her heart that she had to tell her best friend the truth but did she have the courage to do it? Surely it would destroy Erica. What if Erica killed herself after she told her of Gerardo's deception? Her head was beginning to hurt and she quickly rushed down stairs to grab some breakfast before the dentist. Maybe she thought that after the dentist she won't be able to speak and so would not be able to talk to Erica. Her dilemma about what to do came to an end by her mother's questions to her.

"How's Erica settling in her new home?" Susan Grant asked her daughter. "I haven't heard from Karis as yet. You must miss Erica terribly." Sofia's mother paused as she looked at Sofia's face which certainly looked unhappy. "Are you feeling ill Sofia?" Her mother asked worriedly.

"I am just thinking about the dentist's appointment. Erica is just fine." Sofia said in a rushed but reassuring voice. Who was she reassuring? Neither she nor Erica was fine.

"How did the dinner go last night?" Sofia tried to shift the conversation away from her and Erica by asking this question.

"It was good. The food was amazing." Susan replied.

"The butler couldn't keep his eyes off of your mother." Sofia's father piped in as she looked up from her cereal.

"Yes. I did feel somewhat uncomfortable by his constant gazes. What was his name again?" Susan asked her husband.

"I've actually sealed it in my mind. It was Gerardo." Tim stated in a sneering way. Gerardo strikes again! Sofia thought.

"See you guys later." She kissed them both and quickly went off to brush her teeth again before leaving for her dental appointment.

Susan now turned to her husband and asked, "What did you make of the Gagnon brothers?" Before he could answer she went on saying, "I thought you were going to give the game away with too much deep questioning.

"They are too arrogant and self-assured." Tim's answer was obviously emotive. "I know what our main objective is but it is more than our simple trap to expose money laundering which is very closely in our sights. Its moral purpose is also foremost in my mind." Tim lamented.

"We have to tread cautiously if we are to win their trust." Susan replied, tapping him on the shoulder.

"Their property has a vast spread of immaculate grounds. Hasn't it? The Lady of the Night plants had such an exquisite aroma, uhmmm. I can still remember the fragrance." Susan said as though she could still smell the fragrant plant.

"Yes indeed Susan." Tim agreed.

"The grounds were amazing but what did you make of that ringing phone?" Before waiting for an answer Susan rushed on. "That was very strange considering that the grounds despite the hedges are enclosed by a fairly high fence. Don't you agree?" Susan said questioningly.

"Did you not notice the way Lee Gagnon brushed that Gerardo fella aside and turned the other one away from searching? Then hurriedly went off to investigate it himself? Something's not right there." Tim said inquisitively.

"Well we could get it subtly looked into Tim." Susan said.

"Exactly what would we be subtly accusing the Gagnons of? Having a discarded mobile? Any type of subtle snooping may expose us. Tim cautioned.

"Putting my professional thinking aside and using my female intuition, I still think that there is more to that ringing mobile than meets the eye." Tim hugged his wife and laughed at her final explanation.

Chapter Twenty-Six

Meanwhile back on North Caicos, Karis could see that Erica was going through all the motions of living but she knew what her daughter was experiencing was not life. It was just not death. Sensing her daughter's emotional decay, Karis had several conversations with Erica about her education on the island.

The summer holiday was quickly coming to an end and her mother now admitted that she had not been given enough information about Erica's college provision. She said that she was sorry. Erica could see that her mother was under pressure from the divorce. Unfortunately in some ways she and Emma got left behind. They were not in the finer details of things.

Karis openly gave Erica some choices. She could attend college in Miami where she could get the selection of subjects which she wanted and return to the island each weekend. She could return home to Panama City and go to the college which she had originally chosen.

Should she go back home, then Karis would ask Tim and Susan Grant if she could stay with Sophia. Another option was to remain on the Island but go to College on the Mainland. She would be flown there each day by Ethan Miller. It would be forty minutes flying time. Despite feeling that she instantly knew what her decision would be, she somehow felt some sadness and could not explain it to herself.

This could not be in any way easy for her mother she thought but she was considerate enough to give her choice. She also knew that her mother would miss her dreadfully if she left. Even though Emma was difficult and could be a right pain in the donkey, she felt guilty about thinking about leaving her too.

"Please think about all of the options. You don't have to answer immediately there is still time." Karis said very softly with a tinge of sadness. "I love you very much and I want what's best for you. That's all that is important to me, your happiness." Her mum concluded.

"I love you too mum. I will think about all of the options and then let you know what I decide." Erica told her mother and then went on to say, "I am going to my first Karate lesson with Ethan Miller. He is in charge of the Karate club here. Will see what he is made of today. See you later." Erica hugged and kissed her mother goodbye.

When Erica reached the Karate club house she heard a strangely recognizable voice.

"Hi Erica, Ethan is going to be teaching me Karate today also." It was unmistakably Jessica Winsome!

"I thought that you only liked Squash?" Erica smilingly asked.

Erica certainly knew it was obvious why Jessica had now suddenly taken a liking to Karate. This was one of the reasons why she needed to make her decision quickly. She was grown up now and childish rivalry had no place in her world. However deep inside she felt uncertainty looming. Gerardo or family, which would she choose?

Chapter Twenty-Seven

Reflections of the dinner party crossed Gerardo's thoughts and he just could not get Susan Grant's face out of his mind. He did the usual cleaning up and suddenly remembered that ringing phone that was behind the green house hedge. He also thought that as the butler for the evening and the perceived house servant, Lee was too instantly willing to do the task which would have been assigned to him or to even allow Pedro to do so by investigating the ringing phone in the bushes.

He felt that Lee was edgy and was lying about teenagers frequenting the area. There were never ever any problems in that area with vandals or pranksters. The property enjoyed an excellent suburban position in a respected area with high fencing.

His further recollection and evaluation of the night's events were interrupted by Lee as he entered the room and said to Gerardo, "We need a few items bought from the pharmacy. Last night has left us very tired. When Josephine is finished take her home and get these." Lee said and handed the pharmacy list to Gerardo.

"Will do but you need to transfer some money to the household account because the funds are getting low."

"What the heck have you been spending? Thought I topped that up not too long ago?" Lee retorted.

"The bank statements are in the study you can see what I have spent." Gerardo really wanted to say a few nasty things to Lee but kept them to himself and went to get the car keys.

When there is a late dinner party Josephine usually spends the night because she doesn't have her own transportation. Pedro on the other hand left around 2 am and drove off in his relic of a car. Pedro just could not afford to replace his car even though it had become a mechanical trouble shooting master piece. The mounting child support bills which he had to pay were preventing him from getting a newer vehicle.

However before he left, he and Gerardo had an intriguing conversation. He had told Gerardo that while alone on the grounds clearing away he took a chance to search in the Sedums behind the green house for that ringing phone. He thought that if he found the phone, it just maybe of good quality and taking it to a pawn broker could help to pay off some of his court charges.

Gerardo had listened closely as Pedro explained that as he hurriedly walked towards the back of the green house he stumbled on unexpected turned up soil which made him trip and fall. His face landed in the adjacent Blue Spruce Sedums. He said that he remembered when Gerardo had planted the beautiful Sedums but they felt like offending enemies on his face as he hastily attempted to find the mysterious phone.

Pedro recounted that his jaw rested painfully within the Sedums on something smooth and rigid. He got to his knees, wiped his face and felt within the Sedums. His fingers made a firm grasp on an object which was unmistakably a mobile phone! He told Gerardo excitedly.

He hurriedly retreated and resumed his clearing away, putting the phone inside his jacket pocket. Passing through the kitchen and entering the laundry he could not help, he looked at the mobile phone. It had a significant number of missed calls on it. He listened to the voice mail messages and quickly read the texts which were all the same. They said and read, 'Jasmin I love you. Where are you? Please, please come back or call me.'

Pedro said that he briefly wondered who Jasmin was. Why was her phone in the Sedums? Should he reveal his find to the Gagnons? While he was thinking all this, Pedro said that this was the moment that Gerardo startled him. Indeed Gerardo recalled being right behind him. Looking over his shoulder and also reading what Pedro was reading on the mobile phone. Gerardo felt that Pedro's find and the messages on the phone were very intriguing and mysterious.

Suddenly the sound of Josephine's voice now brought Gerardo back to the morning's events and from his encounter with Pedro.

"Mr. Lee I am ready to go." Gerardo heard Josephine say as she waited but Lee did not budge.

"Mr. Lee I am sorry but you have not paid me as yet." Josephine knew that Lee had to be urged to part with money so she waited as he now moved to the study to get his wallet to pay her for last night's work.

"Here you go. I will let you know when we next need you." Lee Gagnon handed Josephine the cash. Josephine counted it since often Lee had paid her short of the total amount due. It was correct this time.

"Many thanks Mr. Lee see you again soon." Gerardo observed that Josephine's gratitude was not acknowledged by Lee as he kept on drinking his coffee. Josephine however had grown accustom to the Gagnon's behaviour. She had to earn a living and that was all that was important. She left the house and got into the sedan with Gerardo.

Gerardo knew that Josephine did not want any small talk but could not help himself. Too much silence was building throughout the journey.

"What did you think of that ringing phone?" He asked.

"I mind my own business. I am not paid to think Gerardo but only to cook." Josephine quickly responded to get Gerardo to stop talking.

"You don't give hints do you Josephine? You just tell people off right away! You know what? That's the kind of woman I like, direct and to the point!" Gerardo said and laughed as he pulled up in front of her house. Josephine looked at Gerardo and jokingly said to him, "There's hope for you yet to become a real gentleman. Thanks. See you."

"Bye Jo," was Gerardo's teasing response.

The drive to the pharmacy seemed long since many things crossed Gerardo's mind. He felt uneasy and did not know exactly why. No news from Guyana as yet for the day. The Grant woman's uncanny familiarity still unnerved him and not to mention Lee's suspicious behaviour and oh yes, Pedro's find!

Chapter Twenty-Eight

Time can be a friend or an enemy, sometimes it passes too swiftly or too slowly. Erica had yearned for this day to come. The day when she would be travelling back to Panama City, time had seemed to stand still but now, here she was ready to leave the island. She had made her decision.

She would miss her mother and Emma but they would see her again on college holidays. Sofia and she would catch up. Mr. and Mrs. Grant had agreed to Karis' request of allowing Erica to live with them. This had been Erica's choice. Karis had no doubt that the Grants would take good care of Erica.

As she sat and waited for her flight her father came into her mind. They still had not had a voice call from him and she felt that something bad had happened to him. Maybe now when she got back to Panama City she could speak to the police. Just maybe, she could find out what was happening if only for Emma's sake.

Emma had started to settle somewhat she seemed to enjoy spending time with John's daughter Marie. Marie was ten and her mother had died when she was only one year old. John had never remarried.

Why he spent the rest of his years on this island Erica could not understand. In reality it had taken his wife away from him. Jessica had told Erica that while swimming John's wife had got into difficulty and that there was no life guard to assist her. She drowned. Erica somehow felt John's pain. She had been torn apart from Gerardo. This she knew would now change in a matter of hours.

"Here's Ethan now he's flying the passenger four seater plane, his very own aeroplane. His father gave it to him for his birthday. This four seater will also enable him to carry back all of Erica's things. Erica you can sit up front and be his co-pilot." John said in his usual happy manner.

"I thought that someone else was flying with him, a co-pilot?" Karis asked worriedly.

"There's nothing to worry about Karis." John assured and went on speaking, "Ethan has successfully completed a course requirement of forty hours of flight time. He passed seven written exams. Completing an extensive solo cross-country flight of ten hours and he has successfully demonstrated flying skills to an examiner during a flight test including an oral exam. He is a fine and capable pilot." John reassured and went on in his explanation of Ethan's capabilities. Karis listened attentively.

"He has done seventy hours of flight time to complete his training. The lowest age for a private pilot certificate is sixteen for balloons and gliders and seventeen for powered flight airplanes, helicopters and gyroplanes. Ethan is nineteen." John concluded giving Karis Ethan's extensive resume.

Karis still appeared somewhat worried but Erica was impressed. He never talked about his accomplishments during any of the Karate club training sessions she thought. Erica did not want to admit it but Ethan was very modest and unassuming. She did not want to acknowledge it but if she tried really hard, she also found him to be friendly and handsome. She did not mind at all flying with Ethan since Gerardo was the center of her world and she could not wait to see him.

Karis did not respond to John but she would have felt more at ease if Ethan had a co-pilot who was older. As John and Ethan loaded Erica's luggage there was a tearful goodbye. Emma hugged Erica and Karis hugged all two girls as though she wanted a bond to exist between them irrespective of space and time.

"As soon as you land remember to call me." Karis pleaded.

"That is if you get a signal to receive my call!" Erica said sadly.

"We'll hold the phone outside the window like you did Erica." Emma said tearfully.

"Don't be telling mum my secrets!" Erica joked and then turned to John. "Thank you John. Please look out for mum and Emma."

"I will Erica. I will. Now take good care of Mr. Miller's son." John joked with Erica.

Erica boarded and watched them all from through the window of the plane. Looking through the plane's small window was certainly déjà vu at its best. She next turned her focus to Ethan as he skillfully mastered the controls of the plane. She didn't want to talk to distract him and she didn't want to be rude either so she quietly asked, "Is talking allowed while you fly?"

"Well we can't spend four hours in silence. That would be cruel and inhumane punishment." Ethan said with a smile.

"How did you learn to do so much with so few years? You are nineteen aren't you?" Erica was amazed at Ethan's skills.

"Well my father always told me never to waste one minute of my life because you will never get it back." Ethan firmly stated.

"Well I guess that your father spends lots of time with you." Erica said with a tinge of remorse.

"Well yes and no. Dad is very set in some of his ways so I humour him and do most of what he wants. It's not hurting me to fly a plane and captain a yacht. I actually enjoy it all." Ethan looked at Erica as he said all of this. "Is everything alright with your daughter father relationship?" Ethan next asked Erica.

"Let's not talk about that right now. Can you learn to fly at any age?" Changing the subject was better than wearing her heart on her sleeve.

"If you ever return to North C if you like, I can teach you how to fly. We can start with a glider!" Ethan joked, which Erica got laughing. Their light conversation rambled on and Erica was beginning to feel less guilty about leaving her mother and sister behind.

"You won't think me rude if I get a cat nap?" Erica asked Ethan.

"Make yourself comfortable. You are in good hands." Ethan reassured.

She closed her eyes and thoughts of Gerardo filled her mind. She had missed him so. She drifted off to a light sleep and an image of her father at the theatre with that dark haired lady flashed before her. That woman's face continued to haunt her. She was sure that she had seen her before but where and when? What also was happening with the missing Sidney Durr?

Chapter Twenty-Nine

The mystery mobile phone with messages and pleas to Jasmin Gerardo recalled was a toss-up between himself and Pedro. Not once did the two think of handing it in to the Gagnons. All that mattered was who would keep it for the pawn shop. Pedro again just briefly thought about the voice mails and messages which were all the same, desperate pleas. He was also desperate too. He was extremely frantic to get money to pay his mounting bills.

Gerardo had recognized the origin of the mysterious phone's missed calls. The telephone number was unmistakably a Guyana listing. Gerardo also badly wanted a chance to go behind the Gagnon's greenhouse to do some searching but the brothers were sober at night and watchful by day. He kept to garden maintenance alone but strongly felt that something was up. How really ruthless were the brothers he thought?

With errands to run about town he took the opportunity and went into a back street phone shop and bought a pay as you go card and a cheap mobile phone. This would become his second mobile phone but a very private one. As he was about to leave the shop he bumped into Pedro at the entrance.

"It seems that you are following me around Pedro. That won't do at all." Gerardo said with a smile on his face but followed by a more serious warning. With a stare right into Pedro's eyes he said, "I haven't forgotten that you still owe me money."

"Man give me a break. I ain't forget. Things are tough!" Pedro replied and hurriedly went into the phone shop.

In the distance Josephine who was also running errands for one of her other employers watched Gerardo and Pedro. She had overheard their conversation about the mobile phone and she could not help but think that they were up to no good.

Gerardo left the shop and went for a drive out into the country side. He went to one of the spots where he used to spend time with Erica. Erica! He suddenly recalled that he had received a text message from her today. She was returning to Panama City. Well he wished that he could pick right up from where they had left off but he couldn't. He now thought of Erica with relish but needed to put those thoughts away and concentrate on what he came out there to do.

He stopped *black beauty* placed the SIM card in the phone. "Darn!" He shouted. He had forgotten that it needed to be charged first. He started the car and drove off back to the Gagnon's estate. On reaching, he ran an extension power lead from an obscured outlet and placed it under his bed. He plugged the phone into it and left it to charge. He considered what he really wanted to do next but questioned whether it was wise to do so at this time. Just then his scheming was interrupted by the ringing of his mobile.

"Hello." Gerardo said into the phone.

"Hi be at the berth tonight at 8 pm. You must be there. Don't be late." The instructions were direct and they firmly went on.

"Your help will be needed to manage things." The voice firmly stated.

"Ok, no problem. I'll be there to help." Gerardo assured.

"We are winding things up here in Guyana. The *plan* has been successful and is now concluded. See you soon." The call was ended.

Gerardo felt pleased but there was not even a query as to how he was. It was all cold and emotionless. This removed all doubt as to the urgent need for him to execute his very own *plan* and he would.

Chapter Thirty

At Durr Shipping Omar was feeling brilliant at being a master at forgery. He was able to do exactly what Hanif wanted in terms of processing the back log of shipping contracts where Sidney's signature and a back date was required. Sidney was now absent whether missing or otherwise. Business matters had to be dealt with. Hanif had the authority to appoint another Executive Director. He appointed Omar.

The legal papers for this appointment were sent to Elaina, Hanif's sister in Guyana to get a notary public, her close friend to witness that Sidney Durr's controlling interest had been transferred to Omar. The papers were then posted back to Panama City. It was done. Whenever Sidney chose to return to Panama City if he did, he would be working for Hanif or he could leave. It would be his choice.

"Omar you will be running things from here. Vanessa will remain as secretary; no more of Sidney's moaning. No more of his crisis of conscience. No more complaining about the shipments."

"What if he doesn't take this lying down?" Omar asked his brother. "Well it is simple if he does not want to take it lying down, we can make him. Even that ex-wife and his children, we can really make them all lie down!" Hanif coldly stated and pressed on with his justification for what he was doing.

"There is too much at stake here for Sidney's new moral stance. Whatever he has done with himself has worked to our advantage."

Hanif had long been scheming for Sidney's departure from the business. Having him declared missing had worked out well in the plan.

Omar still was not completely convinced that Hanif was not putting on a façade. Hanif was ruthless and was known to be able to force even angels to recant their vows. So what was really happening here with this Durr affair? What was the truth behind the missing Sidney Durr?

Chapter Thirty-One

Ethan and Erica landed safely in Panama City and the Grants were eagerly waiting to meet them.

"This is Ethan." Erica said.

"You are a very young pilot and a very handsome one too." Susan Grant said to Ethan.

"Hello Ethan, I am Tim Grant. Pay no attention to my wife flirting with a younger man." They all laughed at Tim's greeting.

"Great to meet you all, this must be Sofia the best friend in the world, I was told during our flight." Ethan said, as he smiled at Sofia.

"It's nothing short of amazing what four hours flying can do to Erica's brain and conversation. Yes, she is my best friend too." Sofia said and smiled back. All this did not resolve Sofia's dilemma. What was she going to do with her knowledge of Gerardo? Sofia and Erica hugged as they both picked up some of Erica's luggage.

"Gosh! Did you bring back everything?" Sofia asked, struggling with the weight of the bags.

"Well good luck Erica with your studies. Flight lessons are still on offer. I must be off to check into my hotel. I can't fly until tomorrow afternoon. Nice meeting you all." Ethan turned to walk away.

"Now hold on there Ethan. We have a great big house, large enough to offer you a room for the night. Please accept our hospitality. Please?" Tim Grant said it with such a pleading but insistent voice that Ethan stopped and thought about it and then he said, "That's really very kind of you but I couldn't impose. Besides my hotel room is already booked."

Taking up Ethan's overnight bag from the airport floor Tim said, "We insist." Joined by Susan's, "We won't hear of it. You, staying in a hotel room after bringing Erica this long way, never!" That settled it. Ethan was staying at the Grants.

Somehow Erica and Sofia seemed oblivious to it all. Sofia's mind was impaired by too much information about Gerardo which she did not now know what to do with. Erica's mind was also absent from the conversation. She was tired but very anxious to see 'her Gerardo.'

Chapter Thirty-Two

Meanwhile back at the Gagnons Lee paced up and down like a frantic gazelle staring at his mobile phone. "Jim! Look at this. Who is this?" Lee shouted.

"First if you calm down and let me see your phone then I may be able to answer your questions." Jim looked at Lee's phone.

The text message across the screen said, 'I know what you did and if you don't want the police involved then wait for where and when to leave $50 000.' Jim read the message again but this time out loud.

"You jackass shut up!" Lee whispered with a frantic look on his face.

"Lee there is no one else about but I agree that we must keep our heads on and think this through. Who could know exactly what we have done or do?" Jim asked puzzled.

"Mr. Big, but would Mr. Big try this on?" Lee asked.

"For crying out loud we are attorneys, analytical people." Jim retorted and silently pondered.

"We should be able to work this out." Jim concluded.

"What would Mr. Big have to gain from blackmailing us and besides that's chicken feed being asked for." Lee commented derisively.

Jim looked at Lee and said coldly. "Like it or not, we've got trouble."

"Big trouble!" Lee worriedly added and walked away.

Chapter Thirty-Three

It was now 7:30 pm and Karis waited anxiously for Erica's call. She and Ethan should have landed in Panama City since 4 o'clock. As she reached for her phone her doorbell rang. It was John and Marie. "I thought that you may like a nice pot of stew all freshly made." John said.

"Hello Miss Karis. Is Emma upstairs?" Before Karis could answer Emma came running down to greet Marie.

"Can we go walking down on the beach?" Emma asked excitedly.

"If it is ok with John then it is fine with me." Karis said and John nodded approvingly.

"Please come into the sitting room. Let me take the stew. This is very thoughtful of you." Karis said as she smiled at him. She hadn't prepared one single thing for dinner so this was great.

"I know how it feels when a loved one leaves." John said looking down at his feet and continued, "Have you heard from Erica as yet?" John asked.

"No. I was just about to call the Grants." Karis replied.

"Give it a few more minutes. Give Erica a chance to show her responsibility." John said smilingly.

"Alright John, I will wait." Karis agreed.

Karis and John chatted about everything and nothing. Karis was getting the impression that John was a devoted father and husband before his wife's tragedy. He was doing a great job as a single parent because Marie was a delightful girl. Their conversation was interrupted by Emma and Marie who came running into the room.

"Look mum!" Emma held her mobile phone so close to Karis' face that she was unable to read the text message.

"I can't see to read it so close up." Karis said. Emma gave the phone to Karis and she read the text message out aloud. 'Hello Emma, I will be back in Panama City tonight, coming home by the yacht, say hi to Erica and your mum. Lots of love dad.' The text message read.

"See mum, Erica didn't believe that dad was fine." Emma said loudly.

"Calm down Emma. You can forward the text to Erica." Karis said. "Come on Marie we have to go back outside to get a signal!" Emma said in an anxious state to forward the text to Erica, followed by Marie.

Just then what Emma said about getting a signal on the phone made Karis spring up and go to the window and hold her phone outside. John looked on and smiled. Sure enough, Karis' mobile sent out a notification sound indicating that a message was received.

"It's Erica! John, it's Erica!" Karis read out Erica's message with relief and delight in her voice. 'We reached safely. Very tired will call soon, xx.' "I'm so relieved!" Karis started to cry. John held her to his chest and gently squeezed her.

"I'm sorry but it just all came over me. I couldn't help myself." Karis apologized to John but realized that it felt so strange to be hugged by a man, yet so good. She had forgotten what it felt like to be consoled and held. It certainly did feel good.

After a chat with Karis, John now went outside to get Marie.

"Oh Dad must we go now? Emma and I were having such fun. Please dad, must we go?" Marie asked with a sullen look.

"We must not tire out Karis. She has had a long day." John said. Emma and Marie watched both parents with down in the mouth looks.

"If it is ok with John, we all can have that lovely stew which you brought over and then we can watch a film together." Karis said.

"Fine by me," John responded.

"Yipee! Yipee!" Marie shouted as she held on to Emma and spun her around. They all enjoyed John's stew and Karis was really impressed with his cooking.

"You must give me the recipe for all of the herbs and spices which you have put into this stew. It is very tasty." Karis said.

"Dad is the best cook ever and he also makes great cakes." Marie proudly chimed in.

"Marie, you, Ethan and Avery are my only critics so my reputation can now be tested by Emma and Karis." John said as he looked at Emma and she surprisingly gave a nod of approval for his tasty cooking.

John volunteered to do the dishes and the girls agreed to dry up. Karis was told to sit and sip her coffee. She did and could hear laughter between the girls and John. It all sounded great.

For the first time in a long while she felt some amount of relief from the whirlwind of separation, divorce, relocating home, starting a new job, wrestling with her teenage daughter and pacifying the mood swings of her younger child. Somewhere in that melee of emotions she had lost herself. Who was the real Karis now? She thought.

She wasn't sure but she was certainly feeling good about Emma's relationship with Marie. Emma's ASD symptoms seemed to be abating and she was more actively involved, not just on the side lines observing.

"All finished dried and put away." John proudly said.

"Thank you all very much for washing up and again thank you John for that lovely meal." Karis said while waving a DVD box in her hand.

"What are we watching?" Emma asked. Followed by Marie's sneak peep of the DVD box and with her exclaiming, "It's Phantom of the Megaplex!"

"Oh Marie you gave it away! No desert for you." Karis said tickling her. For the first time in a long while Karis felt some measure of happiness but would it last?

Chapter Thirty-Four

Erica curled up on Sofia's bed up in the attic bedroom. She had been given the downstairs bedroom but wanted to chat with Sofia in her room as they did numerous times before. The girls were happy to be reunited. Sofia had just washed her hair and the long thick black curls framed her face. "Oh my, gosh Sofia!" Erica exclaimed with such alarm that Sofia turned to look behind her in a frightened way. "What's wrong? What is it?"

"With your hair down you look exactly like her. Exactly!" Erica stressed.

"Erica what are you on about? Exactly like who?" Sofia asked bewildered. "That woman my father was with at the theatre!" Erica said.

"It would be really nice if I knew what you were talking about. The long flight must have affected you!" Sofia looked very puzzled.

"Sorry but I forgot I hadn't told you about her before. I was too ashamed to tell you, that the night I went to the theatre with Gerardo I saw my father there also."

"Well you told me that before?" Sofia said perplexed. Erica spoke on. "He was there with a young woman. One who looks exactly like you now that you have your hair let down!" Erica exclaimed.

"Well for sure it wasn't me. Sidney Durr is not my type!" Sofia said smirking.

"Anyway let's forget it. I am waiting for Gerardo to text me. He knows I am back in Panama City. I can't wait to see him to be in his arms." Erica said.

"Don't you think you should 'cool it off' a bit from Gerardo? My parents are now responsible for you. Your mum would be horrified if you got pregnant while living with us." Sofia said all this with a very serious voice.

"Sofia, what's the matter? You sound just like my mother. Even your voice is stern. Thought you were my friend please do not act like a parent." Erica said pouting and then carried on, "Please don't let's fight we are best friends and I missed you." Erica hugged Sofia and this made it even harder for Sofia to tell Erica the truth about Gerardo!

Sofia dried her hair and the girls went down to the sitting room to join the others. Sofia watched as all that Erica did was continuously look at her mobile phone, no doubt looking for messages from Gerardo.

"Ethan what time tomorrow do you leave?" Erica finally pulled herself away from her phone and asked that question.

"I fly out at midday. Thinking of going back?" He asked her jokingly. Erica gave him a cheeky look and excused herself. She went into the Grants' solarium and closed the door. She just had to make a voice call to Gerardo since all her texts had gone unanswered.

"Gerardo, I'm back in Panama City. I miss you dreadfully. Please call or text me." Erica spoke softly into her mobile phone leaving a voice mail message for her only love.

After dinner everyone at the Grants retired to their respective rooms. They all had had a long day. Susan and Tim sat on their bedroom balcony deciding their next move. They felt that they had made some head way with the Gagnons.

Their next move was to get the brothers to link them up directly with the owner of the Guyana mining company. They were getting close but not fast enough. Tomorrow they would call on Lee and Jim and try to get an agreed date to visit the Guyana mine.

Chapter Thirty-Five

The ground floor back bedroom which was now Erica's led out to the Grant's east side of the garden. It meant that in the morning she would get the beautiful rays of the sunlight reflecting on the palm trees and on the elegant bougainvillea which were spread around outside of her room. That beautiful morning scene was however yet to come.

Right now it was dark and she was in the dumps. Just maybe that would all change. She sat sullenly on the patio chair and stared into the darkness. After quite a while of solitary engagement with the night suddenly she felt her phone vibrate. She looked and did not recognize the number but the words in the text were unmistakably Gerardo's!

'Hi Babe glad you're back. Meet me in 20 minutes the usual place.'

Her heart leaped and she ran into her room and quickly dressed. Clothes seemed to be falling off rather than staying on such was her eagerness to be held by her Gerardo. She debated whether or not to tell Sofia about this meeting but decided that this time she won't. Sofia seemed agitated and not her usual self. Probably PMS, Erica reasoned. She'll leave her friend alone this time.

As she was about to sneak off Ethan's voice startled her. "Going somewhere Erica? You look really smart."

She could not believe it, he was becoming a pain and before she could answer he carried on, "I'm taking in some fresh night air. Walking in the garden is quite exhilarating." He said.

The last thing Erica wanted right now was company but she had to humour him. No need in arousing suspicions.

"I'm missing my mum and sister a bit. I just wanted to be away from everyone for a while. Do you mind if I just sit out here alone?" She turned and sat on a nearby garden bench.

"Of course not, I won't intrude on your solitude but just be careful." Ethan looked steadily at Erica and then calmly walked away.

Erica watched as he re-entered the house. She didn't give two monkeys what Ethan Miller thought and beside how would he know where she was going? She thought. Pushing all this to the back of her mind she sped off through the garden dodging the palm trees and exiting through the back gate.

She ran very fast until she reached the side street where Gerardo would be waiting for her. To her surprise *black beauty* was not parked and waiting but Gerardo was sitting in a small green car, a Yaris.

Gerardo smiled as Erica approached the car. It had taken him longer than he had anticipated cleaning himself up but he was still on time. His ribs felt like they had been squeezed by a laundry clothes ironing machine. They may very well be broken, he worriedly thought.

His mind briefly recalled being assured that, 'It would be simple, just helping out.' Nothing could have been further from what actually took place! Gerardo quickly brought his mind back and welcomed Erica.

"Hi babe, how's things been?" Gerardo asked. While opening the car door and quickly sliding his arm around Erica, as she got into the car.

"I miss you, I miss you! I love you so!" Erica was all over Gerardo. "Easy babe, have to drive." Gerardo felt more pain from Erica's hugging his sore body than the need to be able to drive.

"Why did you not text me?" Erica asked accusingly.

"I did babe a couple of times. I just kept getting a report of message not delivered. Guess that there is no good signal out in that place." Gerardo felt that he could get away with this excuse.

"Yeah that's true. Have to hold the phone outside the window out there! So did you miss me and what's with this car?" Erica piped on.

"Of course I did, dreadfully!" He didn't respond about the car.

"While here you're living with the Grants now? Does anyone know that you are not in bed but out with me?" Gerardo cautiously questioned while handing her an opened bottle of cola.

Erica laughed and nibbled his ear. "Not a soul! I'm yours for the night." She was thirsty and drank all of the cola. She nuzzled up against him while he drove for what seemed like an eternity and then he stopped the car.

"This is not our usual spot." Erica glanced around a bit uneasy by the look of the run down vehicles. "Are you sure this is safe to park out here?" Gerardo did not reply but pulled her close and kissed her on the lips.

Erica lost all trepidation about the place and surrendered herself into Gerardo's embrace and advances. Just the touch of his hand made her heart race and react! She felt as though she was floating away. She closed her eyes and gave into this euphoric feeling while savoring every minute of his caresses.

Chapter Thirty-Six

Hours had passed with Erica and Gerardo now returned to *black beauty*. He sped back to the Gagnons. He had been thrown off. The *plan* had to be immediately adjusted. He needed to collect only the essentials and leave as scheduled. He looked at his mobile. Several missed calls. Reports had no doubt gone back on all that had gone wrong.

He pulled the sedan slowly and as quietly as possible into the back entrance to the property. It was 3 am. The brothers would be asleep. As he walked softly to his quarters he contemplated that his new scheme which he only just started could still be pulled off.

He had put in for his holiday as from today. That was part of the original *plan* so there would be nothing strange in him leaving. He lugged out his strong box which was hidden in a recess of his bedroom floor. He had three passports. Now that things had altered the *plan* which one would he use, Guyana, Mexico or Columbia? His thoughts were jarred by his ringing mobile.

"Yes." Gerardo quickly answered with tension in his voice.

"What happened?" Was a direct question coming from a voice which was devoid of emotion.

"What the hell do you think happened? You must have been told. You must know." Gerardo said and was fuming but minding to keep his voice down. He was also livid for what he had endured this night and now also for how he was being callously treated with no question as to how he was.

"All I know is, that this is big trouble. How did you manage to make such a debacle of things?" The angry voice asked.

"All of a sudden everything is my fault, eh? Why did you all not ensure that all was calm, quiet and subdued? That was your end of things." Gerardo stated accusingly.

"It's too late now for blame. How have you dealt with it all? Closure is needed on this. We have to move on quickly but with caution." These were uneasy questions.

"I've fixed things to ensure they do not fall back to us and I hope that you have handled all of the things at your end especially the money." Gerardo stated.

"Things have been done properly. Wrap up your end and leave in keeping with the *plan*. Get over here quickly so that all looks legitimate! Have you heard me?" There was insistence for full closure and assurance in these questions. More brusque orders and questions continued but they were also masking doubts.

"Again I ask, what have you done about shielding us all?" The voice was persistent. There was steely silence. Then Gerardo said resolutely, "Will you stop drilling me. I can handle things you know."

"Who are you to tell me to stop drilling you? Don't try to dismiss me!" The angry voice retorted. Gerardo quietly listened to the tirade. He was in pain and needed to recover not engage in another battle.

Of all the times in the world this was not the time for squabbling and accusations. He held the phone away from his ear as he listened to why he was indebted to them and the need for reassurance.

"Leave no trace that can come back to us." This was a direct order. There was still silence from Gerardo. "Are you listening to me?" The voice was firm and demanding.

"It's all under control. I've fixed everything. Don't worry." Gerardo replied in an exhausted and irritated voice.

He just wanted to get off the phone. He finally said, "I will call you when I am leaving." Without a response Gerardo disconnected the call. He had lots to do and needed to calm down. His adrenaline was still pumping. Flashes of the night streamed across his mind. They were scenes which he wanted to quickly forget.

Chapter Thirty-Seven

It was a rainy grey and cloudy morning. It was one of those days when it would have been great to be at home and in bed. Instead Inspector Frank Milton was faced with managing the Georgetown Police station with a skeleton staff. Three officers had called in sick. The flu was raging and it had no regard for age or gender.

It seemed especially virulent this year and flu inoculations were expensive so not many vulnerable people got them. Well Milton hoped that today crime would just have pity and take a break. His station certainly could not handle any major incidents with so few staff at work.

"Good morning. How may I help you?" Milton asked the clearly distraught woman who had just rushed into the station. He looked at her eyes and the lids were heavy. It was evident that she had been crying and was on the verge of beginning again.

"Please take a seat. Would you like a glass of water?" Milton offered. Without speaking the woman shook her head to indicate yes. Milton retreated to the back of the office and got a glass and filled it with tap water. Unfortunately his station did not have the luxury of a water chiller. Guyana was rich in gold and diamonds but this richness did not seem to transcend in the value of human life. Things were still hard for the average man and worse yet for the poor.

Accepting the glass of water the woman sipped it and then through tears she gave her reason for visiting the police station.

"I am to blame. It's my fault. It's all my fault!" She started to say in a tear-filled shaky voice and continued.

"I could not give her all that she wanted." She stated. More uncontrollable tears poured as the woman continued to self-accuse. Milton got her some tissues but no matter how many he gave her they just weren't enough to dry the deluge of tears. Milton waited for her to settle down. He didn't rush her. When there was a significant enough amount of calm, Milton said, "I'm Inspector Frank Milton and you are?"

"Clara Bowman, Jasmin's mother." The tears resumed with more ferocity at the junction of saying the name Jasmin. "Oh my Lord something bad has happened to her. I just know it!" Clara exclaimed.

"Ok Mrs. Bowman, is it Ms. or Mrs.?" Milton wanted to get it all right he did not want to upset the woman further. "Just call me Clara, I am not married."

"Now please tell me what is wrong." Milton had been a police officer for over ten years and he knew that it is never easy when people are in a high emotional state. "Let's start at the beginning with why you are here this morning."

"I have six children and Jasmin is the oldest. Six months ago I sent her to live with my aunt and they promised to look after her. I work for very little money and the help which they offered sounded really good but Jasmin called me and said that they were working her like a slave. She ran away." The upset mother said and kept speaking with a shaky voice.

"Sometime later when she called again I told her to come back home but she said that she was at a place which helped girls." Clara explained.

"Did Jasmin tell you the name of the place?" Milton asked her sympathetically.

"No. She did say that mobile phones were not allowed but she had hid the one she had bought. I wondered how she was able to buy a mobile phone and I felt that she would be getting into trouble." Clara said through the beginning of more sobbing.

"When was the last time you heard from Jasmin?" Milton asked. He continued to take notes from Clara.

"Last week she text me to say that she was getting a job in America. That everything was being arranged and that she would be paid well for babysitting. Oh my Lord! Jasmin is only a child herself. She was just only sixteen last month!" Clara wiped her eyes and carried on.

"She said that she would get paid enough to send money back home. She was not allowed to talk about anything else but she would be leaving soon. I knew that something bad would happen!" Clara wept openly in the station so much so that another officer looked into the room.

Milton allowed her time to compose herself. "Would you like to go to the ladies?"

"No, no." Clara replied. "I want you to find Jasmin!"

"I need to get more information from you Clara. How do you know that Jasmin is missing?"

"She has not text me since last week and she has not answered her phone or my text!" Clara was shaking as she went on. "Yesterday I got this message from her phone, here you look at it!" She handed Milton her phone with hands shaking.

Milton looked at the message which showed what looked like symbols. Before he could say anything, Clara said, "It's all symbols. Bad luck! Bad luck! I know that something bad has happened!" She cried.

"Clara, Clara." Milton softly said. He needed Clara to calm down. "May I take your phone? I need to copy this message so that we can examine it. May I?" Clara shook her head in agreement.

Milton turned to the on looking officer and said, "Sergeant please forward this message to the station's phone and see if it can be deciphered. Also please record the phone number and the time and date of the message. Thank you."

"Clara are you sure that this message came from Jasmin's mobile?" Milton asked. "Yes. That is the mobile number which she has been using all the time."

"Would Jasmin play a prank on you by writing a message using symbols? Is she that kind of girl?" Milton wanted to be sure that games weren't being played to waste valuable police time.

"Jasmin is a good girl. She wouldn't do anything like that. She is also asthmatic and gets ill sometimes!" Clara's tears returned.

"Excuse me sir." The sergeant interrupted. "Can I please speak to you in the office?"

"Please excuse me Clara I will be right back." Milton said as he got up to go with the sergeant.

"The message was written and changed to Webdings font. This is what it reads when changed to Times New Roman, 'Your little Jasmin is gone forever. RIP.'

"Strange, very strange, what do you make of it Sir?" The sergeant asked but did not wait for an answer. He gave his own explanation. "It is just a young girl playing a cruel prank on her mother, that's what I think." He dismissively said.

"We have very limited resources so we can't even put a trace on where the phone's location is. See if you can find out where the phone and SIM card were purchased? I will interrogate Clara further. Don't know how much longer for since she is very distraught." Milton stated.

"This has to be just a prank hence the lady has nothing to worry about." The sergeant wanted to convince Milton that this was wasting police time but Milton was feeling differently.

"In my evaluation of things right now, we need to look into this even if it leads nowhere." Milton returned to Clara who had an expectant look in her eyes. "Have you found out what that message means?"

"Clara we need to look over the message more to get to the bottom of things." Milton said since he did not want to distress the lady any more than what she was presently going through.

"Oh my Lord, I knew it! It's something really bad, isn't it? Tell me please." Clara was at such an extremely heighten state that Milton decided to withhold the contents of the message until Clara had support.

"Clara. Clara." Milton called softly to the despairing mother. "We need to examine the message in more detail before we come to any conclusions. Can we keep the phone and try contacting Jasmin ourselves and then get back to you?" Milton had to try desperately to console this mother who was in agony over her daughter.

"Yes you may keep the phone. I'll do anything to get Jasmin back." Clara held her head in her hands. When she raised her head her eyes were swollen and red from crying. She was distraught.

"I have taken all of your details and the information which you have provided. Now please go home and leave it to us. We will contact you tomorrow with any information we collect. We will need to speak to your aunt and we will try to find out where Jasmin went to stay after she left your aunt." Milton explained.

Milton was well aware that there were large numbers of children right there in Guyana without parental care and these children become victims of abuse. Poor family circumstances placed them at high risk. Too often children were left disregarded, ignored and without vital care and support to roam the streets.

As Clara had said, there was a sinister feel to all of this. Despite the sergeant's trivializing of the situation he would start investigations into Jasmin's disappearance as a missing person's report.

Chapter Thirty-Eight

Like the weather was in Guyana, Panama City's was no different today. It was also gloomy and rain was pouring down. The Grants had prepared a sumptuous breakfast for their guests. They knew that Erica watched her weight but one day off the diet couldn't harm. Ethan was bright and cheery and came into the kitchen to find out if he could help. He was promptly ushered out by Susan who thought it would be unheard of for a guest to be helping out.

"I am accustomed to cooking and making dishes. Dad has always made me watch and learn from our housekeeper." Ethan said to Susan.

"Your dad is a wise man to make you self-sufficient and also into a fine and very skilled young gentleman." Susan said approvingly and went on to ask, "Now where are Sofia and Erica?"

"I'm here mother. I knocked on Erica's door and did not get an answer. Guess she is in the shower. I'll give her a few more minutes since she may not want to have breakfast."

"Tim it is like the morgue in here, so very quiet. Please switch on the TV. We'll all hear the usual depressing news!" Susan joked as Tim switched the television on.

"All is ready buffet style. Please come and help yourselves." Susan called out. Although raised in Canada she liked South American dishes and so had created *hojaldas*, salty dough which is then kneaded into flat round shapes and deep-fried with *salchichas guisadas,* a sausage stew. It all looked deliciously mouthwatering.

"Where is Erica? Sofia can you please get-" Susan trailed off as she saw that everyone's eyes were glued to the TV and listening intently.

The news presenter was saying, 'A man has been killed last night on his yacht. His name has been with-held until next of kin are informed but unconfirmed reports state that his daughter has been arrested on suspicion of his murder.' Flashing across the screen were images of a yacht. An extremely familiar yacht! Susan, Sofia and Tim all instantly knew the owner of that yacht!

Susan swiftly left the dining room immediately followed by Sofia. She knocked on Erica's bedroom door. There was no answer. "Erica! Erica!" they both called out. Not a sound came from the other side of the door. Susan turned the door knob. It was locked.

"Get your father." Susan ordered. Sofia ran and got her dad with Ethan following close behind.

"Break this door open." Susan commanded her husband. "Why? What's wrong?" He asked. "Is Erica not in there?" Tim was not connecting.

"Something's wrong. Erica's not answering." Susan replied and continued, "That news' story, you do know who that victim is. Don't you?" Susan's voice quivered. Without answering his wife's questions Tim rested his shoulder on the door and was about to knock it in when Ethan said, "Please let me."

Ethan pulled a small utility pack from his pocket and used the smallest screwdriver to pick the lock. The door opened without damage to the wooden frame or more significantly to Tim's shoulder.

"Erica! Erica!" Sofia called out as the four entered the room in single file their eyes searching the room. "She's not here mother. She's not here!" Sofia anxiously declared. They all looked around the room and then retreated to the dining room. Everyone had lost their appetite. No one ate anything.

Tim broke the silence of the room and said, "Ethan I know that you have to fly back today but this is a crisis. We need to contact Karis. We need to also go down to the police station to find out what is happening and to ascertain if they are holding Erica. Can you take a cab back to the airport, please? Sorry." Tim regretfully said.

"Do not worry Mr. Grant." Ethan quietly said. "It's Tim, please." Tim Grant touched Ethan's shoulder to exhibit friendship. Ethan next said that he understood the urgency and seriousness of the situation.

"I will delay my departure and see if there is anything I can do here to help you." Somehow he did not want to say that he had seen Erica about to sneak out last night. He needed to hear more about the situation. It seemed very grim!

Chapter Thirty-Nine

Karis awoke to a beautiful day. The sun was shining brilliantly and there was a gentle breeze which seemed to make the waves dance and sway as though music was playing and they were keeping tune. The view from her bedroom window was fantastic. It spanned the sea where she could see boats and ferries go by. North Caicos was indeed a beautiful place.

She had really enjoyed John and Marie's company last night. John was great with children. He was also a friendly and good natured man who would be great to get to know, Karis thought. Emma was getting on superbly with Marie and this was brilliant since she had had such a turbulent initial start to high school. Marie had stayed overnight with Emma.

Karis felt that things seemed to be reaching an even base within her life. She was still somewhat worried about Erica. She had given her choice in deciding what she wanted to do and so she had to respect Erica's decision to return to Panama City. Karis knew she would miss her but she was also confident that the Grants would take good care of Erica.

"Good morning! Good morning!" Emma and Marie shouted as they both burst through the open door to Karis' room. "What would you like to have for breakfast mum?" Emma asked. Before Karis could answer she went on. "Marie knows how to make scrambled eggs and she will show me how!"

"Well thank you two girls very much. I will come to the kitchen and watch on." Karis was so very happy and delighted to see Emma engaging and interacting in this way. All thanks to Marie.

"Marie I forgot but your dad is on his way to collect you. I don't think that he knows that you are being the head breakfast chef!" Karis said jokingly. Just then John's car pulled up. "See, there he is."

"Oh darn! Can I not stay to show Emma how to make the eggs?" Marie pleaded.

"Good morning John." Karis said as she opened the door. In a flash Marie and Emma were all over John. "Can I just stay and show Emma how to make scrambled eggs for breakfast? Please! Please Dad!"

"Whoa!" John said to Marie. We must not over stay our welcome. Karis and Emma I'm sure have lots of unpacking still to do." John said looking at Karis.

"Please mum make John say yes!" This was a first for Emma. Karis was really impressed that Emma was interacting at this level.

"Well John I'm afraid that you are outnumbered three to one! Please join us for scrambled eggs by Marie and Emma!" Karis said with a smile to John. The two girls hugged and kissed Karis and flew into the kitchen.

John and Karis sat down and reflected on the bond that Marie and Emma had made. They seemed good for each other. As Karis and John awaited their scrambled eggs and toast specially made by their respective daughters, Karis suddenly remembered that she needed to call Susan and Tim Grant. She hadn't spoken to them since Erica had arrived at their home.

"Please excuse me a minute but I need to hold my phone out the window to get a signal to make a call to the Grants." Karis jokingly stated. As she placed the phone out the window just then it rang before she could attempt her call to the Grants.

"Hello. Yes, speaking. This is Karis Durr, um Karis Palmer speaking. Sorry didn't catch that. You are detective Henriquez." Karis thought it strange that the police were calling her again and said to Henriquez, "I did tell your office that Sidney was not missing." What the heck do they want now? She irritably thought.

"Can you please get a friend or someone you know to come over to your house?" Henriquez asked. What a strange request Karis thought and asked Henriquez, "What for?" Anyway she thought to make a long story short, she just said to Henriquez, "Someone is with me right now, a colleague from my work."

"Ok Mrs. Durr-" Henriquez started to say but Karis interrupted, "It's Karis. Karis Palmer." For God's sake she thought I am no longer married to Sidney Durr! "What exactly do you have to tell me?"

"I am very sorry to inform you but your husband is dead or is he your ex-husband?" Henriquez asked.

To Karis what Henriquez was saying was not sinking in! "Dead? How? When? Where?" All in one breath Karis asked the four questions while a sinking feeling took hold of her. The phone fell from her hand right through the window into the Aloe Vera plants beneath. Karis then sank to the floor.

John then leaped up and ran over to Karis. "Karis! Karis!" He said lifting her head up. "Karis what is the matter? What's happened? Who was that on the phone?"

"The police from Panama City, Sidney my ex-husband is dead!" Karis said in a wailing voice. At that very moment the two girls came through with the plates of scrambled eggs and toast. They froze in their tracks as they saw John trying to revive and comfort Karis who was still on the floor.

"Girls can you please go up to Emma's room and eat your breakfast. Karis just got some bad news and she needs some space. Thanks girls." Emma and Marie quietly complied.

"I'll get your phone from outside. Sit here. Don't try to move." John went to retrieve the phone, the caller had been disconnected.

Karis sat motionless. Her face stony white and her lips clenched. She could not come to terms with what she had just been told. How did Sidney die and when? She needed answers.

John tried redialing the number of the police. There was no signal even when he held it outside the window. He knew what he had to do.

"I will go and get my housekeeper to come over and stay with Emma and Marie. Then I will take you over to my house where you can use the land line to make all of the calls you wish." John said and hurriedly went on. "Get dressed. I will be right back."

Before John left he told the girls what was happening but omitted the news about Sidney. Karis would need help in breaking that news to Emma. This was very unsettling but John had faced crisis and tragedy before. He was well equipped and experienced to deal with the death of a loved one. He knew that no matter what, death is a shattering blow and can break or make you. It had done a little bit of both to him but he was a better man for it. He would give Karis all the support that she needed.

Chapter Forty

Lee and Jim Gagnon watched the morning news with interest. They knew that sometime back in passing that Mr. Big had let it slipped that Durr shipping was involved in work for McLloyd Mining and for helping with the processing of the prospective employees. They had ensured that they kept out of the sensitive aspects and intricacies of operational practices. They had interests in McLloyd but that involved earnings not policies and practices.

They clearly were aware that the company was indeed destroying the rivers in which they were working in but that was not their concern. It was a matter for the government of the land to look at the environmental impact. McLloyd knew that anything could be bought for a price. That even meant that so called environmental officers could be bought to compile reports which favoured McLloyd.

The brothers certainly did not want any back lash from this Durr man's death to be in any way linked to them. They had enough on their hands right now.

As they continued to watch the news the door swung open and in walked Gerardo. "Good morning." Gerardo did not expect a reciprocal greeting and he didn't get one either. Lee Gagnon looked at Gerardo and said, "Yes?" He acted as though Gerardo had interrupted an important event.

"I just came in to say that I am leaving now for my two week holiday." Gerardo calmly stated and was glad that they did not notice his bruises. "What holiday? You know that you don't go on holiday when we are here." Lee firmly stated.

"Well I did get the go ahead from Jim since last month." Gerardo emphasized looking at Jim.

"Oh sorry I forgot to tell you that I did sign off Gerardo. It's fine Lee. Stop the fussing. Go Gerardo." Jim's dismissive voice signaled Gerardo off.

Lee looked at Jim as though he were mad. He then turned on him by saying, "So who the hell is going to clean up around here and see to the grounds for two long weeks eh, Jim?" Lee was an annoying fuss ass and Gerardo could not help but think that he would be glad to see the back of him.

"Be sure to leave the keys to the house and the car." Lee ordered.

"They are all here." Gerardo placed the keys on the coffee table. "I'll be going now. See you in two weeks' time." Gerardo said openly but inwardly he said to himself, 'Yeah right, it'll be when the devil resigns from his post!' He breathed a sigh of relief as he walked through the gate, "The stinking bastards." He muttered to himself.

"I won't even ask you how the hell you let Gerardo off when we are here." Lee said furiously. "But you did ask me just now!" Jim said smiling. "Do you not think that it has worked out well? That Gerardo is gone since we have trouble on our hands?" Jim pleaded for some reasoning to come into Lee's thoughts.

Grudgingly Lee conceded. "We have to get cracking. We need to rent a van, no trace to us and shift things fast. There is still no trace of that phone. That worries me." Lee concluded.

"What worries me most is who the hell knows anything about this business?" Jim whispered as though someone was listening. He went on guessing as to the identity of the blackmailer.

"Let's look at the people who could know." Jim said. "Mr. Big, we ruled him out but just keep him in for a moment, the woman who runs things back in Guyana."

Before Jim could go on, Lee interrupted, "She was never told who we are Jim." Lee stated with a measure of confidence.

"How can you be so very sure?" Jim asked doubtfully and went on, "Our only real connection is Mr. Big but it does not make sense that it is he." Lee next asked about their clerk but Jim had told him the same story that he had given the other two girls.

"Yes, what about those two girls?" Jim asked and quickly answered his own question. "But they are out of the country now." Jim was speculating wildly. He was getting to a point of panic and he was not waiting for answers from Lee.

Lee looked at him puzzled since panicking was his distinguishing mark, not really Jim's.

"Have you checked your phone for the morning?" Jim asked while staring at Lee, a stare which was designed for Lee's action, for him to go and get his phone.

Lee returned with the phone in his hand. His eyes had a steely angry stare and a painful scowl on his face. His phone showed a new text message. Instructions of where to leave the $50,000 glared at them from the screen.

Fifty thousand US dollars was no problem, they had money stashed. No problem at all but as lawyers they however knew only too well that blackmail does not stop with a one time payoff. They had to think and act very carefully. They had to immediately end it all.

Chapter Forty-One

Vanessa shook Omar to wake him. He was never an early riser. He kept on snoring. She knew that Omar hated early mornings and moreover hated being awaken. It was after 8 o'clock however and this was serious. He had to be told what she had just seen on the news. She herself was still in shock and could not believe it all.

Sidney had been a good boss in most respects. In the early days she was his mistress. It was all kept very discreet and Karis never knew. When she got married to Omar she believed that Sidney feared Hanif and their illicit affair stopped.

She did rather like Sidney as a boss and no more but felt that she had to submit to his advances otherwise he may have told Hanif that she was not working out as a secretary. This assumed threat had kept Sidney's lust fed.

Recently he had picked up with a new young woman. She was kind of a mystery. Many of her calls came through from Guyana and Vanessa knew that after his divorce Sidney and she *'took on the town'*. Now he was dead.

"Vanessa what the heck is it?" Omar grumbled. "What can be so important that you are disturbing me?" He rolled back over on his side and attempted to resume his sleep. Vanessa tapped him hard.

"Omar sleeping or not the morning news just showed Sidney's yacht and it said that he was dead!"

"What? What? You are kidding me. You are kidding me?" Omar asked stunned. He sat up in bed and said, "Tell me again?" Omar started to rub his eyes to become more alert and also get control of his thoughts.

"What's there to tell again?" Vanessa was getting agitated. "The morning news said that Sidney was dead. They did not identify him as yet, his name was not mentioned but it is him." Vanessa explained.

"Does Hanif know of this? And how did Sidney die and when?" Omar was now completely awake. He got out of bed and did not wait for Vanessa's reply. He started pacing and wondered if Hanif had had a hand in this. Did Hanif orchestrate all this without his knowledge?

He phoned Hanif immediately. "Hanif have you heard the news on TV?" Omar had forgotten that Hanif had returned to Guyana and it would not be instant breaking news there and before he could rephrase his question, Hanif as his indomitable self, calmly asked, "What news is that?"

"Sidney! Sidney is dead!" Omar knew that nothing shook Hanif Osman. "Well that solves matters to a large degree for us. Doesn't it?" Hanif's cold response was to be expected and Omar wasn't surprised.

Hanif and Elaina his sister had taken charge of the family and business matters for as long as he knew. The two never showed any emotion, neither love nor hate. They were solid and resolute at decision making which made them both artful and skilled at whatever they did, whether legal or otherwise.

"I will stay well away until I am notified officially. How did it happen and where?" Omar passed the phone to Vanessa who filled Hanif in on what she heard on the news. It wasn't much.

Hanif instructed her to contact the police to learn more. That would be the normal course of things as Sidney's secretary. No need to draw unwanted suspicion to themselves. Hanif told Omar to accompany Vanessa to speak to the police since Omar was now the new director of Durr Shipping.

What a lucky stroke of fate. Hanif thought. No need to force Sidney into accepting relegation. It had obligingly been done for him. Hanif still wanted to know how exactly Sidney met his death, it could impact on him. Vanessa had said that it was unconfirmed that his daughter had been arrested.

Could Sidney have been abusing his own daughter? It certainly was not uncommon. Was he capable of stooping so low? He did mess around with young girls so nothing was inconceivable.

Hanif had to wait on Vanessa and Omar to see how things were panning out surrounding Sidney's death. No doubt he would be 'facing off' with Karis. In terms of Sidney's younger daughter, Karis would probably be seeking after the child's interest. Karis he thought was however a small fish in a big pond. He could handle her if and when the time arose. For now he'd wait.

Hanif put these thoughts aside and looked out of his bedroom window. The weather at this time of the year was quite changeable. The morning had started out dark and miserable and now it was worse. Clouded over and beginning to rain. He had to see Elaina. She did not like discussing problems over the phone and he also had to tell her this news about Sidney. He decided that a good walk in the rain may be quite exhilarating. He put on his raincoat and set off to see Elaina at the Centre.

The Centre had been running for quite a few years mainly funded by McLloyd Mining. McLloyd wanted to ensure that they were seen to be contributing to the community. It worked out very well for all concerned. To make themselves look good to the world, the government also had to be seen to be addressing the problem of abandoned children.

They therefore supplied some support and guidelines which set out operational standards that on paper looked good. These were to ensure the safety and well-being of the children but it did not have the capacity to adequately monitor and quality assure the Centre. It therefore became an excellent earner for all of its investors.

His walk took him past streets which had sporadic scores of children begging. This is why he felt that the Centre was actually making a difference. It at least kept some girls off the streets of Georgetown. Hanif now dodged the beggars and wished that this 'inconvenience' did not obstruct his path. He thought if you start giving it does not stop, they just keep coming. Therefore he didn't give.

As he was about to dodge what he thought was yet another vagrant child, a woman pushed a piece of paper into his hand. It was a photocopied picture of a young girl. At the top of the piece of paper in badly written handwriting, it read 'Missing, have you seen Jasmin?' He didn't want to take it but the pleading look in the woman's eyes pierced his. As he reluctantly took the paper the woman asked, "Have you seen my child? Have you seen her?"

Looking directly at him, she next said, "Please sir if you do please ring that number!" The woman kept his gaze while tears rolled out her eyes and she said, "She's my child, my only girl...!" Her words trailed off as tears and loud crying replaced them.

Hanif never got shaken by anything but somehow this woman's pleading seemed to hit a tiny, just a small, slight chord within him. Possibly because he knew that parents just simply abandon children frequently. They give them away. Very little parenting skills existed. Poverty in his country replaced moral resilience and conscience.

Hanif although not formally educated had a sharp mind and a keen sense of inquiry. He read varied materials not only newspapers to keep up with current events but he also read and studied financial journals. He read magazines and books on social issues too. There were certainly many social issues in his country.

He knew that within many families right there in the capital Georgetown that numerous children arc very deprived. They come from extremely dysfunctional homes. Often they run away and they are not looked for. But here's a woman, a clearly distraught mother actively looking for her child. He was astounded.

However anything that attempted to disturb Hanif's emotional equilibrium he would stifle. He stuffed the paper into his rain coat pocket without further thought and walked on. He didn't want to litter. He was nearing the Centre and needed now to get out of the rain. He didn't interfere in what Elaina did at the Centre that was her domain.

Elaina welcomed Hanif. She hadn't seen him for a while. Elaina did business the old time way, face to face. "Hello Hanif. How are you?" Without waiting for a response Elaina went on. "We are being watched more carefully now. One of those welfare workers has been in and was snooping around."

"Well you've always been careful. What's all the worrying about?" Hanif calmly asked. He knew that Elaina was very competent and he trusted her. She had managed the family and she had helped to ensure that all the brothers stayed out of prison.

They had street hustled but none of them ever went to jail. None had a prison record even though the things they did merited one. They were smart. Extremely street wise and very clever in their dealings that is why they had come this far.

"I have girls who should be moving on. I can't go over the allotted numbers. Welfare Services as I said are prying, looking at records. It's a new woman in charge and she wants to make her mark. I have to be careful. Also there are two girls who are giving a lot of trouble." Elaina said somewhat worriedly.

With all the moaning from Elaina Hanif had almost forgotten to mention Sidney's death. "By the way Elaina, Sidney is dead. Omar told me this morning. Don't know all of the details as yet."

"Well that takes care of us wondering what to do about him and his newly acquired conscience!" Elaina said sharply. She had no emotion whatsoever about the news of the death.

At times Hanif felt that her veins were blocked. Ice filled. He guessed that living hard on the streets made you tough and emotionless since his emotions were almost identical to hers. In their younger years they certainly were very much like the unfortunate children he saw earlier. He and Elaina were the 'one percenters' of society back then. They had however risen above poverty and had become self-made flourishing entrepreneurs. He and Elaina felt safe and comfortable in their lives but now Durr's death may very well shake that security.

"What do you reckon we should really do in terms of Sidney's death?" Elaina queried. "I think we should wait it out. See what repercussions result. Oh I forgot to mention that his daughter has been arrested on suspicion of his murder." Hanif said uneasily and went on speaking, "Not sure that Sidney would stoop so low to abuse his own but-." Elaina sharply interjected before Hanif could complete his sentence.

"Oh don't try to defend Sidney." Elaina was piqued in her retort to Hanif. She didn't mix matters. She carried on her angry spouting, spewing out all that she felt about Sidney. "He was no saint but suddenly he seemed to become one and wanted out!" Elaina stated and carried on.

"Well Omar is in his place now but we still have to watch it. That Karis his now ex-wife may cause trouble. Also if there is more to his death than an abused daughter's anger, just if it is not her, what are we looking at?" Elaina's questions and comments were bringing uneasiness into Hanif's mind.

"Yes we have to watch out for anything now. We have to keep things quiet for a while until we know for sure what happened to Sidney. That is our best bet." Elaina concluded. Hanif knew that Elaina always made sense. He could trust her to come through.

Elaina had quarters in the Centre. She often staycd overnight there. In fact to keep a tight and close eye on things she was more at the Centre than at her elaborate home. Like Hanif she was not married and she had no children.

At the Centre she made it point to ensure that only the right staff was hired; those who were desperate in dire need of a job. Their trust was gained and allegiance followed at all costs. They knew that keeping their mouths shut was aligned with keeping their jobs and possibly their lives.

Many who had over-extended themselves and had mounting bills Elaina settled these, hence it was hard for her staff to be disloyal to a 'saviour' such as Elaina. She had their sworn secrecy. The Centre's head cook knocked on Elaina's office.

"Ma'am is Mr. Hanif having lunch here today?" She asked politely. Turning to Hanif Elaina smiled and said, "Of course he will. He can't resist your splendid cooking. Now can you Hanif?"

"Well my alternatives are either a restaurant by myself or my very own pathetic cooking so I'll settle for lunch here." Hanif said with a smile.

Amidst the current issues at the Centre along with Sidney's death Hanif still enjoyed his visit with his sister and his lunch. It was now late afternoon and it had thankfully stopped raining. He wanted to do some shopping but decided against it as he would be lugging around a heavy raincoat. As he walked along he mulled over the day's events and concluded that there was uncertainty in the air.

Chapter Forty-Two

The Grants had telephoned Karis without success. Her phone went immediately to voice mail. They definitely could not deliver negative and distressing news on her voice mail. They had left Sofia and Ethan at home. It was best that they alone went to the police station. It was good that Ethan had volunteered to stay, Sofia they thought needed someone to be there with her. Her best friend was in deep trouble if the news report was accurate Erica must be under arrest.

They now arrived at the police station and Tim spoke to the desk officer. "I'm Timothy Grant and this is my wife Susan. We are here concerning reports of Sidney Durr's death. Can we please speak to the officer in charge?"

The station constable asked them to have a seat. He then rang through and relayed what Tim had told him to the officer in charge. "Inspector Henriquez will be with you shortly." The officer said.

The wait seemed protracted but Tim and Susan were fully aware that in times like these when names were given they were then put through the police database so the police could ascertain exactly who they were dealing with. At least that was how it was done in Florida. The Grants knew the procedure well.

"Mr. and Mrs. Grant is it?" A deep voice greeted them. "I'm Inspector Bill Henriquez. What can I do for you?" Henriquez shook the Grants hands and led them into his office to hear what they had to say.

"We heard the Channel 11 news this morning that a man is dead. We saw the yacht and we know that it belongs to Sidney Durr. Is the deceased Sidney Durr?" Tim continued without waiting for an answer. "He and his wife are friends of ours and their daughter is in our care." Tim said to Henriquez.

"We haven't been able to properly notify his next of kin, his ex-wife and his younger daughter as yet. Our telephone conversation was prematurely disconnected when I called Mrs. Durr earlier and haven't been able to get a connection to her as yet." Henriquez explained.

Henriquez's statement verified it for the Grants. It was indeed Sidney who was dead! With urgency in his voice Tim Grant asked directly, "Are you holding Erica, Sidney's daughter?" Tim watched Henriquez.

"We do have a young woman being held for questioning but-." Before Henriquez could finish Susan Grant interjected. "Erica is just a child. She is only seventeen. Did you allow her to call for her mother or for us? She shouldn't be questioned and held in this way!" Susan's face flashed red but she remained calm and resolute.

Henriquez quickly observed the legal awareness of this couple but he had acted within legal protocols. Erica was over sixteen.

"Mrs. Grant we have asked Erica repeatedly if she wanted to call anyone. She refused. We called her mother, at least we believe that Karis Durr is her mother but the phone line got disconnected before I could inform her that Erica was being held." Henriquez responded.

"Please can you fill us in on the situation so far?" Tim Grant asked Inspector Henriquez. This was not looking good at all, Tim reasoned.

Henriquez recounted the events and stated their reasons for arresting Erica. He also said that the results of urine and blood tests taken, had shown drugs to be in Erica's system. Susan Grant fiercely objected to the tests being carried out on Erica.

"The police can only conduct tests if the young person and their parent consent. Erica certainly did not have a parent present so we are raising objection to the tests." Susan said somewhat calmly. She had to remember that Erica's rights needed protecting but also they needed to have the police as an ally if Erica was to be helped through what seemed like a horrific predicament. Tim Grant backed his wife by stating that, "Erica has the right to have a lawyer and to talk with us on her own in private." Tim emphasized.

Inspector Henriquez listened closely and the Grants further aroused his suspicions that they were no ordinary run of the mill people. The quick checks he ran on them showed them to be model citizens not even a traffic ticket. Well to do Canadian expatriates but he was certain that there was more to them. With this running through his mind he tried to allay their fears and assured them that Erica's rights were not being ignored or violated, that she was seventeen and what they did was within the rule of law.

"Do you know if Erica was a drug user? Heroine along with Diazepam was found in her system." Henriquez looked at their faces for a response but got none. He went on explaining. "It is suspected that it is possible that Erica could have been sexually assaulted but we will first seek permission for full screening from Erica and her parent. If this was positive then it could be a motive for what happened last night." Henriquez was speculating.

Looking for some early answers but if the Grants had any they were not volunteering.

"Thank you for sharing that information with us. Can we please see Erica now? She must be terrified!" Susan said with a sound of urgency in her voice.

"Yes you may speak with Erica. Please let me tell her that you are here to see her." Henriquez left the room and spoke to officer Myles, who subsequently went to the holding cell.

Myles while unlocking the door looked through the bars at Erica who seemed to be nailed to the wall. Erica appeared to be deep in deep thought, more precisely a trance like state...

"Erica, Erica, the Grants are here to see you." Officer Myles repeated this twice because there was no response from Erica. She seemed as though she was completely out of it.

Officer Myles' forceful calls jolted Erica into pulling herself away from the wall and away also from her mind's journey of the past. She was now facing reality. She was under arrest. Officer Myles held Erica by the arms since she seemed unable to full stand.

Erica sauntered from her cell and into the small room where the Grants were and sat down. On seeing her in the prison jumper Susan got up and quickly embraced Erica in an engulfing hug which seemed to say, 'you will be safe.' On release, Erica broke into floods of tears.

"Ok, ok, it will be all sorted." Susan tried to pacify the inconsolable Erica. All Susan could see was a young girl she knew and loved. A girl now in very deep trouble!

"Erica." Tim softly said. "Can you tell us what happened?" Tim really did not understand it at all since Sofia his daughter did not present any known problems, he thought Erica was the same. Inspector Henriquez' account of the events on the yacht was certainly baffling and disturbing. This was not the girl they knew.

Erica repeated her exact version of the account which she gave to Henriquez. 'She did not know what happened. She did not know how she got on to her father's yacht. She did not kill her father.'

"Can you recall what happened before you found yourself on the yacht?" Susan pressed her for more information. "Who did you go out with?" Susan watched as Erica held her head low and did not answer.

"Erica dear, you are in some very serious trouble and we want to help you. We need your cooperation." Tim said this as he tried to get Erica to see how grave her predicament was. She was in custody and the next step could mean that she would be tried for her father's murder.

"Please Erica, Tim is right. This situation is grave and we need to find out what really happened to your dad." Susan

Grant urged. Erica held her head up slightly enough for the Grants to see a very distraught and frightened girl.

"Erica who was it that you met with last night? Please tell us?" Susan leaned over the table and held Erica's hand. Through tears Erica mumbled. "I went out with my boyfriend." She paused and tears tumbled down her red cheeks. Her eyes were almost swollen shut from crying.

"Who is he and what is his name?" Tim said softly while looking at Erica sympathetically.

Within, Erica felt ashamed of herself. She had betrayed the trust of two of the kindest people she knew and now was causing them tremendous worry and embarrassment. She had no choice but to reveal who her boyfriend was but on the other hand she thought that she would be getting him into trouble. She just couldn't.

"I am sorry but I cannot tell you the name of my boyfriend. I just can't! I am sorry, very sorry. I did not kill my father. I didn't!" Erica's voice trailed off and she started weeping loudly. Officer Myles looked into the room and asked, "Is everything ok here? Can I get you some water Erica or anything else?" Erica did not answer. She just kept crying.

"Can I get any water for you, Mr. and Mrs. Grant?" Officer Myles asked while watching Erica.

"Nothing for us thanks. Can we speak with inspector Henriquez please?" Tim Grant asked. Myles closed the door and went to get Henriquez. Tim and Susan looked at each other and knew that Erica needed a lawyer and fast.

After a few minutes Henriquez came into the room followed by another inspector whom he introduced as Inspector Carl Martinez. They indicated that they would be holding Erica for another twenty-four hours and then they would decide if she will be charged on suspicion of her father's murder. The Grants reiterated that Erica was in no condition to be questioned and that they would be providing her with a lawyer.

Before Tim and Susan Grant could continue Erica collapsed to the floor. Susan promptly demanded that Erica should be taken to the hospital and be seen by a doctor for a full physical and mental assessment. They said that they wanted Erica taken to San Christian Hospital a private medical facility. They would foot all of the medical charges.

Henriquez and Martinez agreed that Erica should be medically evaluated and consented to her being taken to the hospital. The Grants followed the police vehicle in which Erica was a passenger to San Christian Hospital. They waited until Erica was admitted and promised her that they would be in contact with her mother and would be back to see her. Officer Myles was stationed at Erica's room.

As the Grants left the hospital they drove frantically in an attempt to get back home to first contact Karis and to start their own 'private investigation' into what had gone so horribly wrong with Sidney and Erica Durr. They were very baffled by Erica's misplaced loyalty in not revealing the name of her boyfriend. Surely Sofia must know who he was and most definitely she would disclose his identity to them.

They needed to get back home with speed but downtown traffic was relentless and so were their thoughts of a justice system where if murder more reasonably manslaughter, was proven, then Erica's life would be hanging in the balance. They couldn't believe that this very young girl whom they knew was now in deep trouble.

Chapter Forty-Three

Sofia and Ethan had been in conversation and were thinking about what was happening to Erica. The time since her parents left to go to the police station seemed like an eternity but Sofia had just taken a call from her mother indicating that Erica was at San Christian Hospital and that they were on their way back home.

Sofia filled in Ethan on all that her mother had told her and it all seemed incredulous. Ethan listened and decided not to reveal the little that he knew from last night's events but remained silent. Sofia did not think anything of his silence and was glad that he was not bombarding her with questions. Just then her mother's car came up the driveway. The Grants didn't bother to park around the back in the garage but such was their urgency that they stopped abruptly outside the front door. Susan flew into the house and immediately set about questioning Sofia.

"Who is Erica seeing? Where does he live and who is he?" In rapid succession Susan threw these questions at her daughter. She looked directly at Sofia and said, "Your friend is in some deep trouble and we need to piece together last night's events." There was urgency in Susan's voice to her daughter as she sustained her pleading to Sofia. "Part of last night's events may have involved Erica's boyfriend who maybe the only person who can account for what she did or did not do. Do you know who he is?" Susan Grant asked this question and stared at her daughter for an answer.

Ethan and Tim watched Susan and Sofia in what seemed like a staring match. Their eyes were locked on each other but Sofia's lips remained sealed. Sofia wanted Erica to be the person to identify her boyfriend. She did not want to place more trouble on her friend and she certainly did not want to be disloyal to her.

"To be honest mother, Erica has never introduced me to her boyfriend." Sofia quietly responded.

"This is serious. Extremely serious and it would be wise to tell us all that you know." Susan tried to cajole her daughter. She felt that Sofia knew more than she was revealing but Sofia kept her silence. With an exasperated sigh, Susan walked away stating that she had to contact Karis and their lawyer.

Sofia and Ethan were left alone in the sitting room and just then Sofia took a gamble and softly said to Ethan, "Will you go with me to San Christian Hospital?" Without a verbal response Ethan took up Susan Grant's car key and walked towards the front door followed closely and quietly by Sofia. The car started immediately and Ethan quietly coursed it down the front drive and skillfully reversed out onto the street.

"Thank you Ethan. Thank you." Sofia softly whispered. Ethan nodded his head and then reminded Sofia that she needed to give him directions to the hospital.

As they drove along Ethan was not sure what he was getting himself into but felt that the need to help Erica seemed right. Ethan did not picture Erica as a killer, just probably a misdirected teenager and underneath it all she appeared to be a lovely girl.

"Somehow even though I hardly know you I feel that I can trust you to help me to help Erica. There is something about you which is different from every other spoilt rich kid." Sofia stated.

"Should I take that as a compliment?" Ethan asked and half smiled at Sofia. He then asked what the plan was on reaching the hospital.

"Not sure. Just know that we have to talk to Erica and possibly get her out of there, until more information can be had on this murder. She needs help. Surely Erica would not kill her father!" Sofia was half expecting Ethan to say something but he didn't. He just drove as quickly as he could while following her directions.

They reached the hospital and could find no space to park at the front so Ethan drove around to the back of the building. Before he could find an available space Sofia tugged on his arm with her eyes fixed on some shrubbery. As hers and Ethan's stares locked on to this foliage, there crouching low in the shrubs was Erica! Sofia jumped out of the car and ran over to Erica. She put her arms around her friend and hustled her into the car.

Chapter Forty-Four

Ethan had driven miles under Sofia's directions which were mingled with comforting words for her friend Erica, who throughout the journey was overcome with uncontrollable weeping. There were now at a property in the countryside owned by the Sofia's uncle, her father's half-brother who lived in Montreal.

Sofia now went to the back of the house and retrieved a spare key which was taped to the bottom of an old bucket of a wishing well. She hugged Erica and gave Ethan the key for him to try to unlock the door. After three attempts and lots of pulling the door finally opened with spooky creaking. Thankfully the utilities were still on. A quick flip of the light switch gave birth to radiant light. The house was in a state of disuse. Her uncle Chester hardly ever spent much of his time there since his divorce.

They had briefly stopped along the way at a service station to get fuel and had collected a few food items. Sofia and Ethan pulled away the dusty sheets which covered the furniture and they all sat on a rather large corner sofa.

"I didn't do it! I didn't! I didn't kill my father!" Erica blurted it all out in a one breathless monologue to the two listeners. Tears started flowing again and followed by another monologue. "I just had to escape. I just had to. I am innocent!" This time Erica looked at her audience, a look which seemed to seek endorsement from them about her innocence.

"Ok, Erica you need to regain your energy. You probably haven't eaten for a while so let's all have something to eat from the food we got at the service station and then we will all be able to focus better." Ethan made this statement but the reality of what he was doing was now setting in. What the hell he thought, he had led a safe and comfortable life so far so he could think of this as an adventure. However he inwardly reasoned all this, to justify his actions in aiding an escapee who was suspected of murder.

Putting these thoughts aside he now took out some sandwiches. "White or brown, which do you want?" Ethan asked Erica holding up the ham sandwiches.

"Any, I don't care." Was her soft reply while accepting the white bread ham sandwich which Ethan gave to her. He was trying very hard at being a good host in this alien house, comforting two clearly very upset girls.

"Perhaps a bag of potato chips also?" he offered as he rummaged through the shopping.

"No thanks." Erica declined Ethan's offer and was about to break into more tears when Ethan joked.

"You really do not need this bag of chips. It will not go very well with the bags you are creating under your beautiful eyes from all that crying. What you really need are shoes to match those bags, not potato chips!" The two girls shared brief laughter at Ethan's remarks. Although it was only mild laughter it was enough to help Erica to hold back the tide of tears which were about to erupt.

As they ate their sandwiches Ethan suggested that Sofia should text her parents to quell their anxieties over their absence. She should for the time being not disclose where they were. She should not let on that Erica was with them. She should only say that they were trying to find out what had happened.

Thirty minutes later sleep, even though an unwelcomed guest came to Erica whether she liked it or not. Her exhaustion had finally caught up with her body clock and she fell asleep on the sofa with an unfinished soda in her hand. Ethan removed it and covered her with a blanket he had found in an upstairs bedroom cupboard.

Sofia watched on and her thoughts about the entire situation proved too much for her so she beckoned him into the next room. They had to think and think fast as to what their next move would be.

"What did your parents say in reply to your text?" Ethan did not want the Grants to think that he was a negative influence or worst yet a man who wanted to manipulate their young daughter. He waited for Sofia to tell him but she didn't. "Please read the text yourself." Sofia calmly said while handing him her phone.

In front of the stark white back light the text message across the screen said, 'Sofia, please come home and leave this to us and the police. We do not want you or Ethan to be caught up in matters which are beyond you. Please do come home. Love Mum and Dad.'

Ethan read the text message and handed the phone back to Sophia. He left her and went to look around outside. He needed to clear his head and he also needed to check in with his father. The property was an interesting mix of vast fields and in the middle of one there appeared an exceptionally long tarmac, probably used for bike or car racing.

Ethan made the call to his dad and as usual it went to voice mail. "Dad I'm fine but a bit delayed. Will let you know soon when I will be back." His dad knew that he was responsible and Ethan knew that he would never let that trust down but somehow he felt compelled to try to help Erica. It started to rain and Ethan returned to the house rather soaked.

"You are about the same size as uncle Chester look upstairs for a change of clothes." Sofia advised, seeing the drenched state of Ethan.

"That's one suggestion I will take up." Ethan said shaking off his wet shoes and climbing the stairs with long deliberate strides. On reaching the top he darted into the privacy of uncle Chester's room and made random selections of just what he needed to be dry. He changed and darted back down again.

"Fill me in please on Erica's story. I need to understand exactly what we are up against." Ethan stated.

Sofia gave a summary of Erica's family life and asserted her belief in Erica's innocence. When Sofia was finished Ethan looked at her with his piercing eyes and calmly said, "Are you not leaving out a significant figure?" Before she could reply, he went on by firmly stating, "The boyfriend."

Sofia exhaled loudly and said, "The least I can do is not withhold information since you have been so kind to try to help Erica clear her name." Sofia said to him.

"Mind you, I haven't done anything yet but I will try. So who is this mystery boyfriend of Erica?" Ethan asked.

"Erica and I used to call him Prince Mysterious. We never really knew anything about him. All I know is what I was told by the daughter of the cook where he works and by my own intuition. It all screams trouble!" Sofia went on to reveal what little she knew about Gerardo. Ethan listened attentively and then asked for a map to get his bearings of the locality they were in.

After a careful study of the area and how it connected with the airport and the Grants' address, he left to return the Grants' vehicle to a safe pick up location. Get more food and cash. He warned Sofia against using her phone or leaving the property. Both girls were to await his return and speak to no one. Without another word Ethan walked out of the door and drove away.

Chapter Forty-Five

It felt like an eternity since Karis had spoken to Susan and she was now boarding a plane en route back to her home in Panama City. Like the first journey she was not alone but this time the flight was different. John and his daughter Marie were with her and Emma. This was comforting but it did not remove the anguish which ripped through her heart over her older daughter Erica.

Karis did not know which pain was worse right now. Her deep suffering emotions over the arrest of her daughter were competing with the dreadful and awful feelings of the murder of her ex-husband.

All that was happening was like a terrible nightmare. How her ex-husband could be dead, indeed murdered and her daughter be found at the scene and arrested? This was a life shattering experience and she did not know how she would survive it.

She was so grateful to her new boss Avery Miller for his kindness in letting her return. To go to the aid of her daughter, who so desperately needed assistance. She could not help but think that she must be a dreadful mother. How could she have failed Erica so badly that she had fallen into this mess?

"Are you ok Karis?" John asked, jolting her from the grave yard of her thoughts.

"Oh John my mind is in chaos, filled with worry, fear and anxiety. Why have I dragged you into my sordid affairs?" Karis' tearful response was filled with emotion.

Putting his arm over Karis' shoulder he said, "I will be here with you and for you, as long as you want me to be."

John had asked for time off, his holiday, to accompany Karis since he felt that she needed support. He also knew that having had tragedy in his life and survived it, that he now had the strength and know-how to help.

There were into the last hour of the four hour flight and the children were asleep. John wished that Karis would close her eyes and rest but he knew that she wouldn't so he was just content to sit quietly beside her and stay awake to keep her company. It didn't take much to make John happy. In fact he was happy with all the simple things of life.

On landing the Grants were to meet them at the airport and hopefully this entire situation could be cleared up quickly and Karis and the girls could start to rebuild their lives. Karis anxiously thought but had severe doubts.

"John please stay with us at our home. I know you were considering staying at a hotel but please do stay with us. Marie's company will be great for Emma. I still cannot believe how well they get on." John agreed wholeheartedly and snuggled up to the softness of Karis' hair as she leaned on his shoulder which seemed strong, like a fortress protecting her from these rocky unstable times.

They both waited eagerly for the flight to come to an end but waiting in times like these always prove to be uncannily lengthy and more often than not, quite fear provoking.

Back at the Grants Susan took the strong black coffee Tim had made and looked at him searchingly. It was more like strong Whisky which was needed, she thought. "Have you touched base with the agency?" Susan asked her husband. She was ever mindful that they needed to still keep perspective on their case at hand and not lose focus. So much seemed to be happening, diverting their attention from their case but they could not neglect Erica. They had to help Karis as they had promised over the phone.

"Yes and I am awaiting some more information on the Gagnon brothers." Tim said, while gulping some of his wife's black coffee.

"Please call again and have them also run a check on Sidney. There has to be more to him than we knew." Susan felt uneasy about this entire affair. Sidney's death, Erica's involvement and now their own daughter's reckless actions, linked with a young man they hardly knew! Before Tim could pick up the house phone Susan's mobile beeped indicating a message had been received. She looked at the phone and sighed. "It's from Ethan thanking us for the hospitality and letting us know that our vehicle has been safely left at Tyco Garage.

"But that is miles from here where are they going to?" Tim Grant asked all in one surge of agitation. "Is Sofia still with him?"

"Your guess is as good as mine since I really do not know why Sofia wants to play this detective role." While saying all this Susan looked at her watch and reminded Tim that they had to go to the airport to collect Karis so he would have to call the agency when they returned.

"I am not looking forward to this at all." Tim said and looked at his wife for reassurance in being bold and courageous, to meet a woman who not only just lost her recently divorced husband but also a mother agonizing for her daughter. "Come on Tim, we know the drill of pretense. We can do this." Susan was reassuring herself and desperately hoping that she could indeed support Karis who was not a stranger but a friend.

Just as they were about to leave, the house phone rang and Tim quickly picked it up.

"Hello." Tim said with an air of command. "Yes, this is Tim Grant speaking. Inspector Henriquez what can I-" Tim was interrupted by inspector Henriquez's swift fire questioning interspersed with statements.

"Did you take Erica Durr from San Christian Hospital? Erica Durr has left police custody. She escaped from the hospital. Is Erica Durr at your house?" When Henriquez broke for a supposed breath of air and after overcoming his surprise that Erica was no longer in police custody, Tim calmly responded.

"Inspector Henriquez the answer is no to all of your questions and we should have been immediately informed that Erica is no longer in your custody." Susan quickly retreated from the door picked up the hallway extension phone and listened to this latest turn of events.

"When did Erica leave the hospital? Did you not have officer Myles stationed at Erica's room?" Tim's voice had now turned to grave concern.

"Officer Myles informed us that Erica asked to go to the toilet but never returned." Henriquez said and then cautioned Tim that if Erica should contact him or Susan they should immediately ask her to turn herself into the police so that the investigation can continue.

"I must emphasize that an all-points bulletin has been issued for Erica." Inspector Henriquez firmly warned Tim of the seriousness of the situation and implored him and his wife to cooperate with the police if they wished to help Erica. Tim Grant thanked him for calling, hung up the phone and looked at Susan with great disbelief.

"I heard it all on the extension, now this will add more to Karis' worries and to ours. What the devil is Erica trying to do?"

Before Tim could respond Susan said almost in a whisper and as if in deep thought, "Erica is a frightened young girl and worse yet if she has been abused by her father, no one knows what that poor girl is going through right now."

"We need to get to the bottom of all of this and quickly." Tim's solemn reply echoed in Susan's ears. Susan hugged Tim and they walked out of the house to the car, to collect Karis and to be the bearers of more bad news.

Chapter Forty-Six

The curcuma plants were in all their glory. Their deep purple and green colours were beautiful. They seem to grace the bottom of the tall mahogany trees which were in abundance over this vast spread of land. It was a shame that the curcumas were not well taken care of.

Their beauty although looking so very wild and free, could have done with some care. It was also unusual to see such blooms at this time of the year. They bloomed at Easter time. It was such a shame that Ethan had to trample on so many of these lovely plants to make his way back to the house.

He opened the door quietly with the key Sofia had entrusted to him. It was now another day, 6:30 am to be precise and Sofia and Erica were still asleep. He quietly unloaded the shopping he had brought back and set about making breakfast while his thoughts paced about in his mind like an athlete training for a marathon.

Time was of the essence in sorting this mess, otherwise he could be trapped, in over and above his head. For the immediate his mind now turned to eggs, bacon and toast, to satisfy his and hopefully the girls' hunger.

As he turned the bacon over in the frying pan he heard Sofia's voice. "Wow something sure smells great in here." Her voice was filled with delight. As Ethan turned away from the frying pan he saw the two girls standing behind the kitchen breakfast bar.

With sleep and a good rest, Erica now resembled the curcuma plants. Aptly so, since the curcuma was also known as the resurrection plant; Erica now seemed to have a new birth, a divine beauty in this morning's light after a long sleep. Their eyes locked for a moment and as quickly as they had locked, just as quickly as they disengaged by the crackling noise of the frying bacon.

"Ethan, when did you get all this?" Sofia looked at Ethan with raised eyebrows.

"Let's just be glad that Ethan was so very thoughtful to get us stuff to eat. Thank you Ethan." Erica said with a small smile tinged with deep-seated fear. Not fear for Ethan but for her situation and now she had also involved her best friend and this kind new acquaintance.

They all had hearty servings of this great breakfast. Sofia questioned Ethan about his culinary skills and when all hunger was satisfied, Ethan said that they needed to have a 'strategy meeting.'

"I have bought some items for you both. They also include hair dye for Erica." Both girls looked at Ethan with surprise but said nothing and listened on.

"If I may suggest that you take your showers and Erica please dye your hair. Brown I believe would be a flattering shade to match your eyes but will also be a good disguise." Ethan said softly as he continued to explain. "Everything you both need is in the bag at the bottom of the stairs including new clothes." These were deliberate instructions and Erica looked at Ethan's broad shoulders and face which seemed to indicate clear thought which gave her a sense of security.

"We need to piece together Friday night's events. We can't go back to your father's yacht since it is under police guard as a crime scene but we have to check out your boyfriend. I think you said Gerardo was his name?" This was a statement but yet somehow also a question and Ethan needed Erica to understand how serious these events were and give needed answers.

"Gerardo Abram. Gerardo is his name." Erica replied and before Ethan could ask another question Erica quickly jumped to Gerardo's defense.

"You have got to understand that Gerardo would never do anything to hurt my father or me." Erica broke into uncontrollable tears.

"Well this is a good time to have our showers and then comeback to this 'strategy meeting' Sofia anxiously suggested. Ethan agreed and the two girls went off upstairs to their guest rooms where each had an en suite bathroom. This afforded Erica the privacy she needed to compose herself.

Ethan cleared away the breakfast dishes and went outside to rummage through his thoughts. He also did some searching around Sofia's uncle's property. The place was an interesting mix of modern and old. In one of the sheds were a collection of tools from times past and yet another revealed new barely used farm machinery and gadgets.

His best find was in the third of the three garages that were at the back of the property. A virtually new two door Audi A3 car, covered over and in pristine shape. He wondered if Sofia knew where the keys to this vehicle were if she didn't he certainly knew how to get it started. As he was making his way out of the garage he bumped directly into Erica.

"I thought that I should come out and find you and apologize for my…" Her voice trailed off and Ethan waited for the tears but surprisingly they didn't emerge. What came next from Erica was a rather mature summation of her behaviour. Ethan certainly was not expecting this level of advanced thought.

"Sofia is my best friend because she has always told me the truth. She has never joined me in folly, telling me that what I was doing was right. Even though I knew what I was doing was reckless, to the point in deceiving my parents and Sofia's own. My love for Gerardo made it all null and void." Erica looked directly into Ethan's eyes seeming to expect some type of confirmation that love has the power to weaken as it can have the power to strengthen.

With no response from Ethan she continued to pour out her soul to him, recounting how she met Gerardo, leading right up to the last night she spent with him. Ethan looked at how beautiful Erica was and especially so with the change of hair colour. He kept these thoughts to himself and remained an attentive listener.

"Ethan this is why I know that because of my love for Gerardo, he would never hurt me or my father." This time Ethan quietly responded to Erica's affirmation that Gerardo would never hurt her or her father. Even though he knew that at times like these, listening was much more preferred than speaking, he felt compelled to say something now.

"You have mentioned your love for Gerardo, what about his love for you?" Ethan watched Erica. The tears dropped silently without an answer and just then Erica composed herself as she saw Sofia coming from the house towards them. She did not answer Ethan's question.

"Wondered where you two had got to? Uncle Chester's place is marvelous, isn't it, lots of gizmos!" Before Ethan or Erica could reply, Sofia caught a glimpse of the partially uncovered car in the garage.

"Wow! I had forgotten about this! Uncle Chester's car, guess he wouldn't mind if we use it!" Sofia said while looking at Ethan and Erica who stood speechless.

"We need a car to get around in, don't we? And this is the perfect vehicle since it is registered to uncle Chester. I know exactly where he hides things. More significantly the keys for this car! Let's go back into the house and I'll show you." Sofia stated with glee.

As they all retreated to the house following Sofia, she stopped mid-stride, looked in the far distance and asked, "Is that an aeroplane I can see?" Turning to look at Ethan and not really knowing what answer to expect she carried on. "I know that uncle Chester has lots of gizmos but I don't recall him owning his own aeroplane."

"Yes, it is an aeroplane. That is my plane. To cover all eventualities I thought it best to bring my plane here. It is an excellent place, out of the way from drawing attention to my prolonged presence in Panama City. It is also inexpensive since I incur no hangar charges. We might need to fly out of Panama unnoticed." Ethan firmly stated.

Erica could not help but think that Ethan was so level-headed and grounded. Mr. Miller must be extremely proud of his son. She so wished that she could turn her life back, that none of this ever happened.

They continued to follow Sofia and she walked into the pantry where a large chest freezer stood. She lifted the lid and searched through frozen packs of rump steak, salmon and then she took out a pack which was labelled anchovy. She tore open the plastic packaging and retrieved a set of car keys.

She was about to put the keys to her lips to kiss them with joy, when she was stopped by Ethan warning her that the cold keys may stick to her lips. They all laughed and ran back outside to see if the keys would start the car.

"Before we try these keys just out of curiosity why did your uncle choose the anchovy pack to hide the keys in?" Ethan asked curiously.

"Well Ethan uncle Chester felt that a thief was less likely to think that keys would be in a freezer and especially in anchovies! And if he wanted to steal the frozen food then he might just leave the less attractive anchovy pack behind!" Sofia said laughing.

Ethan put the key into the ignition and the car started without a sputter! It was like if the car was waiting for this moment, to be ignited. To be brought back to life! Luckily the petrol tank was full. Ethan turned off the ignition and they all walked back to the house to resume the 'strategy meeting.' However before commencing the meeting Ethan thought that they needed to know what was or was not, on the news and so he asked Sofia to switch on the television which was close beside her.

Sofia turned on the TV just as breaking news from Channel 11 was being streamed. The presenter was bringing news from down at the docks, 'Where a young girl's body was seen floating in the early hours of the morning.' The presenter then said that, 'The police could only say that she was between sixteen and eighteen years of age and had no identification on her. The news then switched to the police station where the daughter of the murdered shipping business man Sidney Durr was being held for questioning. The reporter there indicated that the police had issued a statement which said, 'That Erica Durr had escaped police custody. The police had not denied or confirm that the body found at the docks was that of Erica Durr.'

Erica looked at Ethan and Sofia and then her eyes became fixed on the Vodka bottle in uncle Chester's liquor cabinet. Rising to her feet, holding her gaze and clenching her fists tightly, Erica breathed out and just simply said, "If I used to drink, now would be a good time to get really pissed on that Vodka!"

Chapter Forty-Seven

Some sleep had visited Karis last night in the apartment of her former family home. In some ways she felt guilty about having a good sleep and more guilty about not believing Erica about the text Emma had received from Sidney, when he was reported missing. Erica had insisted that it was not her father who was the author of the text and that he was still missing but she would not believe her. All the remorse right now however could not change things.

With her thoughts back in the present she remembered that Susan and Tim had so very kindly filled them in on all that was happening and had offered to accompany her to the police station at 10 am. There were all up until very late trying to make sense of all that was happening. Karis was so thankful that John and Marie had travelled to Panama City with her and Emma. Marie was proving to be a tremendous support and friend for Emma. To her, John was a new and invaluable consort. He was the strength which she needed right now.

Her thoughts turned to Erica. Where could she be? She had not contacted her, Emma or Teresa. They had heard nothing, neither the Grants. Teresa had prepared breakfast and had allowed Emma and Marie to help with the preparation. Teresa would now be their friend for life.

As Karis and John waited for the Grants to pick them up to go to the police station, Teresa came in, "Miss Karis can I get you and Mr. John anything else?"

"Nothing else thanks but can you walk us back through the period of time when the police came enquiring about Sidney being missing?" Karis asked Teresa. Karis was desperate for anything which might shed light on Sidney's death and clear Erica. They had sat through the morning news about the dead girl down at the docks and this brought new despair to an already frazzled Karis.

"Sorry Miss Karis as I said last night, there is nothing else that I can add." Teresa said and waited to leave the room.

"Thanks Teresa. Can you please keep an eye on the two girls while we are gone?" Just then Karis' phone rang and it was Susan.

"I suspect that you have seen the news? Please do not worry as we have it on good authority that the body was so badly decomposed that it couldn't possibly be Erica. The decomposition is way beyond the time which Erica has been unaccounted for."

"Thanks Susan for that. But are you sure it could not be Erica?" Karis asked with tears welling up in her eyes. John sat on the arm of her chair and patted her on the shoulder. This simple gesture made her feel very comforted.

"Now on another issue, Tim and I do not think that it would be a good idea to bring John to the station. The police may view his presence differently." Susan said softly.

"What do you mean?" Karis asked in a bewildered manner.

"Well they may see John as your new boyfriend whom they may construe that you may have been carrying on with before your divorce. They may assume that Erica was caught up in it all, in the middle, between you and Sidney which may have led to an argument between them resulting in his death at her hands. You can also be a possible suspect."

Karis was too astounded and so kept quiet while Susan described her perspective on John and Karis.

"As far fetch as we all know this to be, we do not want to give the police any ammunition for forming their own misleading theories so can you please not bring John at this time? We'll be there in fifteen minutes. See you soon." Susan hung up before even waiting for a response.

Karis felt even more bruised but knew that it was wise not to take John with her. She was now faced with the task of telling John that she would go alone with the Grants. When she told John he was the embodiment of understanding and said that he would help Teresa keep the girls amused. He hugged and squeezed her and said that he would be thinking of her and praying for Erica to come through this.

When Karis and the Grants arrived at the police station inspectors Henriquez and Martinez wanted to confirm that neither the Grants nor Karis had been contacted by Erica, twenty minutes of questioning ensued to determine this. Inspector Henriquez would not comment on the body found by the docks but reassured Karis that it was not Erica. On hearing this news, Karis felt a mixture of relief but still a large proportion of fear. She could not make sense of all that was happening.

"Mrs. Durr-," Henriquez started out but was stopped by Karis.

"It's Ms. Palmer. I have reverted back to my maiden name. I am more comfortable with being called Palmer." Karis did not feel that she needed to give an explanation but she did.

"Apologies, Ms. Palmer. Can you please tell us what type of relationship Erica had with her father?"

"If you are asking me if Sidney abused any of our girls and in particular Erica, then the answer is no." Karis felt indignant by this questioning but remained calm. Martinez then followed on from Henriquez.

"Ms. Palmer can you describe the father daughter relationship, was it a close one and how much time did they spend alone?" Martinez looked directly into Karis's eyes for the answer.

"Erica and her father had a normal daughter father relationship. They were not close since Sidney spent more time working than parenting so a significant portion of his time was spent away from home." Karis certainly did not want to talk about the way she knew that Erica felt about Sidney and so kept very much focused on how she responded.

"Did Erica sail away or spend time alone with her father on his yacht?" Martinez needed to fully understand the type of father daughter encounters which Sidney Durr and his daughter had.

"Erica and Sidney were never away from home together and Erica was never alone on the yacht." Karis replied.

"Can you explain then her presence on the yacht on the night of Sidney's murder?" Henriquez emphatically asked.

Karis looked at the Grants before responding and could only think of the question herself. How did Erica come to be on Sidney's yacht?

"Frankly and honestly, I do not know." Karis just wished that Erica's name could be cleared from this crime. She just wished that it would all go away.

"Karis has just only recently arrived back in Panama City. She's having a traumatic time and she would be happy to answer further questions at a later time with her lawyer present." Tim stated as he watched the inspectors.

"Should Erica contact any of you please urge her to turn herself over to us. Thanks for coming in. We will be in touch." Martinez said as he showed them the way out.

"What do I do next Susan?" Karis asked as they got into Tim's car. "We have Evans Caine coming in from Florida. He is an excellent criminal lawyer, one of the best. So sit tight and wait for his instructions." Without a doubt Susan felt sure that Caine could help Erica and Karis.

As the vehicle reached Karis's former home, Tim drove around to the back where the adjacent apartment was. Emma came running out to greet them followed by Marie.

Susan was very impressed by the changed Emma who was now no longer a melancholy withdrawn child but seemed filled with eager enthusiasm for life.

"Hello again and bye." Emma quickly said and turning to her new friend she stated, "Come on Marie let's go see what

Teresa is cooking and what we can help her make." The two girls ran back into the apartment in search of Teresa.

"Marie has had such a positive impact on Emma. It is like if she never developed Asperger's." Karis said and was inwardly thankful for Marie's presence and also for John's.

"We are also delighted to see this encouraging change in Marie." Susan said and Tim nodded but quickly apologized for haste in leaving, "Karis and John, we are afraid that we must get back since we have some important phone calls and business to attend to. We will be in touch as soon as Evans Caine arrives and if we hear from Erica we will be sure to let you know immediately. Get some rest and take care." Tim said regretfully as he and Susan got back into the car and then drove away.

The drive back to their home seemed long. The last few days had been turbulent and they now had added to their work, Erica's case. Tim had not gleaned very much information on Sidney since the agency said they needed more time. Coupled with all of this, their own daughter had now involved herself in the midst of it all. They didn't know anything at all about Ethan but knew that Sofia was capable of taking care of herself. Still she was out of her league in taking on a murder case. For crying out loud she was only a teenager!

Chapter Forty-Eight

The A3 was driving like a stealth vehicle smooth quiet and swift. The interior had soft leather seats which cushioned and encircled his back, giving great support. Ethan was careful not to draw attention. He drove within the speed limit and had his driver's license to hand. Sofia had said that her uncle Chester loved his A3.

Ethan felt guilty about taking it, really it could be seen as theft but it was a beauty of a car both to look at and drive. The three were now on their way to Sidney's town house in search of answers. They needed something to help get Erica out of this mess.

"Take the next right turn and we can come in from the back of the town house." Erica instructed Ethan. They had decided that it was too risky to approach from the front. For two reasons, the first the police may be watching Sidney's town house or worse his real killer maybe!

Ethan quietly brought the car to a halt a few blocks away and thought it best that they didn't drive up too near. Sofia was to keep watch from in the car so she got into the driver's seat. As they approached the town house there were no visible signs of police presence or for that matter anyone else.

The night sky was lit up with sparkling stars and a large full moon was rising. It was a scene made for lovers. Both Erica and Ethan looked up at it as they walked on. To create a convincing charade, they held hands and appeared to be the two happiest young people on the planet. Ethan's hands felt strong, yet soft and tender as his fingers intertwined and touched hers. She caught a glimpse of his face in the moonlight. Rugged yet sensitive as his deep set eyes scanned all around for potential danger.

"Dad always had a habit of forgetting the key to the town house so he kept one inside one of those flower pots behind the fence." Erica whispered this to Ethan as they neared the entrance. They emptied the entire set of flower pots and there was no key to be found. Erica looked at Ethan with eyebrows raised in a puzzled what next expression.

"Put on your gloves." Ethan said to Erica as he put his on. He then picked up a large garden stone. "Give me your hat and stand back." Ethan broke the glass to the door as quietly as he could, stifling the sound with the hat. He then put his hand in through the hole in the glass and unlocked the door. They crept in but immediately saw that someone else had been in the town house before them. It was ransacked!

"Whoever was here must have known where the key was because there are no previous signs of forced entry." Ethan stated.

"You are right Ethan, someone else but who? What was dad into?" Erica felt optimistic during the drive to the town house but now she had a really bad sinking feeling of not knowing who her father really was and not knowing what he was into! Ethan saw that sinking look emerge in her beautiful eyes and quickly encouraged her.

"Come on we have just started and we won't be beaten!" Ethan said as he hugged her. She felt a deep warmth of reassurance as his chest touched hers and he lifted her chin and repeated, "We won't be defeated." He let her go but could feel the fear within her.

"Is there any place in here where your dad may have hid things? My dad has a safe hidden in the most ridiculous place ever. Would yours have done the same?" Ethan anxiously queried.

"Dad never really told us much but once when we all were spending the weekend over here and he thought that we were asleep I saw him lifting up the gas cooker in the dead of the night!" They both made a dash for the kitchen and immediately set to work lifting the stove.

"What the hell is this stove made of? Lead?" Ethan's voice was strained with this question as they both tried to shift the stove from its position but it was not budging. They kept on jerking and pulling.

"Was your father Clark Kent? I am getting a hernia, also atrial fibrillation! Something better be under this stove!" Ethan's voice was even more strained, under this pressure. At the last wrench the stove came clear throwing the two of them into the middle of the room on top of each other. Ethan could not help but think that Erica's skin felt so soft against his. He swiftly rolled her off of him and looked at the stove's former position which surprisingly enough revealed a concrete slab.

"Marvelous! All that effort wasted for a concrete slab! How very typical of Sidney Durr. Sorry Ethan." Erica sighed while feeling some dejection.

"Bring me that claw hammer it's in that open broom cupboard. I saw it as we walked passed." Ethan said anxiously. "Don't tell me that you will hammer me to death for making you lift that heavy stove for no reason." Erica joked as she walked to get the hammer.

"Take a good look around you Erica." Ethan said before taking the hammer from her.

"What am I looking for in this mess?" Erica asked with interest.

"The entire floor in each room including the kitchen is parquet, yet here lies a concrete slab. Why?" Ethan asked.

"Well Sidney Durr possibly did not want a gas stove to rest on wood in fear of fire." Erica presumed.

Ethan was using all his strength to hook the slap to jolt it from its position. Each time it slipped from the grasp of the claw hammer. He got up off the floor and started looking around frantically for another implement to raise the concrete slab. His hand was bleeding.

"Oh dear Ethan, you are bleeding let me get some plaster and antiseptic." Before he could say not to worry Erica went off for her father's first aid box. She returned, took his hand and gently wiped the wound and applied a plaster. "There now, no danger of getting an infection. I would blame myself for causing you harm if you did."

"Thanks Erica." Their eyes locked and quickly unlocked.

"Where would your dad keep tools like a crowbar?" Ethan hurriedly asked her and darted about the town house searching as he went.

"My father has a big giant sized tool box down stairs in a guest bedroom." Erica hurriedly led the way.

"That concrete slab is not a fire prevention measure at all. I believe it is concealing something important." Ethan stated. They found the tool box and luckily inside, there was a crowbar. They both breathed a sigh of relief and darted back up stairs to the kitchen.

The crowbar solidly hooked the slab and they were able to shift it away. To their amazement and relief a grey safe stared them in the face. They sat down, looked at each other and smiled. Self-satisfaction was however short lived, since they now had to think about how to open the safe.

"What combination of numbers do you think your father may have used for this safe?" Ethan asked and without waiting for an answer he went on. "If he has this safe linked to a security firm for monitoring putting the wrong combination in can trigger an alert to them, to check at this residence or some are police activated." Ethan warned.

Ethan watched Erica as she started to sweat but he tried to calm her by suggesting that they get some paper to first write down possible combinations before attempting them.

"We need I think, six numbers for this type of safe." Ethan wasn't one hundred percent certain. Erica got some paper and a pen, took a deep breath and started writing. She noticed Ethan's steady gaze on her.

"Believe me Ethan, these are not random combinations I am writing down. I know you think that I am a wild, thoughtless teenager with an overabundance of hormones swelling up in my veins but there is more to me than that." Erica asserted.

"You mean in addition to being a wild, thoughtless hormone driven teenager, that there is more?" His face had a broad smirk and Erica playfully punched him over with a clenched fist. He responded to this playfulness and pulled her over. Again their eyes locked but Ethan broke this gaze by raising himself up and away. Soon Erica had four different combinations on the paper.

"What do the combinations signify?" Ethan knew that his dad had combinations which represented momentous life events, either in his own life, his parents or Ethan's mother.

"Things relating to my dad's parents, Emma, he likes her best, mum and Teresa, our long time housekeeper." Erica said and then she tried the parents' dates of birth first. Both of them hoped that the safe was unmonitored because it did not budge. Next they tried the Emma combination. Nothing!

"Oh God if you exist please let the next try be the right one. Please! Please!" Erica begged.

"Wait. Let's mix the Teresa and Emma combination together. Three and three, as you said, he liked Emma and Teresa is not a relative so this may work." Ethan knew that they were running out of time especially if the safe was monitored. They were also in the town house longer than they had expected to be. They needed to get out before they were discovered.

"Ok Ethan, I have confidence in you. Please choose which double of three we put together." Erica watched with her heart racing as he put together the new combination, 461860. These numbers on their own meant nothing but in this situation their importance could not be quantified.

"So here goes, 461860." Erica called each number out as she punched them into the digital keypad. Both she and Ethan held their breath as she keyed the last digit, 0. Immediately there was a click! They both looked at each other thinking that it was the other's breathing which they had heard but it was not. Ethan pulled the handle of the door of the safe. It opened up, as though to bid them entry.

"Holy sh..." Erica caught herself and refined her language as they hugged each other. Somehow she did not want to swear in front of Ethan. "Holy, Mary! Mother of God we did it!" She said over and over as they hugged. Tears rolled down her face and the memory of her father's death made the situation even more painful. They broke the embrace.

"Please get a large bag quickly! Any bag but preferably a travelling bag to put all this in." Ethan knew that the contents of the massive safe were too much for an ordinary plastic carrier bag. Files upon files filled the safe.

Erica returned with two large travelling bags. They filled the first with documents and what looked like diaries. Then to their shock underneath the documents were stacks of money. They needed a third bag to empty the safe as they had filled the second more money was still in the safe. They had to fill the bags and leave fast!

Ethan had bought three new mobile phones and SIM cards. He rang Sofia on the one he had given her. Sofia was sunk down low in the driver's seat to avoid being seen. She raised herself up and pulled the phone out of her jeans' pocket.

"Drive to us now!" Ethan's terse command was urgent. He and Erica almost had to drag the bags. The weight was more than they had anticipated and a few papers fell out of one of the over-filled bags. No time to pick them up. Someone was shining a light through the front window of the town house. They had to get out. They could hear tugging at the door. Detection was imminent if they did not get out now!

Before Sofia could bring the vehicle to a complete stop Ethan had popped the boot and was throwing the bags into it. He then quickly closed the boot and climbed inside the car.

"Drive! Drive!" Ethan leaned forward and urgently implored Sofia, who responded by flooring the accelerator but mindful of not over revving the car to keep extra noise which would draw attention to them.

"As we were leaving I noticed that a light came on in the town house. Lucky break we got out in time!" Ethan said to Erica as he continued to look back, doing so to ensure that no one was following them.

"I am constantly checking the mirrors no vehicles have been consistently behind us." Sofia said reassuringly as she drove with haste back to uncle Chester's.

"What happened to you two? I thought you had gotten married and were on the honey moon! You spent an incredible amount of time in there!" Sofia chided them as she drove with skill and precision.

"You will never believe what we found. We will tell you all about it as soon as we get back. Just concentrate on the driving." Erica said excitedly. Then somewhat apprehensively, she softly said to Sofia, "I didn't even know that you had passed your driver's test. Guess I was too wrapped up in myself or rather in Gerardo. Thanks Sofia for all that you and Ethan are doing to help me."

They stopped at a service station topped up with petrol and Ethan took orders for what the ladies wanted to eat. He did not want them to get out of the car and was happy to get whatever they wanted. With refreshments and food bought he took over the driving. They speedily headed back to uncle Chester's.

One hour later they reached and parked the car safely in the garage. Each of them took hold of a bag to drag inside. Erica relayed the night's events to Sofia. Sofia felt that it was like watching a late night mystery drama film.

"Let's start with the diaries and then the documents, possibly all this will explain the motive behind Sidney's murder." Ethan said as the girls watched him and listened closely.

"But what are we meant to be looking for?" Sofia asked in a baffled voice.

"None of us can pinpoint or be sure of what we are looking at. Therefore anything from any of these diaries which appear out of the ordinary. Whatever looks unusual or any name of a person or company which keeps popping up in a strange manner then we write it on our own blank sheet of paper. Next try to cross referencing it with other names, to see what connections it has. I am no detective but together all we can do is try to get answers for this murder." Ethan's voice sounded out a mighty great plea for optimism.

Each of them took a stack of diaries. The diaries had names and selected dates of what appeared to be shipments and payments. The frequent places were Panama City, Guyana, Canada and Miami. Some diaries seemed personal and had names of women, payments, meetings, outcomes and notes as to whether to set further meetings.

The documents included, bills of sales for several things including the town house. The shipping office and the ships were listed. Included also were deeds to a gold mine in Guyana; cargo manifests, which sometimes had two for the same date but were different in contents.

"Let's deal with the business diaries first. Whatever name of person or company that keeps reoccurring, that you have written on your individual paper, let us now place that name on the main sheet." Ethan seemed like a drill sergeant but they had to make some kind of sense out of all this.

They took turns in writing on the main sheet and it was some time before they all had written but when they had finished what emerged was just a set of names, only two of which Erica knew.

"Ok we have in the people category Walter Crawford, Hanif Osman, Francisco Gabriel, Omar Newman, Chiara

Moseley, Rafael Ramirez, Elaina Osman and Paul Scott. These are the business references that keep reoccurring each and every month." Erica made this seemingly bold declaration but in the fore front of her mind she hadn't a clue what to do next with the information or what it all meant.

She covered her eyes with her hands but remained resolute that she would not cry. Seeing that Erica was on the brink of despair Ethan suggested a break.

"Thirty minutes to do whatever pleases each of us." He said with a broad smile.

"I am choosing a quiet short rejuvenating nap on that sofa over there. You two can enjoy the lovely sound of my snoring!" Sofia laughed and walked over to the sofa and stretched out on its lush soft fabric. In no time at all she was indeed snoring.

Ethan chose to stand looking out of the French windows. It was indeed a lovely night. Shimmering moonlight and cool air, with the sound of the animal night life of frogs croaking and crickets chirping, these were just all magnificent sounds. As he stood there absorbing it all, he felt warm air on his neck. Erica came to stand behind him, peeping over his shoulders to catch a glimpse of what held his attention.

"What's your thirty minute selection Erica?" Ethan asked her without turning around. He could feel the softness of her body and the fragrant smell of the shampoo from dying her hair was extremely alluring.

"I am just standing here enjoying the night that is if you don't mind me standing here with you?" He turned his head and she looked directly into his dark eyes for an answer.

"Not at all, please be my guest." He pushed opened both doors to make room for Erica. They stood side by side looking out into the peaceful night. There was silence between them.

"A dollar for your thoughts?" Erica softly said to him.

"Actually I am not thinking at all. I am just simply enjoying the night air and sky scene. Isn't it absolutely soothing?" Ethan felt that the relaxing night atmosphere was made even more idyllic by Erica's presence. He however kept these thoughts to himself and they both stood in peaceful silence soaking it all up.

They were soon however jolted back to reality by the sound of the kettle on the stove. Uncle Chester still had a whistling kettle and Sofia was up and about making hot chocolate.

"We didn't realize that our break was up. Time sure flies." Erica moaned. She was enjoying not only the night but Ethan's company. She told herself that her feelings were purely out of gratitude for what he was doing to help her, after all Gerardo was still in the picture.

Ethan now turned to Erica and smilingly asked, "But where did the 'dollar for your thoughts' come from?"

"It is always better to ask for more, a penny can't buy much!" Erica replied as she also smiled at him.

While Sofia made the hot chocolate, Erica and Ethan resumed their search of the diaries. They now started to look at the personal diaries to see if any of the business people overlapped into these.

"Oh my gosh!" Erica exclaimed causing Ethan to stop his searching.

"What is the matter? Have you found something significant?" His eyes looked hopeful but his hopes were dashed by Erica's reply.

"Where in God's name did Sidney Durr have so much time to write in all these diaries? No wonder he had no real time for Emma and me neither for mum, his wife!" She started to cry tears of disbelief and tears of regret for what she felt was a life wasted. Sofia came back in, cuddled her and waited for her tears to stop.

"Erica you can take a break from doing this. Sofia and I can continue the sifting out of this information and then you can tell us what and if anything you know from what we pull out."

"That is very thoughtful and kind of you Ethan to make that suggestion but it will be quicker if the three of us continue to work through it all." She dried her tears and ploughed on.

It was another two hours before they had finished pulling names out and for some trends to start appearing from the diaries.

"Paul Scott one of the cargo ship's captains, is linked to the personal diary and his ship always sail from Guyana to Panama City. Then it seems as though it goes on a roundabout journey to Canada and then Miami." Ethan reported but could not as yet make a connection as to the rationale of the route of this journey. Ethan also realized that it was Captain Scott's ship's manifests which were duplicated but the copy had discrepancies. Captain Scott also had some kind of connection to a Walter Crawford in Guyana but would also meet him in Panama City on regular occasions at a place called Oakes Lodge.

"Well Hanif and Elaina Osman are in the business and the personal diaries but Hanif is my father's partner and Elaina is Hanif's sister so it is reasonable for them to be involved at a personal level also." Erica stated.

"What do you make of this woman? She has the most recent recurrent dates but only in the personal diary." Sofia said but she knew full well what the answer would be but still did not want to rub salt into Erica's wounds by stating the obvious.

"Who is it?" Erica asked looking over at Sofia's sheet of paper and seeing the name, Valentina.

"I can see the numerous entries which must mean his mistress but I have never met her, neither do I recognize the name. But wait, is there an entry for the night of the theatre performance?" Erica asked.

"What date was that again?" Sofia inquired, seeking a reminder as she smiled and looked at her friend. She could not help but smile since she recalled Erica standing almost naked outside her bedroom window, in her attempt to climb back into her house.

"June 12th." Erica replied and went on. "It is amazing that you cannot recall the date but your smiles do say that you recall the night!" Erica now also started to smile remembering that night, where she stood almost naked in Sofia's garden!

Ethan watched the two girls knowing full well that this was a joke which was best shared between only them.

"Yes, this woman Valentina is listed for that night alongside the musical Chicago." Sofia confirmed.

"What we have so far, is a ship's captain who has false manifests which are known to Sidney. A woman, who is possibly a mistress, named Valentina. Walter Crawford who seems to be some type of seller with links to Captain Paul Scott; Francisco Gabriel located in Miami but business unknown. Omar Newman known; Chiara Moseley who is a possible Canadian buyer and Rafael Ramirez is another possible trader here in Panama City." Ethan stopped and looked at Erica to give her a chance to have some time out if she wanted to before he went on.

"We also have lots of money in that third bag, possibly counterfeit or perhaps for laundering! Whatever it is, be sure that it could be part and parcel of why my father was murdered!" Erica said soberly.

"Can we vote on folding it in for tonight? We do need to get some rest and then we can think all fresh tomorrow. I'll put the bag of money out of the way in that cupboard under the stairs" Ethan suggested.

The two girls agreed with Ethan since they both felt tired and their eyes were beginning to feel the strain of reading through all that paper work. Erica especially needed to come to terms with what was emerging about her father and that it could all mean, that he was into illegal dealings. It all seemed too overwhelming.

Chapter Forty-Nine

Black cold coffee and a crumpled cheese sandwich that looked as though the cheese had curdled and could well lighten the coffee, was the only dinner inspector Henriquez was facing. Prospects of anything more exotic were rapidly diminishing as the night grew on. Overtime was one of the major hazards of the job. He had to try to unravel the Sidney Durr murder and this was now followed by the young girl's body which had now surfaced at the docks.

"I see that you already have the coroner's report on Durr." Martinez said as he walked into Henriquez's office. Martinez knew that Sidney Durr's case would be a difficult one, which meant lots of long hours.

"Just as we thought the medical examiner has reported that Durr died from several blows to the head and that a metal object could have inflicted the deadly blows. The report does say that a significant amount of force was used." Henriquez said through sips of his coffee.

"I noticed that it also states that he had a high level of cocaine in his system along with a mix of other drugs some of which were muscle relaxers." Martinez added and continued.

"Could Erica Durr a slim teenager inflict such deadly force?" Martinez queried his partner. "Also was drug abuse a family issue?" Martinez queried.

"Anger can turn people into raging lions and if she got the first blow knocking him to the ground, the rest could have been easy." Henriquez remarked. Still Henriquez remained uncertain. He wanted a motive and he continued.

"Can we also rely on Charlie's witness statement which fingers Erica? Charlie's much like a baby. Goes to sleep on the bottle. Wakes up on the bottle! And it's not milk! Henriquez explained as he and Martinez continued to assess this troubling case where little headway was being made apart from everything being pointed to this young victim's daughter.

"Have you talked to any of her teachers and friends at school to see if they knew of anything unsavory between Erica and her father?" Henriquez asked.

"School is still out but I have contacted the head of the school to get a list of teachers and friends." Martinez stated as he too wanted a motive and then they could either build a case or rule out Erica. For now they had to try to find her.

"We need to keep digging to see if others had motives to kill Durr. For one he was reported missing but that did not supposedly develop further. The blood stains on the deck, did Erica have an accomplice? His business partner in Guyana would there be a motive there? He needs to be interviewed along with Sidney's secretary who already came in to the station." Henriquez said decisively but realized that he had more questions than answers.

"Myles, can you please come in." Henriquez spoke into the internal telecom. As Myles entered his office he knew that she was expecting a reprimand for allowing Erica to give her the slip at the hospital but Henriquez chose to move on in trying to make headway on the case.

"We need to find out Durr's last movements. We need information on where his yacht, The Wind Rush came in from. I also need you to talk to Charlie, the old guy who reported the crime. With time he may have recalled a bit more." Henriquez finished his instructions.

Myles took down all these instructions without question and was relieved that there was no reprimand from Henriquez concerning Erica's escape on her watch.

"Tomorrow our next port of call, no pun intended, is down to the docks to interview one of Durr's ship captains, Paul Scott. He may be able to shed some light on Durr's whereabouts while in Guyana and where his yacht came in from." Henriquez then told Myles and Martinez to go off duty since they had worked way past their shifts.

As Martinez was preparing to leave, he noticed that Myles seemed to settle down again at her desk reading over reports, "You have been at work for over fifteen hours, are you not leaving?" Martinez asked puzzled.

"I just need to write up a few reports to ensure that I do not get behind. I'll be leaving shortly." Myles stated.

As he walked past her desk he noticed that she had the *Jane Doe* file open, the body from the docks.

"Thinking on solving that one and making it straight to inspector?" Martinez said jokingly.

"Good night inspector Martinez." Her curt reply given, Myles now read through the brief file on *June Doe*. Nothing much in the report apart from the fact that the body was found undressed with no sign of clothes, jewelry or identification. Initial suspicions were that the body was buried before, near Blue Spruce Sedums and then dumped in the sea.

Henriquez she knew had asked for an urgent post mortem to determine the cause of death. Myles put the file back and called her husband who had come to spend a few days with her since he did not live in Panama City.

"Walter, I will be home in twenty minutes. Hope you have made dinner." Myles hung up the phone and left the station.

Chapter Fifty

Looking through the rear view mirror as he drove away Ethan could only admire uncle Chester's property for its lovely bucolic setting. He had ensured that they had very early breakfast and were now on the road. It was 6am. They were headed to the docks quite close to where Channel 11 news had said that the young girl's body was discovered and he knew that police most likely maybe about.

They however desperately needed to speak with Captain Paul Scott but knew that they had to keep their guard up. His ship manifests were all fraudulent. No doubt he would have lots to hide and Erica had said that she had never seen him before. They had to tread very carefully.

Ethan parked the car a few yards from the ship's berth and as before Sofia remained behind in the driver's seat. Erica pulled the baseball cap lower on her forehead to conceal her face since a few workers were slowly trickling on to the dock. No police were about. The Mistral C was anchored thankfully not too far away from where they had parked. Two deckhands were out and about cleaning.

"Is your captain about?" Ethan shouted to one of the boys.

"What's it to you? He don't want no more help! We two are good enough!" This loud shout back came from the older of the two boys.

"We have a message for the captain from Crawford!" Ethan knew that this might get them permission to board, denied or shot at! He was taking a long shot and a big gamble. He hoped that it all would pay off. Erica nervously kept her eyes lowered.

He took the bogus note out of his pocket which was encased in a sealed envelope and waved it. He had written it up before they left the house. He prayed that Scott did not know Walter Crawford's handwriting. From Sidney's documentation they gleaned that Captain Scott knew Walter Crawford and met him regularly but they didn't know exactly why therefore this was a tremendous gamble. What they wanted was to get Captain Scott off the ship, in a neutral meeting place to talk with and question him if they could.

"Ok Marco," came a croaky voice, the rumble of which signified years of smoking. "Let them board." Captain Scott gave his permission to board the Mistral C.

As they climbed on board, their hearts were thumping but Erica kept a silly smile on her face, faking a brainless clumsy persona. While Ethan's walk and mannerisms, were almost identical to hers as they walked gingerly past the two deck hands.

Captain Scott lumbered from his seat, an overweight man in his sixties, possibly seventies, with receding white hair. Years of drinking and smoking made him look much older than he possibly was. Captain Scott kept looking at them with what seemed like a suspicious eye.

"Yeah, I'm the captain. What's the message?" Scott scowled. His looks now turned directly to Erica and his eyes were filled with lechery. He walked around her and smiled. This revealed an almost empty mouth with some remnants of broken browned discoloured teeth.

"Crawford said to give you this." Ethan handed Captain Scott the envelope and he tore it open so fiercely that it almost ripped the note inside. He lowered his eyes as he read the note. Surprisingly not silently but out loud.

"Meet me tonight at 9 pm at Oakes Lodge. I have in my possession documents that your boss had stashed away, things that could implicate you." Captain Scott crumpled the note in his hand and shoved it into his pocket without saying a single word.

Ethan and Erica both held out their hands as an indication for payment for delivering the message but instead Captain Scott started a fit of laughter and coughing. Then his eyes became slits and he glared at them and started to push Ethan.

"Get the hell off my ship you lizard guts of a boy!" Captain Scott shouted. Ethan started to back away when Captain Scott suddenly grabbed Erica.

"I'll have her for lunch! Fine feel! Just right!" These words felt like they had come out of the Grimm Brothers' fairy tale, Hansel and Gretel but were so obscene that Erica cringed! There was absolutely no doubt that Captain Scott, was a dirty old man!

Erica pulled away and then Marco the older of the two deckhands tried to restrain Ethan, while Captain Scott tried to push Erica below deck. Ethan threw a flying chop to the boy's jaw and punched him. A big scuffle ensued and he held Ethan from behind by the neck. Ethan gained a firm hold on his shoulders and flipped him over so high that he was thrown overboard.

Erica gave Captain Scott a midline punch, followed by a kick below the belt. He gasped for air. Lost his footing and Ethan ran over and pushed him to the deck floor. He was groaning in agony and holding his groin. Ethan then quickly threw a life ring over the side of the ship for the deck boy, who was screaming in the water.

Erica and Ethan both scampered and climbed off the ship as fast as they could. Their feet hit the deck boards causing them to creak and groan from their intense running. Above all this noise, they could distinctly hear the other deck boy shouting but his shouting was getting closer and closer as they ran.

"Man overboard! Man overboard!" He was loudly screaming along with "Wait! Wait up!" He kept calling out.

Sofia saw them in the distance and also saw that a boy was in hot pursuit behind them. She started up the engine and eagerly waited. Ethan glanced over his shoulder, perspiration bathing his hot skin. He could see the boy closing in on them.

They rounded a bend on the dock which was lined with several containers.

"What the f…!" Erica was about to say as she could see that the boy was chasing after them but chose, "What the hell?" Ethan heard her and dropped back his pace and pulled her in behind a large container. It was good that they had come to the dock very early since it was Sunday and luckily not many people were about to witness this scene.

As the deck boy slowed down, looking to see where they had gone, Ethan took him by surprise and pulled him into their hiding niche.

"Wait! Wait! Don't hurt me!" The boy begged. "I was glad that you did old Scott and Marco in. Those Karate moves man were awesome! It serves them right. Old Scott and Marco hurt people". The boy declared.

"So exactly why are you chasing us?" Ethan asked with a menacing voice, while staring the boy in the eyes. Not answering the question the boy went on speaking.

"Oh I know your girl." He said, looking at Erica. "Yes. I know her. *Miss Posh* is the name we called her." The boy said.

Erica stared at him with some surprise but she did feel that she had seen him somewhere before but could not put her finger on it. She also wondered how he recognized her with her change of hair colour and the clothes which she was now wearing.

"Well where in the hell do you know me from?" Erica asked, keeping her stare on him.

"You used to go to that Café on east side every day after school. You walked past my school gate to get there." The boy explained and Erica quickly remembered that he used to be with a bunch of really annoying immature boys but she admitted nothing and just looked at Ethan. She was however relieved that he had not recognized her as fugitive!

"I want to join your shake down gang. That was a shakedown you two were trying to pull on old Scott wasn't it?" The boy's face beamed as he asked this question.

"No it wasn't a shakedown and we need to move on so what is it that you really want?" Erica asked with annoyance.

"*Miss Posh* from the looks of you and him you seem to have fallen on hard times and with those Karate moves you put on old Scott, man we could form a real super gang!"

"You mean like robbing and stealing and all that horse shit?" Erica snapped at him. There was certainly great delight and eagerness to be part of whatever they were into. In that short space of time this boy had become a business negotiator. He had it all worked out it seemed, for a career in crime.

Ethan stepped in before Erica could rip him to pieces or he her since he could see the glares she was giving the boy. "Now you seem clever but we want to do more. We've got big plans to solve a murder and possibly you can help us."

"I just want immediate money. I ain't no detective. You see, a man gotta survive." The boy calmly stated.

Ethan had to call upon his powers of persuasion and the knowledge that this boy possibly wasn't just greed driven but was focused on a fundamental sense of deprivation; a need for the basic things which were lacking or unavailable in his life and offer some to him.

"What if we give you a share of the reward for solving the murder and in the process keep you topped up with some cash for survival. How does that sound?" Ethan asked enticingly.

"Pretty neat, I've got some info on old Scott though, so how's about an advance today?" He eagerly asked rubbing his thumb and fingers together, gesturing that he wanted money now.

"First we need to get away from here so come with us please." Ethan said as they started to walk towards the car. Ethan thought that it was best that he drove while the girls sat in the back to keep an eye on the boy. He dare not trust him or disclose their names or identities to this boy.

"Bloody hell! What a cool car! Who's she?" The deck boy asked hastily while looking at Sofia and the A3. Ethan did not answer but explained the seating arrangement, except the part of keeping an eye on him. He knew the girls would. Erica softly told Sofia who their unwelcomed guest was.

It was a good thing that Ethan had been studying the locality and surrounding areas. He now drove to a secluded park and they all sat down on the grass with the refreshments he had loaded in the boot that morning while the girls were still asleep.

"How much you gonna give me, if it is information you want on old Scott? I can deliver the dirty!" He said all this between gulps of cola and chomping on his third ham sandwich. He seemed to have a voracious appetite and just kept eating. The three wondered how much and what he really knew which could impact on solving Sidney's murder or was it just bits of information about illegal dealings?

"Now before we go any further we need to get to know you a bit. First, what's your name?" Ethan looked him over and knew that he may possibly lie about his name but he waited for the reply.

"Carlos is my name. Carlos Carrillo, that's me." Ethan did not expect a full name and he really didn't care what name the boy gave. He just wanted to gain his trust and get whatever information he had.

"Thanks for that Carlos. We'll get right to the point. Here's $100 as a deposit for all information which you can provide on Captain Scott. When we hear what you have we will work out how much more money will follow." Ethan took the five twenty dollar bills from his back pocket and gave them to Carlos.

"Thank you. Thank you." His eyes gleamed as he counted the bills and rolled them away into this boots. He said thank you as though he was really grateful. Actually Ethan wasn't expecting any courtesy from Carlos and was somewhat surprised by it.

"Now you two don't be looking at where I stash my cash." Carlos jokingly looked over at Erica and Sofia as he said this.

"How's about your names, you know mine what about yours?" His eyes flitted from Ethan, to Erica and then to Sofia.

"Well Carlos let's leave the introductions until later. For now let's deal with the Captain Scott business." Ethan knew that they could not exert trust. It is earned and so for now they had to play this game very cautiously.

"Well suit yourselves. I ain't making any demands apart from our financial agreements, eh." Carlos laughed. It seemed to indicate that he was a hardened and seasoned street wise player.

Looking at him he was tall, around 5' 10', slim, with dark brown eyes and black hair. His clothes had certainly gone past their sell by date and it was clear that he was experiencing a harsh life. However underneath all this, he seemed to have a tiny aspect of kindness about him.

While gorging his sandwiches in between bites he asked Erica if she was hurt by old Scott's *manhandling* her and he politely passed around the pack of fruit, taking care not to eat all of it. There was something, a thoughtful side within him that needed developing. Ethan could not help but feel almost sorry for this boy.

"Now I been on the Mistral C with old Scott for some time now. I left school early, too much effort and no money!" He laughed out loud. The three listened closely.

"The Mistral C she sails from Guyana to here every other month from here to Canada and then to Miami but there is a time gap for each of the Canada sailings and it is not a logical journey." Carlos stopped to drink more cola. He seemed to love this beverage.

"Now also what is written on the ship's manifest is never what she carries. On each and every journey, the cargo should have been a mix of any of these, rice, cereals, paper, machinery, paperboard and tools also vehicles and pharmaceutical products, only these, nothing else!" Carlos said this and stopped.

He had the undivided attention of the three. They were attentively listening and were somewhat irritated by the whistling of the loud wind as it howled through the coconut palms making it difficult to hear what was being said. The weather was gradually changing and the blue skies were turning gloomy. It looked like rain was coming but they listened on while keeping an eye on the sky.

"Aha! What the manifest does not show are the stashes of gold! Yes gold, smuggled out of Guyana and shipped with compliments to Canada!" Carlos emphatically stated.

"So how did they get pass customs doing this? Surely the cargo would be checked." Ethan asked and did not have to wait long for an answer.

"Remember I told you that the Mistral C sails but in a round-about journey to Canada. Well there is good reason for that. Don't draw attention and, and!" Carlos exclaimed looking at Erica. "What else? What else do you think?" He asked looking from Erica to Ethan, then to Sofia. None of them spoke they waited anxiously to be told since none of them had a clue why!

"Chiara Moseley!" He exclaimed with a broad smile and watching the three as their faces looked baffled at his declaration but only knew the name from within Sidney's diary.

"Explain please, Chiara Moseley, who is she?" Erica asked with urgency in her voice which was caused partly by the sight of the impending bad weather and by feeling that she was getting information over load but still felt far away from finding her father's killer.

"Ah, you see, each port travelled to has a customs *'link'* to get all illegal dealings through. Old Scott thinks that my brain is fried like Marco's with the drugs he gives us. He feels that I have no idea as to what goes on but ha, I do!" Carlos said.

He laughed loudly again and opened another cola and took big gulps. Erica looked at him and was thinking, how his bladder held all that liquid was nothing short of a Guinness World Book feat!

"You see the only thing I am addicted to is this!" He held up the cola and carried on. "Cola is my only vice. I don't do any drugs. Marco takes them all! That is why he can't leave old Scott. He has him by the balls! He is hooked! I will never be!" Carlos exclaimed defiantly.

"So what do you do with your portion of the drugs? Sell them to others?" Sofia asked. She felt sure that he did but was pleasantly astounded by his reply.

"Drugs damage minds and bodies. They ruin lives. I flush mine down the toilet and pretend to old Scott that I am stoned! Neat eh?" Carlos boasted seeming to seek their approval.

"Back to the customs woman, now they go when she is on the shift. She clears things as 'prim and proper,' something like *Miss Posh* here." Carlos joked as he looked at Erica while she looked up to the even more gloomy sky, laden with thick heavy dark clouds which were waiting patiently to burst forth showers on them.

"I am getting to the point *Miss Posh* and I too can see those black rain clouds up there. Yes the Chiara woman gets a nice bonus when everything is cleared and the container sent off to the importer."

"Who is the importer?" Ethan asked and was glad that Carlos was making connections with the information which they had sifted through. He too was worried about the rain and also what to do about Carlos.

"Now the importer is always a *'phantom'* company so even though a company name and address exist on the manifest, the bill of laden, it is never really the true importer! So I don't know!" Carlos bluntly stated.

"Canada *'runs'* always have gold and token commodities, just in case but the *'runs'* to Miami and here in Panama City, freight far more than gold!" Carlos paused, went silent and solemn, lowered his eyes to the ground and then looked at the ever increasing blackening sky.

He stood up paced and looked at the three. Their eyes staring up at him expectantly and before he spoke a large rain drop fell on his face. It was as though the sky shed a tear. He didn't wipe it away. He sat back down and slowly and softly spoke.

"The Mistral C's voyages to Panama City and Miami traffics people. Captain Scott traffics young girls!" Carlos held his head in his hands and said no more. After coming to the end of his alarming statement the clouds emptied themselves. Water poured out from the dark black clouds as if this was a cry for help from the sky. They all scampered to the car and sat in silence as the heavy showers pounded down on the car. Mother Nature seemed to be weeping.

Chapter Fifty-One

When they arrived back at uncle Chester's they were wet, cold and felt very uncomfortable. More so from the news they had been filled with by Carlos Carrillo, than from the heavy rain that had fallen on them and was still continuing to fall. Was it possible that Carlos was telling tall tales? They all wondered.

Ethan had bought him a mobile phone, topped it up and said that he would call him soon to meet again. After making the purchase they had dropped Carlos off in quite a rough area. Before he got out of the car he said that he was not going back to old Scott and would lie low until Ethan called.

After each of them had had their showers they met in the sitting room and could see that there was no relenting in the rain. It was coming down in torrents. When Ethan asked if anyone wanted to have dinner the answers were all the same, no. Carlos' disclosures were so incredible that their appetites were all suppressed by them.

They had to think fast and carefully as to what their next move would be. Carlos had said that it was futile in going to the police since you could not tell whom you could trust, corruption was high.

In some ways it was good that Carlos' focus was primarily on survival since he was unaware of Sidney's murder and did not know who Erica really was. They finally decided that they had to eat and settled for a plate each of plain oven chips.

"If Carlos' account was true then this could be part of the motive or the motive, for Sidney's murder." Sofia reasoned and continued, "It could be that Captain Scott wanted a bigger share of the illegal gains and Sidney was reluctant to give and Captain Scott murdered him in an argument."

"Erica sorry, but I know we've been through this all before but can you remember anything you saw on your father's yacht that night?" Ethan knew he was touching on a sore point for Erica but he had to continue. "What about Gerardo? He was the last person whom you were with did he drop you off at your father's yacht?" Ethan looked at Erica as he asked this question and waited for her response.

"Ethan, all I can say is that I have absolutely no recollection of what happened after I met Gerardo but please don't try to involve Gerardo in this." Erica strongly reiterated, clearly defending Gerardo.

"He is not saying that Gerardo is involved but we need to know what happened that night. Are you not wondering how you got on the yacht and how you got drugs in your system?" Sofia asked while becoming agitated because she just wanted to blurt out all that she knew about Gerardo to bring Erica out of this love trance!

"Are you accusing Gerardo of drugging me?" Erica said with irritation in her voice. The two girls stared at each other. Ethan stepped in to diffuse the situation and brought hot chocolate in for everyone.

"Was there anything different about the night you spent with Gerardo?" Ethan asked as they sipped the hot drink.

"Well now that you ask that, we did go to another place that we had never gone to before somewhere over by Moss Grove." Erica slowly said. "How did you get there?" Ethan asked.

"Gerardo drove us in a Yaris. Come to think about it I had never seen that car before." Erica continued.

"From my looking at the map isn't Moss Grove just three miles from where your father's yacht was berthed?" Ethan probed. There was silence and Erica got up and looked out at the rain. It was now getting dark and the showers were still pelting down.

"It was dark that night and my memory of it all is still very fuzzy, maybe it was not Moss Grove. I could be wrong." Erica said softly. It was evident that Erica did not want to come to terms with the fact that Gerardo could be in anyway involved.

"Gerardo does not know my father and Gerardo's name is not listed in any of my father's diaries or documentation so there is no valid connection to my father's murder." Erica said defensively.

"Would you object to asking Gerardo where you both went that night and where he dropped you off?" Ethan looked to Erica for confirmation to doing this.

"He must be going mad out of his head in not hearing from me. He must be really worried about me if he has been listening to the news." Erica stated her concerns about Gerardo and consented.

"Do you know his number out of your head?" Ethan asked since Erica's phone had been seized by the police.

"I am good with phone numbers. Here is his usual mobile number and the one he last called me on." Erica said calling the numbers out as Sofia wrote them down.

Ethan handed Erica one of the new mobile phones he had purchased and told her to ring Gerardo and ask if she could meet up with him. In turn each of the numbers which she rang went to voice mail. She left a message on each asking Gerardo to call her ASAP.

While waiting for Gerardo's call they went over Sidney's diaries and documents again and were now able to make connections with Captain Scott and Chiara Moseley. They still had the others to find links for and knew that they had to meet with Carlos again.

Their browsing of Sidney's files was abruptly interrupted as they all listened to the ringing of the mobile which lay on the table. Undoubtedly it was one of the numbers listed for Gerardo which appeared on the screen. Erica's heart beat increased and her face became flushed.

This time she somehow did not experience the same emotions she had had in earlier times. This time she felt somewhat fearful and apprehensive. What would he say to her? Ethan had told her what to say to Gerardo but how would he feel about her as an escaped fugitive?

"Hello Gerardo!" She said this with heightened enthusiasm probably a bit too much given her situation.

"Hello Erica." His greeting was flat and nondescript.

"You know what has happened but I first want to say that I am not guilty. I did not kill my father!" Erica exclaimed and then went on. "Can we meet at your place so I can ask you about the last night we were together?"

There was a pause of prolonged silence from Gerardo and then he said, "Can I call you back?" Without waiting for Erica's reply he disconnected the call. Erica felt bruised by Gerardo's coldness. "Well I'll have to wait. He must be busy." This was Erica's excuse for the callous dismissal by Gerardo.

They silently resumed their browsing of Sidney's files and then decided to turn in. Ethan kept all of the phones with him but said that he was a light sleeper and if Gerardo did call that he would bring the phone to Erica. Ethan however knew from past experience that Erica had a habit of sneaking out in the night to meet Gerardo so he had intended to keep watch and had again advised her against disclosing their location.

Erica went to bed thinking that she was happy to hear the sound of Gerardo's voice but she was worried that he might be afraid to get back with her now that she was in this trouble. She felt that he may feel that it might ruin his reputation.

She could not help but remember the good times they had had and knew that she needed to protect Gerardo from any repercussions which may come from being involved with her. A teenager and now a suspected murderer, sadly she thought, that all this could very well all mean the end of Erica and Gerardo. She was ever confident that Gerardo would want to help her and that in the end he would stand by her.

Chapter Fifty-Two

By now Gerardo had anticipated that he would have been out of Panama City but he wasn't. He hadn't listened to the news since the initial broadcast which indicated that Erica was in police custody so he reasoned that she must be out on bail. Where he was holding up was in a grimy no frills bed and breakfast which did not have the luxury of a television or radio. There was growing impatience as to his delayed returned to Guyana and so he had to move quickly. Erica was now throwing a spanner in the works. Had she told the police about her meeting with him on that fateful night?

Did they know about him and her? He had no idea and now needed to talk to her again with a view to finding this out. She had suggested meeting him. This may very well be expedient, he thought. However he was somewhat unsure as to what he really wanted to do now. Should he or shouldn't meet Erica? After a brief internal deliberation, he finally thought that indeed Erica could very well help him in his scheme of things. He wasn't leaving anything to chance though.

Very soon Gerardo made a phone call and went out to the back of the bed and breakfast. He pulled a roll of money from his pocket and palmed it. He walked off and intentionally bumped into a man wearing a hood. The man slipped him a gun as Gerardo slipped the money into the man's hand. .Gerardo suspiciously looked at the man.

"Sure this piece works? No fucking messing me about now would you?" Gerardo questioned.

"On my mother's life! Would I be shitting around with you?" The man replied.

"You ain't got no mother, sick Sammy did her in long time. So try your own life! Cause I will fucking kill you if this is shit!" Gerardo said through grit teeth.

"That piece is top grade man! All loaded at no extra charge." The hooded man reassured.

Gerardo hastily walked away leaving the hooded man as the man counted the money. Suddenly the hooded man dashed after Gerardo. He pulled on Gerardo's shoulder and abruptly stopped him in his tracks. Gerardo spun around and the hooded man shook the money at Gerardo. Gerardo squinted his eyes as a scowl appeared across his face.

"Hey man this is short! Where's the rest of my fucking money man? The hooded man angrily asked.

Gerardo grabbed the hooded man's throat and pushed him up against a dumpster. Gerardo pulled out the gun and pressed it to the hooded man's temple. The hooded man wobbled and tried to draw back from Gerardo.

"Shall I see if this works right now? A test run maybe? Eh? Eh?" Gerardo angrily questioned.

"Man! We cool! You can owe me. Just point that thing away from me!" The hooded man pleaded.

Very slowly Gerardo backed off and put the gun away. He eyeballed the hooded man, and then patted him on the face. Gerardo stared at the hooded man and smiled.

"Bill settled? Yes? Paid in full!" Gerardo sly stated. And walked away.

Chapter Fifty-Three

The sun had finally regained its position in the heavens. The rain clouds were now pushed back to reveal a blue sky, radiating warmth after yesterday's and last night's heavy rain fall. Erica had not slept well at all and Ethan was tired from his night vigil of keeping watch. What Ethan did not know was that Sofia also was secretly watching out, in case Erica had decided to sneak out.

They had their breakfast and watched the morning news where someone had leaked to the press that Erica was a drug user and that her mobile phone, which was in the possession of the police, had an incriminating text on it which was sent to her father. The news reporter went on to say that the text possibly suggested that Erica was blackmailing her father and that may have been the reason why she killed him. It also said that Erica was still not back in police custody and gave a description of her. Thankfully they did not show a picture of her.

The presenter then switched to news about the unidentified dead girl's body found by the docks, *Jane Doe*. It stated that the police were appealing to anyone who had information to come forward. The police said that the girl did not drown and that an autopsy had revealed that she had been poisoned, possibly also buried and then dug up, before being placed in the sea. Unconfirmed information leaked to the press also said that it was possible that the body was buried in close proximity to Sedums.

As the news broadcast was coming to an end, the mobile rang and startled the two girls. Erica sprang to her feet and they all glanced at the screen. Unmistakably it was one of Gerardo's mobile numbers which appeared across the screen. Erica picked the phone up with shaking hands. "Hello Gerardo I really miss you." Was Erica's greeting. Sofia pressed her ear on to the phone to hear Gerardo's response.

"Hi babe, meet me at eight tonight. I will send a text with the address. Don't be late." Gerardo was unemotional and he quickly disconnected the call. Sofia breathed out loudly, with a big disapproving sigh and repeated out what she heard Gerardo say to Erica. She then looked at Ethan with a frown on her face, indicating contempt for Gerardo. Ethan as usual showed no expression and said nothing.

"He did call, so I will wait for his text." Erica said with a hint of jubilation. She did not have to wait very long because the text followed almost instantaneously with the address. His text also read, 'Come to the front door of Riverview bed and breakfast and I will be there to meet you, come alone.'

Ethan and Sofia looked at the address and immediately noticed that it was in an area very close to where they had dropped off Carlos in Colón. On hearing this, Erica recalled that she had never been to Gerardo's house before but she somehow did not expect that he would be staying in such a rough slum.

"We are all going with you and we need a plan." Ethan firmly stated. Before Erica could object he took the mobile phone from her and called Carlos.

"Carlos we need to meet tonight at seven, same place we dropped you off." Ethan spoke into the phone like a commander and waited for Carlos' reply.

"That's fine *Chief*, no problem. I'll be waiting." Carlos eagerly said to Ethan. Ethan felt that Carlos would be a good person to have along with them on this occasion. He was street wise and he knew the area.

Sofia was however hoping that they could indeed trust Carlos and that there would be no unpleasant surprises waiting for them from Carlos or for that matter Gerardo. Indeed she hoped that neither Gerardo nor Carlos had called the police to turn in Erica. How could they tell if Carlos, by now had worked out who Erica was? Therefore there was a high possibility that the police could be waiting for them. Sofia shared all these concerns with Ethan and Erica.

Ethan agreed and said that those adverse possibilities were also occupying his mind. Erica was pensive and silent for a short while but again re-affirmed her trust and faith in Gerardo and said that she felt confident that Gerardo would not betray her and contact the police.

Ethan took the street map and studied it carefully with Sofia his co-driver. Erica looked on. There was an open park it seemed small but it had a community club house so it offered seclusion and if there was a community event then more people may be about.

He and Sofia also studied the connecting roads to ensure that if they had to make a hasty retreat that they wouldn't be driving down a blind alley. They worked out possible exits from the street and alternate routes. After going through all this, Ethan then turned to Erica to go through a partial plan.

"We will let you out of the car on an adjacent side street out of sight of the B&B. Sofia will park a safe distance away but still within sight of the B&B. I will stand on the corner looking over at the entrance pretending to be just having a smoke and waiting on someone." Ethan said all this in as confident a manner that he could use but he really did not know how things would actually play out.

"Whatever you do, stay outside. Do not go inside." Ethan emphatically urged Erica. She listened to him without a word leaving her lips.

"We will continue and tighten up the plan better when we meet up with Carlos." Ethan felt that Carlos could have an input since he knew Colón better than they did. They would be sure to go early to scan the vicinity in case the police were about.

Outwardly Erica was listening to everything Ethan was saying, she admired his decisive planning and his kind help. However inwardly her soul was in turmoil; coming back to

Panama City was to be the solution for her wretched separation from the man she so dearly loved but so far her return had been an absolute horrific episode. She had been arrested and is under suspicion for her father's murder!

She held her head in her hands. "Why, why is this happening to me?" Erica screamed and ran outside. Ethan followed her and when she stopped he just calmly held her close. She leaned on his shoulder and cried, until she had no more tears left.

He gently took her by the hand and walked along the path which was lined with small shrubs. The cool air and the smell of the wet grass seemed refreshing. It calmed her. They turned around and headed back to the house. Erica was glad to have a friend like Ethan, who was a firm tower of strength to lean on when the times were rough.

"Thank you Ethan. Thank you for being my friend." Erica said and squeezed his hand firmly before letting it go. They went inside to get some rest so that they would be alert later that night. They needed all their energy and wits about them for whatever awaited them.

Chapter Fifty-Four

Today Lee and Jim had received the final instructions from their blackmailer as to where to make the drop. The blackmailer emphasized that Lee was to make the drop, no one else. Detailed instructions outlining that the bag with the money was to be placed in a manhole and left, were all written up in a scorching text message.

Jim was to sit on a bench a few feet away from the drop site, where he would be watched by a sniper in hiding. Should things go wrong or if the police came to the drop site, then Jim would be shot. This was explicitly stated by the blackmailer.

The Gagnons however had a different plan to this. Lee thought that the Gagnon brothers didn't take orders from anyone and they sure as hell were not about to start. They were going to use a reliable and trusted business associate whom they preferred to call Jack of Spades. This was his gambling name. Jack of Spades would make the drop instead of Lee. He was roughly the same height and build. In the dark and distance he would not be easily recognizable as not being Lee.

Jim also had Jack of Spades seek out and pay a homeless man, who was also given clean and expensive clothes to wear, to match what Jim wore, to impersonate Jim. The homeless man would be the one sitting on the bench not Jim. After the drop, Jack of Spades would walk away after placing the bag in the man hole and Jim's impersonator was to be instructed to stay on the bench and wait for Jack of Spades to tell him where to go to be paid the remainder of his money.

Jack of Spades would double back and wait in hiding to see who was retrieving the bag. The Gagnons firmly instructed him that he was to ensure that he was the only person leaving that scene that night and with the money. They had packed the bag taking care to place right on the top a series of twenty dollar bills as was ordered.

To the Gagnons that was chicken feed but they hated parting with money and wanted to make sure that they got it back. Tonight at eight they were hoping to put an end to this torturous affair. They did not like being manipulated by anyone and this was serious. This could mean the end of their careers. They were not sure if they could bribe their way out of what they had done and they did not want to find out.

"Did you watch the news this morning?" Lee asked Jim. Jim often did not get out of bed until very late when they were in Panama City. He however kept the TV on even though he slept and this annoyed Lee greatly.

"Why are you asking? Did you not hear the sound of my TV?" Jim retorted. The two brothers could not really get on but still they kept living together. Theirs was an unusual union which couldn't be deciphered.

"Well if you listened to the news how come you have not mentioned the news report about the body that was found?" Lee was aiming for Jim to become concerned but he wasn't budging.

"It really should be left alone and not discussed." Jim warned.

"Watching and listening to developments surrounding it can be useful." Lee softly said as though someone was listening. Lee's urge to always be in control of situations made him nervous when he couldn't be and he was becoming nervous now.

"Let's deal with one issue at a time. Don't call trouble before it comes. Leave it alone Lee!" Jim exclaimed and walked off to get the bag with the money ready for collection. He placed it close to the door.

"Bloody mess this all is!" Lee exclaimed.

Meanwhile Jack of Spades had noticed that the day had passed painfully slow but the sun was now quickly setting and darkness was closing in. He checked his watch to ensure that he was on time to collect the bag from the Gagnons. He also placed his Beretta inside his jacket pocket.

He was dressed immaculate. He looked in the mirror and thought that he did indeed look just like Lee Gagnon but could he pull it off? He reckoned that the blackmailer possibly didn't care really if it was indeed Lee Gagnon who made the drop and possibly only cared about getting the actual money.

Suddenly the thought of why the Gagnons were being blackmailed entered his mind but it left sooner than it entered. So long as he got paid nothing else mattered. He had commitments, several, and more bills often times than money. He had worked hard but gambled harder. Tonight's business had helped him to repay a good portion of his gambling debts. He closed his door behind him and got into his vehicle for the drive to the Gagnons.

Chapter Fifty-Five

The time had come for Erica's meeting with Gerardo. Carlos eagerly greeted Ethan with a cheerful hello and a nod and smile for the two girls. Ethan quickly briefed Carlos on why they were there. He limited his explanation and took care not to reveal the true reason for Erica's meeting.

Carlos confirmed their suspicions that the area was filled with dubious transient people and that that particular B&B was known to the police for drug dealing happening there. This information did not at all inspire confidence in dealing with tonight's events but they clearly knew that there was no other alternative but to face it all.

"Carlos I want you at the back of the B & B watching for anything or anyone that may appear out of the ordinary, including the police."

"Well *Chief,* it depends on what you call out of ordinary because around these parts everything is out of the ordinary! My eyes will be peeled though!" Carlos reassured.

"It's two whistles for the police and three for anyone else and I'll come around since a phone signal may not be present." Ethan said to Carlos and was glad that he was willing to help out.

"But where abouts exactly will you be?" Carlos smilingly asked Ethan. "I will be standing at the corner opposite the B&B. While our girl my co-driver, will be at the top of that side street, watching and waiting in the car."

"So it's *Miss Posh* that we have to make sure nothing happens to? Ok." Carlos asked and answered his own question. Ethan still held back all names and thought that Carlos was quite hilarious in his references to Erica and to him. Ethan reminded Carlos and Sofia to keep the mobile phones which he had given them, on vibrate but ready to communicate with him. He was hoping that they would have a signal and that nothing would go wrong.

The time had now come for their plan to be put into motion and Carlos left them and took up his position. Erica walked down the street to the B&B with her heart racing. In the past, meetings with Gerardo made her heart miss beats but those times were times of joy. She wasn't sure how to interpret these heart beats and feelings right now.

Her head was generally over ruled by her heart when it came to Gerardo but this time, some how she felt a measure of anxiety. What would he say to her and how would he feel about all the trouble she was in? She was sure that he would be able to explain the last night they spent together, the night her father was killed. Surely he will help her.

As Erica got closer to the B&B she could see Gerardo. He didn't look his usual self in terms of how he was dressed. She had never seen him in a track suit and he never wore a baseball cap before. Erica reasoned that he had to dress like that so as not to be robbed in an area like this. He had to blend in. He probably met her here because it was less conspicuous.

"Hello babe. Your hair looks different." Gerardo greeted her as she threw her arms around him and held him so tightly that he had to force open her arms to get her to release him. Ethan watched on as he stood aimlessly opposite pretending to light up a cigarette.

"How are things? What have you been up to? Did you tell the police about us?" Gerardo asked.

"Of course not Gerardo I would-." Before she could finish answering he opened the door of the B&B and gently shuffled her inside.

"Damn it!" Ethan muttered. "What did I tell her? What did I tell her?" He muttered again and text Sofia and Carlos. 'She's gone inside!' Ethan was not sure what to do next but told Carlos and Sofia to hold their positions and he would hold his.

Erica was glad to be away from the public view of her and Gerardo's meeting and knew that she was changing the plan but felt that the privacy of the B&B would give her that closeness to Gerardo. He would be able to talk to her more freely. Gerardo walked her briskly up to his room and closed the door.

"You look great babe. Have you been missing me?" Before Erica could respond he held her close and kissed her and continued speaking.

"A friend of mine has left me some money. You know, the funds you don't want the government to know about but when he came to me to deliver, I missed him by a few minutes and the silly fool has now told me that he left it down the manhole out back." Gerardo kept kissing Erica and nibbling her ear all the while he continued talking.

"Now I need a favour. I want you to go with me to get the bag and then we will come back and talk all about you babe. It won't take a minute to go out back." Gerardo cupped her face in his hands and looked into her eyes and said, "Please Erica."

Before she knew it, Gerardo opened the door to the room held her hand and guided her out and back down the stairs. As if on automatic, Erica walked and kept pace with him and quickly found herself outside but at the rear of the B&B which backed on to part of the park. Carlos spotted them and whistled three times. He was very surprised to see *Miss Posh* being led by this man.

Ethan heard the whistling and covertly went around to the back. Carlos now spotted Ethan in between the trees who motioned to him to also follow Erica and Gerardo. It was five minutes past eight o'clock now and growing darker by the minute. As they walked on, they couldn't help but notice how quiet and deserted the park was. Apart from them, there was only one old man sitting on a bench in the distance.

They watched as Gerardo stopped and whispered into Erica's ear. Then he stepped back to the side of a dumpster, which was filled with building rubble as if he was hiding.

Erica walked on for a few more yards and then quite surprisingly, she bent down in front of a manhole, lifted the cover and retrieved what looked like a rather heavy bag.

As she turned and started to walk back with the bag in her hand, towards the dumpster where Gerardo had retreated to, suddenly a gunshot rang out and barely missed her head. Erica dropped the bag and also dropped to the ground. Hyperventilating, she slowly raised herself up but another shot aimed at her whizzed by, missing her head again. She kept low and made a run for some trees.

Carlos' senses were sharp and he quickly realized that one of the shots had come from Gerardo. Armed with a broken plank he had picked out of the builder's dumpster, Carlos crept up behind Gerardo and knocked the gun from his hand. Before he could strike again, Gerardo sprinted out picked up the gun, ran and grabbed the bag.

Ethan saw Gerardo but out of the corner of his eye he also saw a tall figure moving between the trees and before he could get a closer look almost immediately, this tall figure stepped out of the silhouettes with a gun in his hand. The man aimed and fired several shots at Gerardo. Crouching low and running, Gerardo returned fire. There was a volley of gun shots as the noise pierced the night air.

Erica could feel insects crawling up her legs but she dared not move since she felt certain that her life would be ended by a bullet. She cowered in the bushes which were a mixture of stinging nettles and waited for an opportunity to run.

In the blackness of the night Gerardo was a cheetah, he moved with speed. In the flashes of movement it was evident however that the weight of the bag was beginning to hold him back. The distance was closing between him and his pursuer.

Erica took this opportunity to slither away further in between the shrubs and thorn bushes which pricked her face and caught her clothing. She kept still and endured the stings of all the ants that had attached themselves on to her legs and were attacking them with ferocity. Ethan had by now joined Carlos in hiding behind stacks of garbage and they quietly watched the unfolding drama.

To lighten his burden and increase his momentum, they watched as Gerardo threw the bag over the top of another dumpster. The assailant kept up the chase. Then suddenly a single shot was discharged. The noise was deafening, more so because it was fired virtually from in front of where Carlos and Ethan were hiding.

Gerardo's knees buckled and he fell flat on to his face groaning and writhing. His assailant deliberately walked up to him and shot him a second time, right in the head. The gunman now turned towards the dumpster where Gerardo had thrown the bag but a voice was heard from a window in the B&B.

"What's happening out there? What's going on? I need to fucking sleep!" The shouts from an irate guest rang out.

These shouts seem to startle the assailant into fleeing mode for fear of being discovered and caught. He put his gun away and ran off into the night. His feet thumped the ground so loudly that it sounded as though it would break. One more gun shot rang out in the distance and then there was silence.

Carlos and Ethan waited quietly to confirm that the attacker was gone. They cautiously crept out from amongst the stacks of garbage, looking around guardedly and seeking out Erica. Ethan quickly ran over to Gerardo bent down to him and felt his wrist for a pulse. He looked up at Carlos and shook his head indicating that Gerardo was dead.

Ethan searched through Gerardo's pockets and emptied them of their contents. He stuffed these into his own pockets. He stood up quickly but now Carlos was nowhere to be seen! Ethan frantically headed in the direction of where he thought Erica was hiding but she was not there. Desperately, Ethan quietly called out her name.

"Erica! Erica!" Was she shot too? His mind was not thinking. It was just spinning. Turning in shock and disbelief as to what had just happened but then he thought again, exactly what did just happen? The entire episode was unbelievable!

Just then he heard foot-steps within the bushes. He drew back into the trees. Was it the gunman? He positioned himself for flight or fight. Panic was creeping in on him and he had to keep focused. He could not let fear overcome him and he was not going to. Just then out from within the bushes, he distinctly heard a soft whisper of, *Chief, Chief* travelling softly on the night wind.

"*Chief, Chief,*" was being repeated by Carlos. Ethan then stepped out of hiding and ran towards the bushes where Carlos was calling out from. To his relief and surprise Erica was with Carlos. As soon as she saw him, she threw her arms around him and then around Carlos who had searched and found her still crouching in the bushes. She was not alright but filled with abject fear and shock! Her body was shaking and her head was splitting open with pain. She could neither think nor walk properly.

"Are you ok? You are not hit, are you?" Ethan asked anxiously and kept looking her over.

"She only has lots of stings and bites from insects and ants and trembling from the shock of being shot at, otherwise she is ok." Carlos volunteered to answer. Ethan breathed a big sigh of relief but still kept looking around and whispering.

"Quick! We must get back to the car and leave here right away before the police and people come."

"Ha! Ha!" Carlos laughed moderately loud.

"What's so funny Carlos, you think this is a laughing matter? This is serious shit!" Ethan said through grit teeth. He couldn't understand Carlos' behaviour and he didn't want to waste time attempting to find out.

"Why I'm laughing is because you well to do folks do not understand poor people. Look around you. Do you see anyone running to find out what's happened? No! No one gives a shit! People get robbed and killed often around here and it's business as usual. That's the reality of it all." Carlos explained in a slow and emphatic voice. As they turned to leave, Carlos picked up a large bag from the bush behind him.

"What the hell! When did you pick that up?" Ethan did not swear as a rule but this night was turning him into a man that he did not want to be. He felt somehow changed and he did not want to be changed.

"Is that not the bag that Gerardo threw into the dumpster?" Ethan looked at Carlos waiting for an answer while Erica looked at them both and said nothing but kept on trembling.

"*Chief* which of your questions do you want me to answer first?" Carlos said and smiled at Ethan. Ignoring Carlos' reply, Ethan started to move him and Erica along by pointing towards the street. Then he stopped them and paused for a moment and then spoke.

"Wait. We must not leave all together. Carlos you go first and Erica and I will follow like a couple taking an evening walk." Carlos swiftly walked off with the bag and Ethan took hold of Erica's hand which was cold and icy and waited to give Carlos a slight head start. He quickly peeped at his mobile and it had several missed calls and texts from Sofia.

He released Erica's hand quickly and called Sofia. He whispered into the phone that Carlos was coming and they were following. Erica was still shaking and her eyes were staring. She may need to see a doctor Ethan thought. She is most likely in shock but more importantly they needed to get away from this place and fast!

As they neared the car he could see Carlos standing outside and waiting. Sofia was still sitting inside getting more and more anxious. Carlos had filled her in briefly while he was waiting for Ethan and Erica to arrive.

"Ok *Chief*, what's next? Inside this bag is money. I peeped in. What do you want to do about it?" Carlos asked Ethan a question which he had to think fast about but before he could utter a response two thugs appeared from nowhere and pushed Erica away from Ethan. One pulled a knife and wheeled it around from Carlos to Ethan then to Erica who was trying to regain her footing. Sofia slipped down into the car seat unseen by them.

"Give me your money! Give me your fucking money!" The knife wheeler shouted.

"Yeah! Come on! Come on! We ain't got all night. Money!" The second thug ordered. His voice was bigger than he was and his lack of height made his demand seem trivial but still yet menacing. The one with the knife moved towards Erica and this seemed to make her snap out of her shock. Her eyes glared at the two men.

Ethan looked at Carlos, and then he looked at the knife. He next looked at the bag. Carlos instinctively knew what he had to do. Very quickly Carlos threw the heavy bag and hit the man who held the knife. It toppled him to the ground and Carlos took up the knife and threw it over the club house fence. As the thug stood up, Ethan backed away and leveled him to the ground with a drop kick. Ethan now maintained his defense with several kicks. Erica punched the short thief and placed him in a firm neck hold. The two thieves were making an incredible amount of noise and another one of their cronies came flying to their rescue.

He pounced on Carlos and tried to pull the bag from him. Carlos wrestled with him and they ended up on the driver's side of the vehicle. Sofia then violently pushed opened the car door knocking the thief over. He promptly got up and stumbled away very fast.

Ethan and Erica landed punch after punch on the other two. When they both found themselves flat on their backs on the ground, with their opponents positioned over them, with their feet on their chests, then they rescinded their earlier demands.

"Please! Just let us go. We won't hurt you. Please." The knife wheeler whimpered.

"Yeah just let us go! We was just having some harmless fun. Sorry!" Short and demanding now offered an apology for his freedom. Ethan and Erica released their adversaries and the would-be thieves sped off. Erica thought that the night was so fraught that the only thing left to happen next was for the police to arrest her again.

"Let's go!" Ethan shouted. He did not have to stress the urgency of that request. Sofia started the engine and Erica got into the car as Ethan was about to get in, Carlos interrupted their departure.

"*Chief! Chief!* What about me? You ain't gonna leave me here, are you?" Carlos looked at him with wide eyed-disbelief. Ethan also felt that he could not leave him but was not sure that he could fully trust him either.

"Sofia let's switch drivers. You ride in the back with Erica. Carlos you up the front with me."

"Pop the boot I still got the stash!" Carlos pushed the bag in the boot of the A3 and jumped into the front seat. Ethan sped off. In the distance he could hear sirens. He didn't know if they were going to the park or elsewhere but he just wanted to get as far away as he could and as quickly as possible. They needed to leave Colón behind.

Chapter Fifty-Six

Martinez and Henriquez had spent yet another long day working on the two most recent murder cases. It was now very close to ten o'clock and they were still at the station. They had visited the Mistral C and had spoken to its captain Paul Scott if he knew anything about his employer's murder he was not letting on.

He had said that Sidney Durr's murder came as a shock to him since he could not think of one soul who would want to harm him. He had described the relationship which he had with his boss as a good one and said that they got on well. He said he knew nothing about Sidney's ex-wife and children and had never met any of them.

Both inspectors were troubled by the fact that they were nowhere close to solving Sidney Durr's murder and were unable to find Erica, the main only suspect. Her phone which they found at the murder scene had had a blackmailing message to her father on it. But what was the secret that she mentioned and who was the elusive mistress the father had?

In addition to all this, they now had *Jane Doe's* murder to investigate and had no leads what so ever. Young girls go missing regularly and are often not reported since many come into Panama City and get involved in prostitution, so where to start was difficult.

"Henriquez is it your usual black coffee?" Martinez called out as he made a drink for himself.

"Yes thank you. Bring it in we'll be here a while." Henriquez replied as he read through the reports on his desk.

"How in God's name did the Channel 11 news get wind of the details surrounding the fact that *Jane Doe* was possibly buried near to Sedums?" Henriquez angrily asked Martinez and went on. "I feel that we may have a *leak* in amongst us, someone getting money from Channel 11." He stated.

"What's puzzling is why bury her then dig her up and then dump her body in the water down by the docks?" Martinez was by now reading over the report again and felt that this may very well be one of those unsolved cases which rested in the filing cabinets. People rarely came forward with information unless of course they were going to be paid for it and even then the bought information often led nowhere. As they read through the file again and looked through missing persons' reports nothing matched *Jane Doe*.

"Yes?" Henriquez picked up his internal line and Myles was on the other end. She was working the night shift and had just come on duty.

"A report just came in that two men have been found dead in Colón." Myles said into the phone and continued, "Do you want me to come along with you and Martinez?"

"Another murder, rather two, this is becoming a bloody joke!" Henriquez said loudly without answering Myles' question.

"What is it?" Martinez asked, raising his eyes from the files.

"Two stiffs over in Colón. Yes Myles you may as well come along." Henriquez stood up and put on his raincoat. It had suddenly started to rain and he disliked getting wet. Martinez and Myles joined him and got out umbrellas. Myles travelled along with another officer in the marked police vehicle while Henriquez and Martinez drove in an unmarked car.

When they arrived the first officers on the scene had cordoned it off to keep back the few onlookers. Martinez noted that one victim was lying on his face on the ground while the other was around the corner a few yards away.

"Who called this in?" Henriquez asked Myles while looking around. His eyes caught the back of the B&B.

"It was an anonymous caller who only said that two men were dead in Colón by Riverview Park."

"What time did the call come in at?" Martinez asked trying to put some sort of time line together to relate it to the time of death, when that is known. "Eight forty-five." Myles said.

"Well we can see that this old guy was shot in the head." Henriquez said as he walked around the body. "He's very well-dressed in expensive clothes to be out here in Colón." Henriquez vocally observed.

"How do these two deaths link or is there no link at all?" Martinez asked.

"No identification on either one of them. The one face down on the ground, his pockets are turned out, possibly robbery but before or after he was dead?" Henriquez asked since Colón was not a reputable place.

"Both have gunshot wounds. A B&B card was found near the body of the younger man." Martinez stated.

"The coroner and the rest of the officers are taking all the evidence they can. Have they spoken to any of these few onlookers to see if anyone has seen anything?" Henriquez enquired.

"One man said that he only saw a very expensive car driving through this area last night but he could not remember the number plate but said that it was a two door Audi. Another said that he saw a gang fighting by the same car but he also did not know the registration number." Myles reported.

"Very interesting this is but useless unless we have a registration number or identification on the gang members. We have nothing to really go on." Henriquez stated. He started to think that this was now four murders in quick succession and he could not help but feel that they had their work cut out for them.

"Let's go into the B&B and speak to the manager there is nothing more we can do here besides get very wet and cold." Henriquez said to Myles and Martinez as they headed towards the B&B. They were intercepted by TV reporters who were firing questions one after the other at the police officers.

"Is it true that these killings were drug related?" The reporter asked. "All we can say is that two males were found dead and we are investigating."

"Officer some people here, say that it was gang related. Is that true?" The reporter was relentless in questioning. Henriquez just calmly said, "I have no further comment to make at this time." They entered the B&B and asked that the reporters be kept outside.

Chapter Fifty-Seven

One by one they clambered out of the car feeling and looking shattered. Their adrenaline was still running high and each one felt that so much had happened this night that they were lucky to be alive. Carlos just stood up and seemed astounded. He looked all around in awe of the expanse of the property and grounds. He wasn't sure if he was more amazed by the sights around him or by what they just encountered.

"Golly this is something else out of the world!" Carlos exclaimed and continued to look around.

"Come on Carlos let's get inside. This rain will not make you grow any taller!" Ethan could feel the showers on his back and was not in the mood for getting drenched.

He had driven like a formula one champion to get to uncle Chester's and he just wanted to get inside and collapse his body on one of the soft arm chairs. The short distance from the garage to the door seemed like running the gauntlet. Every shrub and long thorn bush was either lashing them in the face or sticking to their hands and feet but they finally made it and were now secure inside the safety of uncle Chester's house.

Carlos' eyes were dilated as though he was having an eye test and his head was almost making three hundred and sixty degree turns looking all around the expanse of the immense house.

"What happened tonight? Exactly what happened?" Ethan said looking at the other three. No one answered everyone seemed too shocked to respond.

"Erica do you need to see a doctor because you must be in shock and have you really checked to ensure that you are not hurt?" Ethan wanted to be certain that she had not been physically hurt and that it wasn't going undetected because everything happened so fast.

"No. I am ok just some bruises from falling and a few insect stings and ant bites. I was standing in ants' nests I believe, and this agitated them." Erica's body was still shaking and denying her words.

"Let's try to analyze and piece together tonight because I cannot make any sense out of it. First let's all get something to eat and drink and then we will all be able to think clearer." Ethan urged.

They all went into the kitchen and Carlos was amazed that it could hold the four of them and still have room for about ten more people.

"Wow this is a cool place. Do all of you live here? Man this is more than cool!" He kept on surveying the place so much so that he didn't seem to realize that no one answered his question. Sofia made her usual hot chocolate for everyone and Ethan was helped by Carlos to make toasted cheese sandwiches. He also got out chocolate cream biscuits for everyone.

They took their night's feast into the sitting room and dug into the food. Fear seemed to have heightened rather than suppressed their appetites and they ate like ravenous beasts. With all the food consumed, they looked at each other and smiled. It seemed that then and there a bond of friendship had been sealed between the four young people.

"Thanks Carlos for helping out tonight. I think you probably saved Erica's life. Thank you." Ethan said this with deep appreciation and sincerity.

"Yes Carlos, I am very grateful to you for helping me. Thank you." Erica's eyes fell to the floor since she was feeling that she was the cause of all of this trouble.

"Well we made it out of Colón alive. Now it is open to you Erica to tell us what happened." Ethan said and continued by being direct with his next question. "Why did you go inside the B&B and why did you go out back to get that bag?" Ethan asked.

"Shit *Chief,* the bag is still in the boot of the car!" Carlos exclaimed and jumped up from his seat to go outside.

"Please sit Carlos the bag can wait. It is safe in the car. Please let Erica tell us what happened." Ethan calmly stated but realizing that he had started calling Erica by name. Carlos unquestioningly sat back down.

"I really don't know why. He just has a way of talking me into things. I went in and he immediately said that he wanted to pick up a bag left for him from out back. When we got there Gerardo then asked me to pick it up for him." Erica looked at her feet but she knew that everyone in the room was staring at her.

"Did you not think it strange that he was asking you to do something like that?" Sofia asked Erica and wondered how long she could restrain herself from grabbing hold of Erica and shaking sense into her. Erica didn't answer and just stared at her feet. She felt ashamed of herself and of how she had endangered the lives everyone else.

"Who the hell was that friend of yours? Some friend who was shooting to kill you! What did you do to him, a shake down gone bad?" Carlos asked Erica and looked at not only Erica but at each of them for an answer. No answer came.

"Why did Gerardo want to kill you? Could the reason be linked to what has happened to your father" Ethan asked Erica this but knew that she would or could not supply an answer.

"*Chief,* let me go and get the bag to see exactly how much money is inside maybe this was a payment for drugs and the deal went bad. Colón is famous for drug dealing." Carlos said.

Ethan got up and took the keys and went outside with Carlos. He still did not place one hundred percent trust in Carlos. It was possible that he could drive away with the car and the money if he gave him the keys.

Thankfully the rain had stopped and the night air was heavy with the smell of the lawn grass and the green foliage along the pathway. As they walked out to the garage Carlos engaged Ethan in conversation about the night and said that he felt that they all worked together as a good team. Ethan listened and smiled but his mind was on untangling the night's events and how he would go about handling the information about Erica in Carlos' presence.

Could he bring Carlos into their circle? Could he divulge the present truth about Erica? Ethan unlooked the car boot and Carlos retrieved the bag. It was heavy but Carlos carried it without a complaint. Finally reaching the house Carlos set the bag down and waited for the *Chief's* instructions. They all looked at Ethan to give the order to open the bag. He just simply nodded his head and Carlos pulled the Velcro of the handles apart, unzipped the bag and put his hand inside and took out a stack of what appeared to be money.

"What the hell!" Carlos exclaimed looking at the stack in his hand. A twenty dollar note was on top but the remainder of the stack was all paper! Carlos frantically turned the contents of the bag on to the floor and all the stacks had twenty dollar bills on top but all else was paper! Carlos counted up the twenties and all the money that was in the bag, amounted to only one hundred dollars!

"Well that was going to be some big ass double cross!" Carlos loudly said. "I thought that we was all gonna be big time rich. Oh well, back to the streets!" Carlos said dejectedly. His hopes dashed to the ground.

"Don't worry I will pay you for your help tonight. You've been brilliant." Ethan handed Carlos five hundred dollars and on reaching into his pockets he remembered that he had put all the things from Gerardo's pockets into his. He now reached to take them out but he stopped.

The news at midnight was about to come on. Sofia had turned on the TV to see the Channel 11 news. They watched as the Colón murders took center stage of the news. The report showed covered bodies of two men one behind a wall and the other flat on his face. The news said that, 'these murders were possible gang related drug deals which went bad since residents reported seeing a group of men fighting in the street and reported gunshots being fired.

One of the dead men was believed to be Gerardo Abram but formal identification has not yet taken place. Gerardo Abram was forty and his nationality was believed to be Guyanese but he also held Mexican and Columbian passports which are suspected to be fraudulent. The police are asking for anyone who knew Gerardo Abram to contact them immediately. The other man found has not yet been identified.'

Sofia switched off the TV and sat back in the arm chair. Erica looked at her and felt lower than a snake. She had felt that Gerardo was shot but no one had confirmed to her that he was indeed dead. She had a plethora of feelings, anger, love and sorrow. She could not believe the trouble she was in and held her head in her hands.

Carlos interrupted the solemn silence that pervaded the atmosphere in the room since no one spoke. They all sat steaming in misery so he spoke and made a profound announcement.

"I was busy minding not to be shot but when that man, not *Miss Posh*'s friend, the other one who came out of the bushes, I thought that I recognized him and I believe that I do. He is the one that comes around to old Scott to collect some of the girls. He takes only the *posh* looking ones, three at a time." They all now sat up like Dobermans with their ears pricked.

"Are you sure of this?" Ethan asked feeling that this news could change things and help them make sense of all that was happening.

"I am sure. I will bet my life on it, even though no one cares about my life, that that was him! Old Scott called him Burns." Carlos' reply was unequivocal and his face radiated confidence. They were getting an overabundance of information but had to somehow put it all together. They had to solve Sidney Durr's murder. Erica had to be cleared.

"Carlos you are proving to be of great value to us. If Burns is connected to Captain Scott with the people trafficking and then Burns kills Gerardo but not before bringing him a bag which was supposedly to be filled with money, then Gerardo has to be in some way linked to Durr's death." Ethan reasoned aloud.

"Wait up *Chief*; I am missing part of this picture. Who is Durr?" Carlos asked looking around the room at the three of them and waiting for an answer. There was silence.

"Oh come on! I risked my life, it may not be worth anything to anybody but to me it's sacred man, precious! I know that trust is not given that it is earned but have I not done enough to earn your trust?" Carlos was seeking their approval of him and most importantly their trust to let him into their ring.

Ethan looked around at Sofia and then to Erica seeking her approval to bring Carlos into their confidence after all it was her life that was at stake. Even though no death penalty exists in Panama if she could not be cleared of this crime then she would spend a substantial amount of time incarcerated.

"Carlos, Erica has to call the shots here. Erica do you want me to paint the entire picture for Carlos?" Ethan was direct. He didn't want to dictate but wanted Erica to choose. She looked at each one of them, held her head in her hands and spoke directly to Carlos.

"You helped saved me and you have provided us with a lot of information which I am sure we all will try to piece together. Thank you Carlos." Erica got up and walked over to Carlos and hugged him.

"Never had a hug from a posh chick before, in fact I never had a real hug ever! Wow!" Carlos was beside himself with delight and it showed from the broad smile which smothered his face.

"Now, now Carlos, don't go getting any ideas, that was a platonic hug!" Ethan said laughing and then spoke directly to Erica.

"Does that mean that we can tell Carlos the whole story?" he asked.

"Yes!" she said loudly but held her head down.

"On second thought Erica, it is better that you tell your story. No one else knows it better than you." Ethan himself was trying to piece together this girl's story and was finding it extremely difficult to unravel what seemed like a gigantic puzzle of misfortune.

Carlos sat with eyes wide open turned towards Erica and listened attentively to her background relationship with Gerardo and her arrest for her father's murder. Carlos never flinched nor batted an eye eyelash he just soaked it all in. Erica then introduced herself by name and introduced Ethan and Sofia as her true and dependable friends.

"Carlos you are now welcomed to join in our friendship group if you want to, after hearing all that I have said." As she finished she started to cry and Ethan knew that it was time to stop and get some rest. Sofia showed Carlos his room and told him to help himself to some of uncle Chester's clothes. She knew that Chester wouldn't mind at all. He was a kind and generous man.

Ethan went to his room and emptied his pockets. He saw the three mobile phones which he had pulled from Gerardo's own pockets along with a small amount of what looked like heroine. If he was linked to Captain Scott maybe he set Erica up for her father's murder.

Tonight's events also sure looked everything like a setup. He must have known that if he went for the bag, that maybe he would be shot. He probably decided that one way or the other he would get Erica killed to silence her. The other dead man, who was he? What part did he play in all of this? Ethan speculated but was too tired to think anymore.

"What a fucking nightmare!" Ethan said loudly as he found himself swearing again. He now headed for the bath tub and then immediate sleep. However he realized that they now had more information but couldn't put it all together to make full sense. It was frustrating. He needed to sleep. He needed to recharge for tomorrow but he had agreed with Sofia to take turns to *'watch'* they needed to still keep vigil to see if Erica was sneaking off, despite Gerardo's demise and now to also ensure that Carlos didn't grass them up! Sofia was taking the first watch and him the second.

Erica showered with such extremely hot water that it burned her skin. She felt dirty, used and deceived! She wanted the hot water to dissolve her immense pain and misery right away. The heat was needed to purge and cleanse her soul. Inside her felt frozen and her heart seemed to have stopped. It was numb devoid of feelings and emotions.

She had fallen into the typical mould by being gullible. Trusting and foolish! Love and the desire to be a woman had blinded her. Somehow she could not believe that Gerardo had shot at her! He set her up but why? He had lied about his age too. It was just too unbelievable to comprehend and he had to have drugged her.

Colón the thought of the place made her skin crawl! His respectable façade certainly was brilliant. He had made an absolute fool out of her and she blamed herself. Why had she done it? Why? Are teenagers expected to be this way? Sofia certainly wasn't. Why was she? She wept uncontrollably. She wanted to drown in her tears.

Chapter Fifty-Eight

Last night's rain had helped Jim and Lee Gagnon to sleep well but it was not an easy sleep. Their minds were occupied with the drop. They crawled out of bed and wished now that they had not allowed Gerardo to take his holiday. They sure had a lot of cleaning up to do.

Lee stumbled into the kitchen and found Jim making a feeble attempt at making breakfast. He had dirtied more pots and pans than were required to make scrambled eggs and toast. Lee hated mess and quickly took charge of the breakfast fiasco. With plates in hands they walked into the dining room. Jim switched on the TV to get the nine o'clock news.

They had not heard from Jack of Spades as yet and they were a bit worried by the lack of communication. The Channel 11 news started with an announcement. 'Four murders in a week leave Panama City police baffled. The latest victims were found shot dead in Colón. One man remains unidentified while the other has been listed as Gerardo Abram. Formal identification is yet to take place and police are asking anyone who knows this man to get in contact with them. Sidney Durr's murder still remains unsolved along with that of *Jane Doe* who still has not been identified. Erica Durr is still at large and the police are urging her to give herself up.'

Jim jumped up from his chair spilling his hot coffee on to his trousers and ran to get his mobile phone. He frantically searched through his call log and pressed on Jack of Spades' number. Lee followed him and stood transfixed as he waited for the phone to be answered. It rang non-stop, it didn't even go to voice mail. The brothers were frantic. They paced up and down like frightened ferrets. With no answer, Jim finally pressed end and disconnected the call. They looked at each other with frantic eyes and said nothing for a while. Then Lee broke the silence.

"Gerardo, Gerardo?" He said the name with incredulous disbelief and he turned to look at Jim. "Right under our noses, he knew. He knew and the bastard was the one blackmailing us but worse, we never had him in the picture. Our trusted caretaker! We never suspected him!" Lee was beside himself now with the possibility of being found out.

"Where is Jack of Spades? Where the hell is he? Why isn't he answering his phone? I don't like this at all!" Lee was shouting and Jim needed to calm him down but he too was nervous and worried about this entire situation. It seemed out of their control. Lee carried on with his dooms day speculations and warnings.

"Bet he has pissed off. Told you we should not have paid him until everything was fine. Next thing you know the police will be ringing our door bell and we will be disgraced and in shackles" Lee said nervously. He was beside himself and rattled on. "I could not have imagined that the blackmailing culprit would turn out to be our very own Gerardo! What a shock!"

"We have been bloody fools all along!" Lee ranted and raved with such a scowl on his face that it looked painful.

"Lee! Lee!" Jim shouted. "We need to think this through calmly and not give ourselves away. We should go to the police and identify Gerardo as our caretaker and that would be all that we know. If we don't it will look suspicious as though we have something to hide so let's keep calm and leveled headed." Jim urged.

"Ok but where the hell is Jack of Spades? Where is he and why is he not answering his phone? Can you tell me?" Jim didn't answer but dabbed his trousers to dry off the spilt coffee and reheated the remainder which had gone cold.

He would drink his coffee to soothe his parched throat which was now tight and dry from the revelations on Channel 11 news. He just had to ignore Lee for a minute in order to gather his thoughts. Lee threw his scrambled eggs and toast into the bin along with the plate, knife and fork. He, like Jim had completely lost his appetite.

The brothers questioned themselves as to how they could have missed having Gerardo on their radar as a suspect. The obvious was staring them in the face all this time but yet they failed to see it. They could still pull this off and come up smelling like roses. They reckoned. They had to play their cards right. They had to convince the police that all Gerardo was to them was simply a caretaker nothing more nothing less. But where was Jack of Spades?

Chapter Fifty-Nine

It was almost noon when all body clocks of the four young people still weren't recharged. They were tired and they all seemed still in need of sleep especially Ethan and Sofia, who had kept the night watch. Erica was still in her room chastising herself for being used by Gerardo. They had never really talked about her father at any time apart from when Gerardo made her send Sidney that now damning blackmailing text message and a few queries from Gerardo about him but nothing more.

She remembered that Sofia had warned her sometime back that Gerardo was no good. In her words then, Sofia had called him, 'a predator' and said that 'she was his prey.' How very true Sofia was back then. How will she now face Sofia in the light of day? How will she even face Ethan? He had seen her sneaking out of the Grants' the very same night that she got arrested. How will she face him today?

With all those questions racing around in her head she finally made it down stairs and was determined to put on the best cheery face. Walking into the kitchen the aroma of eggy bread and bacon filled the air. Carlos had made breakfast.

"This kitchen smells great and the breakfast looks delicious!" Erica greeted them with these words of approval for Carlos' cooking while masking her embarrassment and awful feelings.

"I had to do all of the cooking on old Scott's ship and I learnt as I went along." Carlos proudly stated, serving up shares of his culinary delight.

"This is a planning breakfast so listen up while you eat. Last night I looked through Gerardo's mobiles-." Ethan said.

"Mobiles, how many did he have?" Erica interrupted asking this question with a despairing sigh.

"He had three mobile phones. One had only one contact someone called Valentina, only calls were listed no text messages. The other two had no contacts." Ethan was interrupted again but this time by Sofia.

"Hold it! Hold it! That name Valentina, yes Valentina!" Sofia repeated herself while all the others were anxiously waiting for Sofia's disclosure of who this woman was and to inflict more torture on her captive audience she continued by asking them a question.

"Don't you, Erica and Ethan, don't you remember seeing that name?" Sofia's torture knew no end it seemed and Ethan quickly asked to be put out of their misery for failure to recall.

"Would you please tell us who she is so we can get some sense out of all of this?" Ethan exclaimed.

"That name is in Sidney Durr's personal diary numerous times and in particular, on the date of the Chicago theatre performance. You saw that woman Erica. Don't you remember telling me that your dad was out with a young woman?" Before Sofia could go on Erica responded with a quick and confident reply.

"Yes! I shall never forget her face. She was far younger than my father and very pretty. So how is she connected to Gerardo?"

"That is exactly what we have to find out and very soon too." Ethan spoke with urgency. "No doubt the A3 was seen in Colón last night and let's pray that it wasn't reported to the police. We must move fast otherwise we may be accused of Gerardo's and the other man's murder." Ethan told the group. This was a very sobering thought which they had to bear in mind. Therefore they had to be more cautious.

"We will come back to the Valentina woman. There were no text messages, even Erica's were gone. The bag with the money seems to indicate that he was indeed blackmailing someone but whom? And what was the reason of the blackmailing scam?" Ethan asked.

Ethan was baffled by all this and could not let on to the group that he was having serious doubts as to whether they were not all in over their heads. After all, Erica nearly got killed last night!

Maybe he should hand this information over to the police who had the resources to deal with it but then what if it didn't clear Erica? She would face incarceration. Putting this in the corner of his mind he was about to continue when Sofia took the stage.

"I know someone who knew Gerardo." Sofia said, holding down her head slightly and not making eye contact with Erica. This revelation startled Erica who turned to stare at Sofia. Her lips quivered in an attempt to interrupt but she kept quiet.

"The café Erica and I used to go to after school in east side, one of the waitresses, Marrianna gave me the low down on Gerardo and-" Sofia's sentence was abruptly cut short by Erica.

"You knew things about Gerardo and never told me? I thought we were friends Sofia?" Erica sharply addressed Sofia and kept waiting for an answer.

"Erica you had already left the country when Gerardo made a pass at me!" Sofia said defensively.

"Where did this all happen and why did you not text and tell me?" Erica asked accusingly.

"If you would let me explain and not jump to conclusions then you would have a better understanding of what happened." Sofia softly said to her friend whom she knew, had now had all her emotions shattered and would have them completely mutilated by these revelations which would now follow.

"At the Café one evening Gerardo 'tried it on,' I resisted him and left the Café. Then the waitress Marrianna who saw him making a 'play' for me got on the same bus and told me about him." Sofia looked up and saw that Erica had a very distressed look on her face.

"So did she tell you whom he worked for?" Ethan asked Sofia as he tried to diffuse the volatile air between the girls. He could tell that Erica was not feeling very well hearing that Sofia held damning information about Gerardo.

"No but she said that her mother worked for the same people." Sofia answered and decided to look at Ethan and not at Erica, who was still staring at her.

"My parents also went to his employers for dinner but I did not ask them anything about it and won't at this time either unless we absolutely have to." Sofia stated.

"I thought that we shared everything and I am shocked that you knew things about Gerardo but did not tell me. Even at this time before last night when we have been here together, you still did not tell me. Was it to make a darn fool out of me?" Erica asked as she glared at Sofia. She was filled with anger and could not decide if she felt it more for Gerardo, herself or for Sophia?

"Erica please calm down. I know that you must feel dreadful by being betrayed by Gerardo but I did warn you when you were sneaking out with him and all you told me on one occasion was that the very heart of romance was uncertainty." Sofia reminded Erica and left the room.

"Ok I think that this is a good time for us all to have a break. It's no point in going out today. We are tired and it is now afternoon. It also keeps the A3 off the road for a while." Ethan suggested and they all agreed.

Erica left the room and went off to her bedroom. She wanted solitude. She felt like such an idiot and the friendship she had with Sofia seemed to be crumbling. How could Sofia withhold such vital information and sit and look her in the face day after day? She could have shaken sense into her to make her forget about Gerardo, Erica reasoned.

All she wanted to do now was to die! Death would be a remarkably great pain reliever! She was aching all over in her mind, body and soul. The entire affair was soul destroying!

Maybe she should give herself up to the police and let them sort it all out.

She was tired and for the first time she missed her mother and Emma. She wanted to cry in her mother's arms but right now her tears seemed spent. She wanted to shed tears but none came. It was a hollow and empty feeling. A horrible feeling that she did not know how and when it would end, how would she be able to put Gerardo out of her mind? The man she so loved and now the man she so hated!

Sofia was in her room and could not sit, lie down or stand still. She paced the room. Up and down, up and down, seeking answers for why she did not tell Erica about Gerardo. Why she was so cruel in delivering the news to her just now. Was it because she had no love in her life? Was it because she was jealous of Erica and Gerardo?

What the hell was wrong with her? Why did she not save her friend from this trouble? Why? Why? Back then she just helped Erica with her deception. If she was a good friend, would she have played such a significant role in helping her to stage one ruse after the other?

Is that what a good friend does? Help you court misfortune? Sofia felt that she was as much to blame for Erica's mess as Erica herself. This was more than a mess. For crying out loud this was murder!

Chapter Sixty

Yesterday was difficult with all the revelations about Gerardo. Today's meeting was going to be no less painful. The girls still were barely on speaking terms so Ethan made it swift and painless outlining what the day's tasks were. They were to look over the remainder of Sidney Durr's files to see if they had missed anything. They spent hours doing this in gloomy silence. By afternoon nothing new surfaced so they stopped had lunch and a rest.

Later they all got into the car and left the house headed for the café in east side. As Ethan drove the A3 with speed through the country lanes it was hard to keep focused since a lot of the unknown seemed to be still waiting. Carlos sat up front with Ethan. Erica and Sofia sat in the back each looking out to the side without any conversation going on between them. They were taking Sofia to the café to speak to Marrianna the waitress. It was now after five in the afternoon and Marrianna worked into the evening shifts so she should be at work.

The plan was for Sofia to go inside and talk to her to get the name and address of Gerardo's employer. Next Carlos had said that he knew where Burns went off with the girls. A small office building but it did not have up a sign. Old Scott had sent him there once with items from Guyana that Burns had left behind when he came on board the Mistral C. They would check out this place but knew that if Carlos was right in his identification then Burns was a dangerous murderer. They had to watch out!

They now arrived and Ethan parked the car. Sofia got out and entered the café. "Hi Marrianna how are you!" Sofia greeted the waitress who smiled at her and came over to her table. Marrianna immediately started talking about the news and asked if she had seen it.

"Yeah, I saw it. Isn't it dreadful what happened to that Ger… guy, can't remember his name but it's horrible!" Sofia feigned forgetfulness and sat looking alarmed. "Gerardo, yes Gerardo, he was a shady one but my mother said that she was surprised that he was so brutally killed. She thought that he was just a womanizer!" Marrianna declared.

"Oh yeah, you did say that your mother knew him or were friends?" Sofia wanted to be subtle about getting the information which she wanted. She did not want to arouse any suspicions about her interest in Gerardo's employers.

"He, a friend of my mother, never, they just worked for the same people, the Gagnon brothers over in that exclusive area, El Valle de Anton, Cocle Province. They won't like this publicity at all." Marrianna said as she excused herself to serve another customer. Sofia took that opportunity to slip away back to the car where Erica's face was the seat of misery.

There was brief silence then Carlos spoke to Ethan, "*Chief* if you don't mind me suggesting, we should survey that Burns' man place first while some daylight is still left so we can see how it is situated and then go back at night fall. He is a mean SOB and we don't want him to get the upper hand on us." Carlos suggested and Ethan agreed. They now headed for Burns' place as they listened to what information Sofia had received from Marrianna.

They slowly drove through the street. It looked quiet and innocuous but how would it be by night? To wait for nightfall Ethan drove into a multi storey car park and they all wondered what he was doing. For one, he was getting the A3 off the road and he felt that they all needed a slight diversion to relieve the stress which they had been under. He was taking his friends to the cinema.

"We stay together and watch the same film. Then we leave to check out Burns' office." Ethan suggested. He was such a considerate friend Sofia thought. He was helping Erica when none of this had anything to do with him if they got caught he would be ruined but he was still helping.

Erica sat on the first seat followed by Ethan and then Sofia sat beside Carlos. Carlos looked at Sofia and smiled. She smiled back and thought that he was a diamond in the rough and possibly with the right polishing he could be an interesting person to get to know.

Ethan could feel Erica's hand resting close to his on the arm rest. He gently put his hand in hers and held it. She felt some relief and a little less ashamed by Ethan's gesture. This was a good idea to come to the cinema they all thought. Even though more fear lurked in their hearts for what was next to come than complete enjoyment of the film but it was still a little but good stress reliever.

It was now well after eight when they left the cinema. Darkness had fallen like a blanket over the city. Sofia assumed her usual position as co- driver and look-out, while Ethan, Carlos and Erica went around to the side entrance of Burns' office which they had seen earlier. The office had a small apartment on to it. No lights were on inside the apartment or the office. That is as far as they could see.

From outward appearances the office had no security cameras only a burglar alarm. Carlos quickly disconnected this and picked the lock to the door. It opened with a horrible creaking noise and they gingerly entered. Each had a torch they didn't dare turn on lights! However, Ethan thought that this is where their inexperience detective skills were about to fail them. What exactly would they look for? Burns certainly would not record the blackmailer's name and requests!

"Look through the files and see if anything links to Sidney or to Captain Scott. Look for anything that may ring a bell." Ethan whispered but felt that he was steering a ship without a compass. He had to get his bearings fast.

"Got some files with names of what looks like girls and possibly where they were sent." Erica said as she burrowed rapidly through the filing cabinet. "Exactly what does this man Burns do?" She asked as she rummaged and searched more.

"Working as a clerk by day, and an assassin by night!" Ethan joked but knew that that was most likely the truth. "Ah! Aha!" Carlos softly exclaimed. "Look at this diary, these people love diaries. Why do people like to do so much writing? That is why I left school. Too much writing! I keep it all in my head!"

"Will you stop your philosophical oration and tell us what you found!" Ethan quietly said through gritted teeth.

"Sorry *Chief,* you know how I can't stop talking, I just can't restrain my mouth." Carlos apologized

"And will you stop this *Chief* thing for heaven's sake!" Ethan stared at Carlos and wanted him not to think that he was his superior.

"*Chief,* ain't we a team now? So ain't you our leader, the *Chief*?" Carlos rambled on as though they had no urgency at all. Carlos definitely knew that to him, Ethan would always be *Chief.*

"For fuck sake we are losing the will to live waiting to hear what it is that you found! Not to mention being caught by Burns and shot dead!" Erica softly but forcefully exclaimed with exasperation as she recalled Burns' bullets passing her head.

"Now, *Miss Posh,* watch your language." Carlos said with a smile and carried on explaining. "Well Erica, this diary shows the names of the people that Sofia said, that Marrianna the waitress said, that Gerardo worked for, linking them to Burns. We have their exact address which is out in that extremely filthy rich area. We definitely must pay them a visit to see what's in their house." Carlos concluded.

Carlos was long winded about everything he had a way of stretching it out. Ethan and Erica could not help but softly laugh when he had finished his statement and Carlos could not help but join in with them. This was the first time that some light hearted humour had come over them since yesterday and it felt good.

"Let's bring everything we have found with us. Let's take it back and go through it." Ethan told his two team mates.

Just as they were about to leave Erica pulled back the side of a discolored blind and peeped out through a small window. Her heart jumped! A car was pulling up outside. She looked intently as two men got out of the car. Worse yet she recognized the car. The car was unmistakably *black beauty!* The sedan which Gerardo drove! The men were walking towards the building. What would they do? They each had two very large canisters in their hands.

"Quick we have to hide. Two men are coming towards this office!" Erica whispered and looked around frenziedly. Ethan pointed his index finger motioning towards a door in the office, indicating that they were to go in there. They couldn't speak least being heard. The three bundled in through the door only to realize that it led to the apartment!

Luckily there was a row of old filing cabinets with space behind them they needed no directives but each scrunched their bodies behind the cabinets. Quickly they pushed the files which they had found into their inner vest shirts and underwear. Carlos slipped his phone on to record and placed it obscurely on top of the cabinet between two books. Silently holding their breath as they heard the door to the office open they became frightened rodents now huddled behind the cabinets.

"What the hell! This lock has been picked. Look at it Jim." The three could hear the men reveal their discovery of the broken lock.

"Careful now, did that bastard really have a sniper, an accomplice? It could be him who picked this lock. Slow now, slow." Lee warned. They entered the office and looked around. Jim was keeping quiet while Lee as usual was filled with agitation.

"No one is here but still this is disturbing. Who broke in here and where is Jack of Spades?" Lee's nonstop questioning and directives surged on. The three, on hearing the name Jack of Spades, wondered if they were really at the right person's place but they listened on.

"Look for anything which may bear our names and connect us. Put them in a pile here." Lee commanded.

"Lee doesn't Jack of Spades stay here in the back in the apartment?" This was Jim's first question but one which could put the three hidden intruders in mortal peril. The three could hear it all but dare not move a muscle.

"We have to find Jack of Spades. All loose ends must be tied up and tied up immediately!" Lee lowered his voice but the three could still hear him. Their brains were frantically working to take it all in and at the same time trying to think of not being discovered and finding a way out speedily.

"We never told Jack of Spades why we wanted him to make that drop so he doesn't know everything. Obviously he would have suspected that we were being blackmailed." Lee was rationalizing their next move which they had come to find Jack of Spades for and he went on speaking.

"Jack of Spades would by now know that the man he shot was our caretaker Gerardo." Lee said and continued. "He had to have heard the news." Lee carried on with this one sided conversation.

Jim kept silent but now decided to make his observations known. "What Jack of Spades has in here may tie us to that Jasmin, rather *Jane Doe* girl and this entire Gerardo event. It wouldn't be long before the police made connections which lead to us. You already told me that the news on Channel 11 said that she was possibly buried near Sedums before being dumped. What do we have an abundance of? Sedums! What does Jack of Spades, keep? Records! No doubt of transactions of the girls, sums paid and who and where they went to. I don't think he is a fool. Perhaps the name of Mr. Big is somewhere in here also." Jim frantically told Lee.

The three were straining their ears listening and what they were hearing was becoming explosive in their brains but it was also very frightening! Extremely terrifying!

"Look down Lee." Jim said as he switched on another lamp closer to where he asked Lee to look.

"It's blood and there is a trail." Lee observed and he started to walk to the adjoining door to enter the apartment. He was followed by Jim. They kept looking down at the trail of blood stains and passed the hidden intruders. The three had missed the blood trail because they had not turned on any lights.

"Jack of Spades! Jack of Spades! Jack of Spades!" Lee called out and entered into the bedroom area of the apartment. Suddenly a groaning answer could be heard from within the room.

"I'm in here. Lee is that you? I'm in here." A feeble voice which sounded as though the speaker was in great pain called out. The brothers rushed forward into the room with haste.

"Man what happened? What has happened Burns? What happened, Jack of Spades?" Lee asked impatiently, using both the man's real name and his alias. Confirming to the unnoticed audience that they were indeed at the right place, that Jack of Spades and Burns was one and the same person!

"Can't you see I've been fucking shot? Wounded! The man had a gun and was prepared! He also did have an accomplice, a girl not a sniper. I dare not go to a hospital so I have been doctoring up myself. I have been lapsing in and out of consciousness and only just woke up." Burns groaned out loudly in pain, while the brothers listened closely.

"Who was the girl? Did you do her in also?" Lee demanded.

"How the hell would I know who the girl was, oh it hurts, probably the man's floosy? I missed her, oh, oh, the pain!"

"So there is a witness that you let escape? You know what? You should really reimburse us for the botched job. No one was to leave there alive, no one!" Lee shouted at Burns. "Does anyone else know what you did last night?" Lee asked uneasily while looking at Jim.

"Man I don't tell people what I do, ah, ah, pain. I'd jeopardize myself. Can't you see you need to get me a fucking back street doctor and stop questioning me?" Burns was feeling extreme physical pain and his wound was throbbing. He was also in mental agony by the relentless questioning.

"What about that vagrant you paid to sit on the bench? Did he know your identity and did you tell him that he was impersonating me?" Jim asked. "He may have talked to somebody."

"What kind of idiotic questions are you asking me? Ah, ah! Bloody pain! He was a homeless man who would do anything for a quick buck and that is what he did!" Burns groaned in pain but carried on speaking. "Then I eased his pain and put him out of his wretchedness. Are you satisfied? No loose ends! Get me some medical help. Please! I can't walk!" Burns pleaded.

"Is there anything else you may have forgotten about that night? Did anyone see you?" Lee kept prodding. It was excruciating for Burns and also for the three since their bodies were in cramped confinement and it was taking its toll on their muscles which by now were accumulating so much lactic acid that it could be used in a science experiment.

Burns or more familiar, Jack of Spades, was pleading for help but it was all falling on ears that were stoned walled. Without saying another word the brothers turned away from Mike Burns and retreated back into the office space.

"Hey are you going to get me some medical help?" Burns shouted as loud as his shattered body would allow.

Papers were being thrown into a pile in the middle of the room within the office. All the filing cabinets were being overturned and emptied. The three knew that it wouldn't be long before the two men got to their cabinets. It was evident what the men were preparing to do.

"Too many loose ends! Way too many!" Lee shouted at Jim while in the background they could hear Burns calling out and pleading for them to get help. "Shut up Burns help is on its way." Lee shouted back. He was heartless in his drive for self-preservation.

"We still have a loose end, whoever that girl is. Could Gerardo have told her that he was blackmailing us? She must have been in on it with him for a small price or was she his patsy?" Lee was doing all of the talking and analyzing again. He was having the last word.

The three knew that danger was imminent. They could hear the sinister noise of liquid being poured from the canisters the men had brought in and now a strong pungent odor permeated the air. It was the distinct smell of petrol! They had to get out of there!

"Oh, for fuck sake!" Jim moaned loudly at Lee. "You keep going on and on so much that you left the fucking matches in the car!"

"Fire a shot at the pile it will ignite!" Lee callously said!

"You seem to be thinking from your ass right now, that'll certainly call attention to this place and us. I'll go and get the bloody matches!" Jim said. "Fine they are in the pocket of the door on the passenger side. Get them!" Lee ordered. With Lee it was unreal he definitely had to have the last word.

The fact that these two also had a weapon did not do much for inspiring confidence in escaping this doomed situation. Was it best to wait until they lit the place and then make a run for it? Or should they get out now. Ethan didn't know which of the men had the gun or if they both had guns. All he knew was that the lives of others were expendable to these two. They had killed before and they would also kill them all now if they discovered their presence. He had to act fast.

The pile of files, paper and overturned cabinets blocked Jim's path to the office door they had entered through. He had to make his exit through the apartment door. As he came back through the adjoining door and walked towards the exit, Ethan pulled himself from behind the filing cabinet and jumped on to Jim's back flooring him with force! As Lee came running through Erica gave him a punch to the face and as he rocked back with pain, Carlos struck him with a chair. This surprise attack unnerved the two brothers and the three managed to get the upper hand on them.

Carlos, Ethan and Erica levelled an unprecedented assault on Jim and Lee which left the brothers bruised, bleeding and lying on the floor. Whoever had the gun did not have a chance to draw it, for the three surprise was the weapon of use and it worked brilliantly!

Like Olympic sprinters they burst through the door and ran out into the street. Sofia saw them coming like flashes of lighting in the distance. They were running so fast that their legs resembled those of the long-legged racing breed, the greyhound. Papers were flying everywhere as they ran but they kept up their rapidity never once stopping. Sofia could tell that this speed was meant to overcome a predator. She quickly started up the A3. Shifted it into gear and guided the car to meet them. With frenzied panting they scrambled aboard. Ethan and Erica climbed in the back and Carlos collapsed down in the front seat beside Sofia.

Adrenaline in the three was still pumping high. Their fight and flight response had not dissolved. Their bodies were still stimulating their heart rate, contracting blood vessels and dilating their air passages. All of which had them breathing so heavy that Sofia was very concerned about them. Erica's and Ethan's breathing seemed to be making a loud musical rendition in rhythm with each other. They were all shaking and seemed unable to calm down.

"Shall I pull into a petrol station and get you all some water?" Sofia anxiously asked.

"No, no! Just drive!" Ethan said anxiously while still out of breath and gasping for air.

"Just get us out of this area as fast as you can but keep within the speed limit. Don't attract attention." He spoke in an almost incoherent tone and slumped back in the seat waiting to arrive at the safety of uncle Chester's.

Chapter Sixty-One

Sofia made the ninety degree turned into uncle Chester's and immediately gun shots rang out at the vehicle. Everyone ducked and lowered their heads! Sofia swerved from the tarmac drive-way and turned the car rapidly in between the mahogany trees. If they stayed in the car they would be sitting ducks. They all franticly climbed out and took cover as a loud voice came nearer and nearer.

Shots were being fired repeatedly but it seemed that they were ascending into the air and not directly at them but they weren't sure. In the distance a voice was calling out and getting closer and closer to them. They were all crouching low behind the A3 but ready to defend themselves from this unknown enemy. A man with a shotgun now came within inches of them.

"Who the hell are you squatting on my property and driving my car?" The loud voice reverberated through the mahogany trees as the branches blew in the night breeze. Sofia flew out in the open and waved her arms. The others watched on in alarm.

"Uncle Chester! Uncle Chester! It's me! It's me! Sofia! She ran and jumped on her uncle and hugged him. The others slowly came out from behind the A3 and stood to the front of it. Chester looked shocked and baffled as he reciprocated Sofia's hugs.

"Child you almost got shot. What on earth are you doing out here?" Her uncle asked, while now looking towards her stunned and frightened friends.

"Sorry I thought I had squatters who had stolen the A3. I came in this evening just felt like a break and was shocked to see the house in use. I jumped to conclusions and decided to wait to see who was coming back so I could catch them and then call the police. My God you gave me a fright!"

"Giving you a fright? You nearly killed us! It seems to be the shoot first, ask questions later, policy which you use!" Sofia said and hugged him again. She then introduced her friends. Chester now greeted them as though nothing happened and they all walked to the house.

"We need hot drinks and a warm bath just to soak in the tub is what we all need." Sofia said to her uncle. She gave him a condensed version of her friend's dilemma and why they were at his house and using the A3. She couldn't have asked for a more wonderful uncle as in turn uncle Chester bear-hugged each one of her three friends.

Ethan told Chester and Sofia all that had happened in that office and said that they had managed to bring away what may be incriminating evidence, which was left in the car. Chester listened with eyes wide open in shocked disbelief and worry for their safety.

It was now three minutes to midnight and they wanted to see the Channel 11 news. Maybe what was taking place in Burns' office had been completed and was now on the news. They were sorry that they could not have helped Burns even though he was a killer.

All seated with eyes bonded to the TV screen the news came on. It was live at the scene of a fire in Ferdinano, 'An entire immigration office and an apartment were burnt to the ground. A man suspected to be the owner of the building was pulled from the fire by a passerby who heard his cries for help. He suffered major burns, has a gunshot wound and has lapsed into a coma. Arson is suspected in this fire. The police are appealing to anyone who has any information about this fire to get in contact with them.'

"My God! I can't begin to understand what you kids have been going through. As I see it, you need to hand some of the information you have over to the police. We can do it anonymously. I can drop it off without being noticed." Uncle Chester offered.

"Before we do anything let's remember our primary goal is to clear Erica. All we have right now is evidence about who killed that *Jane Doe* girl, really Jasmin and who killed Gerardo. Nothing clears Erica." Ethan stated and next said, "I am going to the car to get the stuff we took from that office."

Ethan rose to his feet followed by Carlos and they tiredly walked slowly out to the car.

"*Chief* some serious shit happened again tonight! This is a big time game! But we handled it. Didn't we, *Chief?*" Carlos asked.

Carlos seemed to recognize the seriousness of the situation but was still eager to praise the team work which got them out alive.

"Carlos we did well as a team but we still aren't any nearer to solving Sidney Durr's murder and clearing Erica." They started walking back to the house armed with the evidence. This they would also have to sift through.

"Carlos." Ethan called in an extremely weary voice and stopped walking just before they were about to re-enter the house.

"Yes *Chief.*" Carlos quickly responded anticipating to be given a task which he was ready to do for his friend.

Ethan looked at Carlos and smiled before speaking.

"If I don't die tonight, I will live forever!" They both laughed loudly and ran back inside.

Chapter Sixty-Two

Brilliant sunshine ushered in the morning as Ethan busily removed the shrubs and buses which he had used to hide his plane. While doing so he had called his dad to let him know that he was alright but wasn't very sure of his return date. He reassured his dad, disconnected the call and continued to wipe his plane down. The others had by now come out to join him.

Chester looked on in absolute astonishment and marveled at the skills of this very polite young man. Chester had got up early and made breakfast for them. A more apt description for it would have been cremated toast! Ethan and the others had had long sleeps. Ethan had to ensure that he had had the required amount of rest since he would be flying out later today.

Carlos was filled with awe! He looked on at the plane as though he was about to kneel down and worship it! It seemed as though he was about to offer up his body as a living sacrifice to the plane! He couldn't help himself. He just had to expound his knowledge about the plane. He loved planes.

"*Chief, Chief,* you have a great plane. This plane, a four seater Cessna Skymaster was used from 1991 through to 2001 by the Cuban exile group Hermanos al Rescat. There were also called Brothers to the Rescue. They flew search and rescue missions over Florida." Carlos took a short breath and then went on, as he kept gently touching the plane. "They looked for rafters trying to defect, by crossing the Straits from Cuba. If they found any they dropped life-saving provisions to them. Skymasters were used because their high wings gave better views of the waters below."

As Carlos said all this, he continued his reverent and religious like scrutiny of the Skymaster, touching it and caressing its wings as though it could recognize and appreciate his ardent interest. Ethan was impressed with

Carlos' knowledge and interest. Chester stood wide-eyed and Sofia and Erica were astounded, that for a boy who left school early that he was so enlightened.

"Let's go over the plan again." Ethan said. "We need to have our heads on at all times. It has been outright luck that any of us hasn't been shot! Even Chester here, tried to do us in!" They had a hearty laugh and retreated to the house.

"Chester you-" Ethan was cut off by Chester, "Uncle Chester, to all of you, if you please! You are friends of my niece and now you are classed as family. That reminds me, he turned to Sofia, your mother must be frantic with worry. I will allay her fears so don't let me down and get hurt now! Uncle Chester to you all, do you hear!"

He sat back quietly to allow Ethan to continue. "Uncle Chester," Ethan rephrased, "Will tip off the police about the Gagnon brothers, sending in copies of Burns diaries and the recording from Carlos' phone. That was brilliant Carlos, great work. That kind of gets the *Jane Doe* and Gerardo cases out of the way but still not completely"

"Who was Jasmin and who supplied her to Burns? We know she came possibly on the Mistral C but from whom? Could it have been your father Erica?" After asking this Ethan was sorry that he didn't say Sidney Durr instead of personalizing it. Carlos saved him and quickly interjected.

"Old Scott was only the transporter but the girls came to him secretly from someone called Mr. Big and I never knew his identity." Carlos revealed.

"There also has to be some place where these girls are found. Carlos you said that some of the girls looked *posh*. Well looked after so they could not be picked up from just off the street like that. Maybe this Valentina woman is involved in getting the girls. Maybe Mr. Big is really a woman." Erica stated and was also hoping that her father was not that deeply involved but it was not looking good for him at all.

Uncle Chester now interrupted them. "All the bookings have been made and things taken care of. Watch yourselves now and be careful."

He followed the four young people to the aeroplane. It would be a five almost six hour long flight to Guyana but they had to make that journey. They just had to clear Erica's name and get justice for her father. Going to Guyana seemed to be the next thing which they had to do to get answers.

Chapter Sixty-Three

Without John and Marie Karis felt sure that she would have had a nervous breakdown. She was worried about her older daughter and could do nothing to help. Evans Caine the lawyer had arrived from Florida and was meeting them later today. The Grants had said that he was a good criminal lawyer and would do all he could for Erica.

Karis was not sure that her daughter would get out of this. She was in deep trouble. Being accused of murder was not to be taken lightly. Where was Erica? She must be terrified and as a mother she felt that she had failed yet again. Karis was trying to be optimistic but it was hard to see the 'light at the end of the tunnel' right now. All that she could see was the light of oncoming train. Therefore she could only use her Catholic belief and upbringing to rely on God to see the family through this and hope and pray that Erica would be cleared and the real murderer found.

Her pensive mood was observed by John. He had been her tower of strength. She couldn't help but think that fate had brought them together for a reason and some good had surfaced from all this bad. Emma had truly improved in her attitude and behaviour. She was also holding up fairly well about her father's death. Emma also seemed to be losing many of the issues she had and had begun to interact more with others. Marie was extremely good as a friend. It as though the two were sisters and Marie even one day joined Emma in calling her mum. She seemed to have lost one daughter but gained another.

Thinking about what Erica must be going through was agonizing and she could not help but shed a tear. This did not go unnoticed. In fact nothing went unnoticed to John. "Oh Karis I so wish that there was more that I could do to help in this situation." He held her close in such a consoling way that Karis felt guilty about being comforted when Erica had no one to soothe and dry her tears. The Grants had hinted in confidence that Sofia and Ethan most likely were supporting Erica and felt assured that all would turn out well.

"Thank you John you are doing more for me than I could ask for. You and Marie have transformed Emma and at least that is one significant aspect of all this chaos that is working out for good. Thank you again."

She squeezed into his chest and he could feel the rhythm of her heart. He hoped soon that one day it would be beating with rhythms of joy and not anguish. Even though they had only just met, he knew that he would stand by Karis. She was awakening emotions in him that had gone dormant and remained so since his wife's death. He felt in the past that no one could have taken her place in his heart but things felt different now since meeting Karis. The telephone was ringing and John broke his embrace with her.

"Miss Karis the police are on the phone and would like to speak with you. It is inspector Henriquez." Teresa said this with strained emotion and handed the phone to Karis. She took it with trembling hands wondering what bad news he would be delivering. Was inspector Henriquez going to tell her that her daughter had surrendered to the police or that they had found her body? She braced for the worse.

Chapter Sixty-Four

The four friends arrived safely in Guyana and were now settled in a small cottage, in a lovely rural and quiet area just a few miles outside of Georgetown. A 4x4 was parked at the back of the cottage for their use. They needed to have a reliable vehicle since road surfaces were more often than not unpaved.

Uncle Chester had made all of the accommodation arrangements and the refrigerator and cupboards were stacked with food. This cottage was owned by one of his friends so there was no need for them to have to show ID to rent it. This had to be a fast turnaround. Time was running out for them to uncover the truth about Sidney Durr's murder. Darkness was closing in so whatever they planned to do had to be done as from tomorrow.

During the hours of flying Erica and Sofia had made up. Erica had apologized to Sofia and Sofia to Erica. They did not want this sordid affair to ruin their friendship and felt that they needed to be strong and pull together and not permit these unfortunate happenings to push them apart.

They had a meal which was prepared and left for them. They hadn't seen the cook. They all thought that it was as though uncle Chester was looking after them remotely but the only difference was that the food was not cremated. It certainly did not resemble road kill! They ate it all gratefully and shared light banter together.

Carlos in his usual style kept up the entertaining atmosphere. He was able to tell them that butterflies taste with their feet and that dolphins sleep with one eye opened.

"So is that why your feet have food on them Sofia?" Carlos mischievously asked while smiling at her since she was taken off guard and started looking down at her feet.

"Oh Carlos you are such a tease!" She threw a paper napkin at him and he chased her outside. There was a full moon and she allowed him to catch her. He held her close and kissed her and then quickly pulled back. "Sorry! I shouldn't have." Carlos softly said while looking into her eyes.

Sofia looked right back with eyes melting, heart pounding and held him by the shoulders and replied, "You should!" She pulled him closer. He then kissed her again with unrestrained passion which he never knew that he had within him. He never felt this way about any girl before. This had meaning. This had depth.

By nine thirty they had all disappeared to their respective bedrooms to get a proper night's rest. Ethan and Sofia felt more able to trust the others but still decided that they had to be on their guard. They were in a foreign place after all and Erica was still wanted. They both studied the street map as per the norm. Sofia would be his co-driver if need be.

By day break as they prepared to set off early. Ethan and Erica couldn't help but notice that Sofia had let her hair down and she was looking radiant. They could also see the admiration for her in Carlos' eyes.

Carlos was taking them to see a man who may be able to help them. Carlos had said that when the Mistral C was docked here, he and Marco had met this fella, a worker of McLloyd mining. The directions which Carlos was giving took them past streets with children begging. It was easy to see how the vulnerability of these young people could be exploited.

"One of Gerardo's mobile phones, which had that sole contact in it, a Valentina, we need to find her and anyone who would know who this woman maybe, is this man we are going to see. If he doesn't know then he will be sure to know someone who knows." Carlos said with confidence.

"Are you sure you never heard about Walter Crawford? He is another Guyana contact mentioned in Sidney's diary" Ethan asked Carlos.

"Only heard the name when you first said it back on the Mistral C, never heard old Scott talking about him but we can ask the same fella I am taking you to see." Carlos replied.

Ethan pulled onto a side road and talked over the decision that they should all stick together. This was unknown territory. They were no longer in a city which most of them knew but in Guyana. He could not trust to leave Sofia alone by herself in the vehicle. Furthermore they were going to McLloyd Mining which was logged in Durr's documentation. They all agreed to stick together. Ethan drove on and soon reached McLloyd. They stopped by the side of the café and got out of the 4x4.

"What is this fella's name?" Ethan quizzed Carlos all the while looking around but before Carlos could answer a big burly guy came lumbering towards the café.

"Hi Jake." Carlos greeted the man. Who took Carlos up and shook him in a frisky way. "Didn't know that the Mistral C was in port, we haven't had instructions to load. Is she in port?" Jake asked Carlos.

"No, I am here with my friends-" Before Carlos could continue Jake interrupted him. "Thought the only friend you had was Marco? Where's he?" Jake carried on speaking not giving Carlos a chance to answer. "Wait, you are looking very good. Expensive clothes! Did you win money and forgot about me?" Jake asked laughingly.

"Be serious Jake. I need your help." Jake then started to look more closely at Carlos' friends. His eyes became stationary when he saw Sofia. He seemed to recognize her. Sofia could not understand why this man's eyes were cemented on to her face. Ethan moved slightly in front of Sofia to break the man's glare.

"Ok what do you want?" He asked Carlos while still trying to get a glimpse of Sofia. "Do you know any floozies around hear named Valentina? Or do you know anyone who may know her?" Immediately after Carlos had said this, Jake's demeanor changed. His eyes and his feet shifted uncomfortably.

"No, never heard the name before. Why do you want her?" His voice was not convincing at all. The three could tell that he was being evasive but why? What did he have to hide?

"Break's over Jake, back to work!" A loud voice shouted out and Jake walked off but not before attempting to look at Sofia again.

"He knows her. Don't you all think?" Erica asked nervously.

"Of course he does!" Ethan said and looked at Carlos for confirmation which he got by a nod from Carlos.

"Why was he so taken up with Sofia though? He acted as though he knew you. Have you ever seen him before?" Carlos asked looking at Sofia for an answer. "Definitely not; I never saw that man before! Are we stumped now?" Sofia asked, looking at the three for encouragement.

"What time does McLloyd close? Carlos do you know?" Ethan queried.

"Raina what time does McLloyd shut off?" Carlos called out to the waitress in the café.

"About five or after. Carlos is that really you? Wow you looking good!" Came her reply.

On hearing the closing time Ethan whispered to the three. "We will go to that Elaina woman next and then come back here when it is closing time and follow Jake. Just maybe something may give."

As they were about to walk away Carlos turned and asked, "By the way Raina, you won't happen to know a Valentina woman?"

"Yeah she is Jake's sister!" The waitress replied.

Raina had made their day and the four turned and hurried into the café looking at Raina intently, who was surprised by their stares.

"You know what Carlos? You and your friends have to buy something if you come in here asking me questions. What will it be?"

They were not thirsty at all for beverages but ordered some none the less. They all now had insatiable thirst for more information and were willing to pay for it. They put down a one hundred dollar US note on the table to pay for the drinks which Raina knew far exceeded their cost.

"Brother and sister they are so when Jake told you that he didn't know her I thought, what a flipping liar! But I assumed that he was lying because it had something to do with her husband's murder!" Raina stated.

"Husband? Whose husband?" Erica quickly asked while looking a bit edgy.

"Valentina's! She was married to that Gerardo fella who got killed in an execution style shooting in Panama City!" Raina said.

The three looked at Erica and could see her face contorting under this heavy news that Raina was dishing out. They were uncertain about how much more Erica could take. Fortunately, Raina turned her gaze to Sofia and made a direct statement and this thankfully took the pressure off of Erica.

"You are the identical image of Valentina! You look exactly like her!" Not knowing what to do about this declaration, Sofia kept silent but realized that that was probably the reason Jake was looking at her.

With this break in conversation, Ethan quickly reengaged Raina. "Raina can you please tell us more about Valentina and Jake?"

"I won't ask why you want this information because I don't want to get involved in whatever is going on but I will tell you all that I know anyway." Raina looked at the four and resumed her information sharing.

"Years ago my mother told me that Jake and Morgan Hawkins' parents owned this land but were cheated out of it by a Canadian woman and her German husband, all helped nicely along by the authorities." Raina stated.

"Do you know if this couple had any children?" Ethan asked, recalling that title deeds to a mine were amongst Sidney's papers.

"I think that she said that they did have a son." Raina went on.

This would mean that this most likely was Sidney Durr. Ethan inwardly and silently speculated. He asked Raina to carry on.

"I think that the couple's name was Durr or something like that. I can't remember completely. But Clarence Hawkins died fighting for his land and Millie Hawkins took her own life. Their son Morgan works very closely in McLloyd as a health officer or something. People say that he is on the take and turns a blind eye to what they do." Raina was conveying and clarifying many of the missing pieces to this series of ill-fated events.

"My mother also told me that the Hawkins adopted Valentina. She was one of those children from an older man, whom they said, took advantage of a teenage girl and it resulted in a child. Valentina was given up and her mother was sent to Canada. I can tell you where Valentina lives." Raina's information had been invaluable. Through her they had been able to connect a lot of dots.

"Here is the address. Jake is very protective of her and does everything she says to do. He won't hesitate to get rough with anyone who may attempt to harm her. Be very careful!" Raina warned.

They thanked Raina and left the café with their minds acting like whirlwinds. The vortex of information seemed too much and they had to find a quiet place to go to, to study the information more.

Half an hour later they were sitting on the grassy area of a community park which overlooked a valley. The four looked at each other and waited for someone to break the silence and speak. Erica was certainly not in any emotional state to communicate so Ethan took the lead to speak.

"It would appear that Sidney's parents had owned the mine, now renamed McLloyd Mining. The Hawkins' children are aware of this and maybe, just maybe, they decided to get even with Sidney through using Valentia to get close to him. Is this sounding probable?" Ethan asked.

"But if Valentina was my father's mistress why kill him? Why not continue to get whatever she can?" Erica managed to ask this while still feeling that some pieces were still missing. Just like the pieces to her shattered heart.

"Maybe she wants as much as can be had but immediately and fast." Sofia suggested as she looked over at Erica's face which showed extreme despondency.

Additionally they still had no idea who Walter Crawford was and Raina didn't know either. If they could only get a clear idea as to who had murdered Sidney Durr then they could have uncle Chester hand over the evidence to the Police. Jasmin's real identity also remained a mystery. Who she really was and where she came from was still a part of this puzzle.

With these things still hanging they now headed for Elaina's. They knew that Erica could not go inside to see her since Erica felt that Elaina couldn't be trusted. Elaina would undoubtedly immediately ring up the police as soon as she could if she revealed herself. They had to decide how to work this one out. Breaking into Elaina's house was also out of the question. Erica said that when they had visited it in the past, it was like a fortress but they still needed to try.

It had by now started to rain. It seemed that the day's sudden change of weather wanted to spoil the progress which they had made in meeting Raina. The dark clouds and the now heavy torrents of rain seemed determined to dampen their mood. Erica recalled that her dad had said that Elaina did some kind of charity work closer in town. A shelter or Centre but she could not remember the name of the place.

They finally arrived outside of Elaina's house. Carlos was great he always found an answer it seemed for every problem. As they sat in the 4x4, a short distance away, just outside of Elaina's property pondering their next move, they noticed a young girl who looked like a worker leave the house. Carlos quickly got of the vehicle and approached her. She stopped and a conversation ensued. The girl then exchanged smiles and continued on her way while Carlos returned to the car.

"Well does 14 Cedrick Street ring any bells Erica?" Carlos had got the address for the place where Elaina helped out. "Yes it sounds like the shelter address but how did you get that out of her?" Erica asked.

"Well what can I say? I turn on my charms at all costs and sometimes for free when I use gentle persuasion." They all laughed and Ethan shifted the vehicle into gear, while Sofia used her brilliant map skills to direct them on to Cedrick Street.

As the car moved slowly down the street they started to feel that they were in a time warp which was transporting them back to Panama in particular back to Colón. As they got closer to Cedrick Street, the roads seemed to be lined with beggars. It was apparent that this was a very depressed area. Very much far removed from where Elaina's stately house sat.

The rain continued and thunder rolled. The homeless lay on the filthy pavements which they had made their homes, under plastic bags and cardboard boxes. Ethan did not know where to park since it was certain that if they left the vehicle in that area it would be stripped or stolen.

He swiftly turned the 4x4 around and headed away from Cedrick Street. He didn't have time to explain, he had to focus on dodging the mass of beggars taking care not to run over any of them. When out of the danger zone, he breathed a sigh of relief and brought the vehicle to rest in a paid parking lot which he had seen when they had first driven past.

"We will have to take our chances and walk there, approaching it from the west which seemed to have less destitute people and children on that side. The vehicle should be fine here." Ethan said this while looking it over. He was sure that all the desperate hands of need that pressed on it, begging as they drove by, must certainly be imprinted in the paint work. They all seemed filled with wretched hunger. Just wanting what most people take for granted, food and shelter. These basic things, these poor children were deprived of.

"Erica we can't leave you behind. Do you think that Elaina will recognize you? How long ago did she last see you?" Ethan asked this since he knew that in this shanti town which by all appearances seemed worse than the dangerous Colón that they had to stick together. The rain clouds had made the afternoon dark and depressed quite symbolic with the area.

"It was some time ago my mum did not like Elaina and Hanif so we never visited frequently, therefore she most likely would not remember me but I am not sure."

They walked the human gauntlet of beggars and finally made it to 14 Cedrick Street. It had a very small sign on the door which said Centre for Homeless Girls and another circular award plaque with a McLloyd crest which read, 'Investors in People.'

The three read the signs and looked at each other. Could this be the place which gives the Gagnons their supply of girls? The McLloyd plaque of 'Investors in People, bore heavy irony if this was indeed the type of place which they thought it was. Also could Sidney be Mr. Big? It was strange but they all seemed to be thinking the same thing.

Ethan motioned to them to go around to the back of the place. The dwindling daylight was a welcoming camouflage. They sneaked quietly around the building and got to the back.

They saw that it was in dire need of repairs. They peered through a broken window pane and saw some girls of various ages talking.

Suddenly Sofia lost her footing on the slippery wet grass and started sliding. Carlos tried in vain to grab her hand but the rain soaked sleeve of her shirt tore off in his hand and she fell through a concealed opening in the ground. She literally disappeared down what seemed like a deep dark hole! The three were horrified and looked down the terrifying opening trying to see Sofia.

"Sofia! Sofia!" Carlos anxiously looked down the hole and called in a strong whisper. There was deafening silence. No response. Their stirring in the grass made the girls inside the room stop to listen and also look out the window. The three fell to the ground and froze. After a while Carlos raised himself up slightly to see if the little girls had gone from the window. His face came directly in contact with the barrel of a gun which a very tall man was holding!

"Get up you three! What the hell do you think you are doing here? Who are you?" Erica knew that voice. The man looked them over and swiftly saw that the quality of the clothes they wore was far beyond what the street hooligans around Cedrick Street wore.

The three raised themselves up and said nothing. Inwardly they were praying that Sofia was alright and not down that hole hurt or worse yet dead! Should they raise an alarm that one of their friends was down that hole? The man hadn't even noticed the opening in the grass. This was nerve racking! What should they do?

"Come on! Come on! Move! Move!" The man shoved them impatiently with the gun as his big raincoat swished in the wind. Ethan knew that if he got them inside that they would be cornered by that gun. Going inside with him was clearly not an option. They reached the door and their hearts thumped as though they were knocking on its panels! A stern-faced old woman swung the door open and stood looking at them as though it was an everyday occurrence to hold people at gun point.

"There was another one back there!" A voice called out from behind the old woman. The gun wielding man turned around sharply to look behind. The three took this divergence as their opportunity to escape. Ethan pushed him back and the gun went off. The man tried to tackle Carlos but Carlos kicked him in the stomach and he briefly doubled over in pain but swiftly regained composure and grabbed Erica as she tried to run off. He had her left arm, holding on to it tightly.

As she violently fought to free herself from his grip, his massive rain coat engulfed her! Ethan and Carlos stopped running and returned to Erica's aid. The boys leveled punch after punch onto the man's head and back.

Finally Ethan backed off and gave him a flying kick into the back which rocked him off his feet. He groaned in pain and Erica broke free tearing his raincoat in the process. As she ran she realized that she had torn off the pocket of the rain coat and was about to discard it but a paper was stuck to it. She held onto it as she ran with speed.

By now it was dark and as they turned the corner to the carpark they stopped running. Completely out of breath, they now became very upset about leaving Sofia behind.

"*Chief* we have to go back! There is no way I am leaving from here without Sofia!" Carlos started to turn around but Ethan held him back.

"We will never leave Sofia but we have to think this out first." Ethan started walking towards the car and Carlos and Erica followed in the most dejected way. They were troubled. Very troubled and frightened for Sofia. As they got closer to where the car was parked they quickly caught a glimpse of a shadow lurking behind the 4x4.

"Quick, go around to the other side!" Ethan whispered to them as they tried to see who or what was behind the 4x4.

Could they have been followed? Unlikely since the old guy had taken a battering from them and they left him on the ground. Could he have sent his cronies after them so quickly? These questions raced through Ethan's brain.

"Ethan!" The unmistakable voice of Sofia came from behind the 4x4. What a relief! She was hiding and with her were two girls!

"Oh, Sofia! Sofia!" Carlos said as he hugged her tightly and not wanting to let her go. Erica and Ethan joined in the group hug. They were so relieved that she was ok and not trapped in that hell hole!

"How did you get out? And who are these girls?" Erica asked her friend.

"The hole I fell into is the 'cell.' They put any girl into it who does not do what they want. I was just told. When I fell into it, I heard you calling out but I did not answer because I could see the girls staring at me. When I heard the commotion above, I waited climbed back up with the help of Naveena and Anneeza, peeped out and we all made a run for it!" Sofia tiredly stated.

"Hello Naveena and Anneeza." Ethan's greeting was hastily and he quickly said. "We have to get away from here and fast before that man's cronies come looking for us. He has to be Mr. Big. Come on let's go!" Ethan urgently requested while unlocking the vehicle and hustling everyone inside. Going to investigate Valentina was now out of the question for today.

The rain had now subsided and the cottage was insight and just like the welcoming feeling they had when they reached uncle Chester's. This same feeling came over them now as they pulled into the front yard of the cottage.

When they unlocked the door the aroma was over powering. The phantom housekeeper had been in and had made them a meal again. Carlos marched into the kitchen and lifted the lid of the saucepan. It was Ginger and Scallion Fry

Rice. He then followed his nose and uncovered a cake stand. Vermicelli Cake, greeted his wide eyes and watering lips. They washed up and sat down to this delicious meal.

Sofia introduced her three friends to Naveena and Anneeza. The girls looked timid and afraid. As they ate, their eyes darted to and fro.

"You can relax with us. We won't harm you." Ethan reassured but this was getting bigger than them. After the meal Ethan excused himself and called uncle Chester.

"Don't go to the police yet we have made some progress here and we don't want to drive the culprits into hiding. I will call again tomorrow. Yes we are all fine," if uncle Chester only knew what they gone through today! Ethan returned to the group and wanted to know what these two girls knew.

"Oh, my, I left a paper in the 4x4 which I got when I ripped that man's raincoat pocket. I will go and get it." Erica interrupted. Ethan accompanied her outside. As they walked, they talked with each other.

"Do you know what Ethan? We seemed to be solving more crimes than the one which I am accused of and I am getting very worried!" Erica leaned on his shoulder and started to cry. He held her closely to comfort her but he too was concerned but he dare not tell her this! Letting him go she waited as Ethan unlocked the vehicle and she quietly said, "That man's voice, the one who held us at gun point at the Centre, I recognized it as Hanif's, my father's partner and Elaina's brother. I bet that he is Mr. Big!"

Chapter Sixty-Five

Erica retrieved the now crumpled paper and they returned to the cottage to sit with the others. She sat at the dining table and smoothed out the paper. When finished she held it up and it read 'Missing, have you seen Jasmin?'

"Oh Holy Mary! Mother of God! This must be the *Jane Doe,* Jasmin from back home!" We need to take this to the police here and tell them what we know!" Erica exclaimed and jumped from her seat.

Naveena and Anneeza were very frightened. These two girls had filled them in with some information on the Centre but seemed too frightened to talk about it all. The Centre it seemed was indeed the supply for girls being trafficked.

"The question still remains, who killed Sidney Durr and why? All this appears to be a very bad case of reverse serendipity!" Ethan said and brought the focus back to solving Durr's murder.

"Wow! Look up there!" Carlos pointed to a camera. The cottage had CCTV and the outside grounds also were being monitored.

"Carlos you are brilliant, just simply wonderful!" Erica got up and kissed him. "Hope you don't mind Sofia?" Erica smiled and started laughing. Everyone kept looking at her. Had she gone stark raving mad? Why was she laughing? Ethan wondered and was about to ask her what was causing the euphoria, when she looked him in the eye and said only four words, "Durr's murder is solved!" She was beside herself with glee! Unfortunately all the others looked on with questioning faces but said nothing.

"Follow me!" Erica commanded everyone. She led the way to a study at the back of the cottage where a computer system was on the table. Uncle Chester had told them the password to it if they wanted to use it. He had said that it had internet access. Erica sat down and switched it on. It powered up but not fast enough for her captive audience who waited eagerly looking over her shoulder. She logged on to a website called Monitor Me 24/7. She entered a password and a screen opened up showing the interior of a yacht!

"Is that what I think it is? Is that the inside of your father's Yacht, The Wind Rush?" Ethan asked in shocked disbelief. The inside had been just as the night the murder took place everything turned upside down and just through the window the police tape cordoning off the yacht as a crime scene could be seen.

"Monitor Me 24/7 was designed with hidden cameras and remote Internet access." Erica explained and went on. "Sidney Durr had had it installed when the yacht was burgled last year. He also had a tiny wireless concealed camera and microphone attached to the pole by the berth. No one else knew about it but him and his family. Sadly in all this I had forgotten about it and mum never paid any attention to things like this. Probably the drugs which I was pumped with caused me memory loss!" Erica said with remorse.

As she started to run through the footage, scenes of her father enjoying himself with a young woman flashed across the screen. As Sidney called her by name within their conversations, that woman, Sidney's mistress, was revealed to be Valentina and now also known to be Gerardo's wife!

Erica paused the video screen directly on Valentina. Everyone was astonished that she did look exactly like Sophia! There was silence from the group.

Raina had said that Valentina's mother who was abused by an older man was sent to Canada. Susan Grant was from Canada. Could it be? Erica inwardly mused over this idea but moved on.

"Can you run the video to the 16th when the murder happened? The police arrested you just after 4 am so run it back a few hours before that time." Ethan instructed and was completely amazed when Erica pointed the mouse at a calendar and selected the 16th that fateful date and then the time. Suddenly she felt a lot of sorrow and grief for her father but she continued.

What the video was about to reveal would be both shocking and heartbreaking not only for Erica but for everyone viewing. What her father endured before he met his untimely death would prove to be very vicious. Erica ran back the video to the berth and she turned the speaker's volume up so that all could not only be seen but also heard. The video played:

Gerardo paced the dock. He mutters, "The Wind Rush is late." He continues talking to himself. "Not sure at all about tonight, not at all sure that bringing Durr back to Panama City is a good idea." He looks out and says, "O good. The Wind Rush is coming." Gerardo helps Jake with the mooring. "How's it been Jake?" Gerardo asks.

"Bloody awful that's why I'm late!" Jake replies. "Ok let's get this moving." Gerardo quickly climbed on board and was led to the below deck by Jake. They were headed for the first cabin when suddenly the door swung open and hits Jake in the face knocking him back onto Gerardo. Before they could regain their footing Jake was hit in the face with the metal leg of a chair and it rendered him unconscious.

"What the hell are you doing on my yacht?" Sidney Durr shouted as he used the metal chair leg on Gerardo. Gerardo blocked as best he could but he was no match for Sidney. "Stop hitting me you bastard! Stop!" Gerardo blocked his face while shouting.

Sidney lurched again to deliver another blow but lost his footing. Gerardo blocked and managed to grab the offending weapon. They scuffled and fell. They rolled onto the floor over and over knocking down everything within their path. Gerardo scampered to his feet. Sidney was punching his middle with all his might. His eyes glared and his nostrils flared he kept hitting Gerardo.

"Stop, you bastard, stop!" Gerardo yelled again but Sidney was like a man possessed.

"You bastards kidnapped me. You locked me up in that old mine!" All said in one breath as he kept punching Gerardo. It seemed that it was retaliate or die! Gerardo's face showed abject fear indicating that he felt certain that Sidney would kill him.

Gerardo raised the metal chair leg up above his head and struck Sidney blow after blow, after blow. Losing complete control delivering blows which were too numerous to count, until Sidney lay motionless and bleeding. Gerardo looked out of breath. He was panting and walking dizzy. He bent down and felt Sidney's pulse. He felt Sidney's wrist again and said in a hopeless way, "Clammy and sticky but no pulse. Oh God what have I done? What have I done?" Gerardo said and immediately dropped the metal chair leg from his hand and ran to Jake.

"Jake! Jake!" Gerardo shook him. He slapped his face and he dragged Jake to an upright position. "Jake! Jake! Wake up!" Gerardo ran and picked up a bottle of water and poured some of it on to Jake's face to bring him round. Jake shook his head and slowly regained consciousness.

Groaning, Jake shouted, "That bastard rushed me. He hit me! Oh my head hurts!" In an agitated voice Jake quickly asked Gerardo, "Have you tied him back up?"

"Jake I think that we are past tying up." Gerardo said.

"What the hell do you mean?" Jake had pain and impatience in his voice. "Go take a look for yourself." Gerardo said in a defeated and distressing voice while wiping blood from his face. Jake stood up and walked over to where Sidney lay.

"Durr is not breathing. Blood is pouring from his head! Did you hear me? Durr is not breathing!" Jake's eyes glared at Gerardo as he said this. "Jake repeating it will not change anything. I know that he is not breathing. I know that Durr is dead!" Gerardo said tensely.

"How the fuck did you manage that?" Jake shouted.

"Like if he didn't knock you senseless and then tried to kill me. That's how I managed that, defending myself!" Gerardo angrily said, with dimmed eyes fixed on Jake.

"Well Gerardo this messes up the *'plan,'* messes up big time!" Jake lamented.

"It was supposed to be drugs, alcohol, tragic mishap of falling overboard and drowning! Which part of that did I mess up on, when you didn't drug him enough!" Gerardo said derisively through grit teeth.

"This will not be liked at all. Your wife will be furious. Valentina will not be pleased. This changes the *plan* completely!" Jake's voice rushed in harshly.

"This is not about a change of the *plan* this is about murder which is plainly obvious and will not be possibly suspected but can be visibly seen! However done in self-defense, it won't be easy to get out of it if we are caught" Gerardo stated and started to pace.

"Think! Think! Think!" He shouted, talking to himself. Jake sat with his head in his hands and was groaning from his bruises.

"Ok let's get back on track to part of the original *'plan.'* Remove all traces of us. Total wipe down." Gerardo quickly ordered.

"I wore gloves all the time." Jake said shakily.

"Next you get out of here. Be careful your rain coat has blood dripping from the end. Go on to the next mooring for the hired boat. A new passport awaits you for re-entry to Guyana if you are challenged by the coast guard. Go! Go now!" Gerardo's orders were swift. He looked as though he was experiencing fear and shock simultaneously.

"What are you going to do Gerardo?" Jake asked and for the first time he looked really scared and spoke softly.

"What I don't tell you, you can't reveal! Go on, go now!" Gerardo pushed Jake up the cabin steps as fast as he could get him. He briefly noticed that Jake's rain coat still dripped blood but too late now. He just wanted him gone. Next in haste, Gerardo took out his new mobile phone and sent a text. Mumbling to himself, "I have to do this. This is my only way out." Gerardo then left The Wind Rush.

Erica pressed pause. The video froze. There were loud gasps from even the two strangers Naveena and Anneeza, who did not know either her or her father.

"There was Jake, navigating my father's yacht, steering him to his death, a death at the hands of Gerardo!" Erica said.

Recognizing how heartbreaking and agonizing this must be for Erica Ethan asked her if she wanted to stop and not continue to watch the remainder of that night's footage because both Ethan and Erica knew what was coming next.

Monitor Me 24/7 resumed at the click of the mouse. The video rolled on to Gerardo's return to The Wind Rush. Gerardo was carrying an exceptionally large duffel bag which seemed extremely heavy and burdensome.

He boarded the yacht again and went down to the lower deck. He placed the duffel bag beside Sidney Durr's battered body. Unzipped it and rolled the bag over to empty its contents. He lifted the bag away and what had filled the duffel bag was Erica! Her arms and legs were taped together in a fetal position.

The tape which bound her limbs was removed and she was rolled in her father's blood. The metal chair leg was used to inflict lacerations on her arms. It was then placed in her hand. She was set to lie beside her father. Gerardo then put her mobile phone on the cabin floor after doing what seemed like deleting all messages to and from him and his number. Gasps were heard from everyone watching and tears were set in their eyes.

Tears did roll down Erica's cheeks but she held back the sobbing. She was relieved. She was not a criminal. She had not killed her father! Everyone in the room hugged her without speaking. Erica downloaded the footage of the events of the 16th on to the cottage's computer. She looked around and found a USB but would it have enough capacity to hold the video footage? It did.

Erica had now come to terms with the reality that Gerardo had murdered her father. Inwardly she was relieved that she was not a killer but only a fool.

Chapter Sixty-Six

Morning came peacefully to Erica. She was prepared to turn herself in. She was crushed and just wanted it all to end, now that she had concrete evidence of her innocence. She also wanted justice for Jasmin too. The Gagnons had to pay. They had Naveena and Aneeza's evidence. Hanif's and Elaina's people trafficking trade would be over. They would take their evidence into the nearest police station. Erica did not relish turning herself into Henriquez in Panama City but wanted to go to a Guyana police station since most of the culprits were in Guyana.

Carlos warned them that he did not trust any police. They all had their price. He empathically said. He felt somehow that Erica should send them with the evidence and not turn herself in yet. Ethan and Sofia also agreed.

"Why not let us fly back to Panama City and then go in with a lawyer?" Ethan urged but Erica seemed very emotionally bruised. Hurt by a lot of things which happened to her and her father. Her mind and soul were smarting from the betrayal, treachery and deceitfulness which both she and her father bore and most of it was at their own instigation, especially her.

"No. I am giving myself up! You my great friends have helped me through all of this. Risking life and limb it is time for it all to come to an end. Ethan, please can you call uncle Chester and tell him he can do what needs to be done at his end."

Erica was both determined and adamant. "Thank you my loyal friends. Thank you." Erica said and walked and hugged the three. They each held her tightly and then released her. She walked to the vehicle got inside and waited for the others to do the same. The drive to the police station was somber. It was like taking a condemned man to the gallows! Naveena and Anneeza wanted reassurance that all would be well before giving evidence. They were still very frightened. They would stay in the car and wait.

The friends entered the small police station and an officer sat at the front desk writing. The four of them stood and waited for him to look up. He did and it was in a surprised manner on seeing the four of them.

"How may I help?" He calmly asked.

"I am Erica Durr and I am wanted in Panama City for the murder of my father Sidney Durr. I am surrendering myself to you but I have evidence in my possession that I am innocent. I also have evidence about the murder of the missing girl Jasmin whose body was found in Panama City. I also want to provide evidence about people trafficking by Elaina and Hanif Osman who goes by Mr. Big." A huge load had been lifted from her as she blurted it all out without stopping or pausing.

The officer looked stunned and was momentarily speechless. Erica however wanted to get it all off her chest. She would no longer feel trapped and imprisoned since her entire being was arrested. She wanted freedom and this declaration she thought, would give her exactly that.

The officer continued to look more and more shocked by Erica's revelations and he told her that he would take down a statement from her and then she would have to be taken into custody. He asked her where her evidence was and she said that her friends had it and would hand it over in due course.

"Are your friends staying until you go into custody? It may be somewhat awkward to have an audience while giving a statement of this magnitude." He seemed uneasy by the presence of the three.

"Ok guys can you please wait outside until I am finished?" She reluctantly told her friends. "Then can you please call them back in to say goodbye?" Erica asked the officer. She didn't want them to leave. They were her life blood for the last set of days. She knew however that they could not go into custody with her no matter how good their friendship was. She had to face this alone. All three kissed her and went outside to wait with the other two girls.

"Officer I didn't get your name. What is your name?" Erica wanted to know who she was dealing with.

"Sergeant Walter Crawford. That is my rank and name. Sergeant Walter Crawford." The police officer repeated.

On hearing these words Erica froze. Her brain shifted into gear and then it went into neutral to console herself. It is possible that this is a coincidence. Two people can have the same name. She was trying to reassure herself but it wasn't working! What could she do? If she ran out to the vehicle they would end up in a police pursuit! Holy Mary! What should she do? She desperately thought.

"Sergeant Crawford may I go to the toilet?" She quickly asked.

"Of course, it is through that door and to the right." Crawford said. She walked calmly not to draw attention and followed his directions. She frantically went into the ladies looking for a window but there was none. Oh God! Her heart raced as she recalled Carlos' words that 'police were not to be trusted.' She should have listened to Carlos. Walter Crawford! The name was cutting through her head!

Try the gents a voice in her head quickly said. She did and luckily a window was there but a very small and horizontal one. She opened it and put her head in what seemed like a crevice and painfully forced the rest of her body through. Her body became stuck! She couldn't move! Erica frantically wriggled and pushed her body with all the force she could muster and suddenly her body shifted! She quickly jumped the short distance to the ground and ran with speed! Turning a corner she climbed inside a huge garbage dumpster, huddling between the rubbish and called Ethan!

"Walter Crawford! Walter Crawford!" Panting for air all she could do was shout out the name.

"Erica! Erica! Who and where is Walter Crawford?" Ethan couldn't understand what was happening and the others stared at him as he quickly listened on to what Erica was saying.

"That policeman, that officer is Sergeant Walter Crawford!" Erica now said slowly and deliberately.

"Where are you now?" Ethan quickly asked.

"I jumped through the toilet window and ran down on a street. Wait I'll tell you the name." She pulled her head out from the garbage and swiftly looked around. "I'm hiding in a garbage dumpster on Flowmont Road! Come and get me quickly! Flowmont Road!"

Ethan coursed the 4x4 quietly away from the station and Sofia looked on the map and found Flowmont Road. They headed there as fast as they could and got Erica out of the rubbish bin. By now they thought that Sergeant Crawford would have realized that Erica had escaped and would be looking for them.

When Anneeza and Naveena heard the name Walter Crawford they immediately cowered and told Erica that he was Mr. Big and not Hanif as she mistakenly suspected. So Crawford was not just in her father's diary as an ordinary dealer but he was a human trafficker!

In his police role the girls said that Crawford would round up girls off the street and take them to Elaina. Then he would forward 'select ones,' the very pretty ones, on to Panama City via the Mistral C. The two girls had said that they had listened in on conversations while they were at Elaina's Centre. Ethan and Erica knew that this was becoming way beyond them.

"Crawford didn't see what I was driving. Thank goodness! But he knows that it was four of us and he saw us. We need to split up." Ethan quickly decided. He pulled up by a taxi rink and hailed two taxis.

He sent Carlos with Erica in one of the taxis and Sofia with the two girls in the next. They all were to head to the hanger off the airport. He was flying them back to Panama City immediately! They would arrive by 14:50. He knew exactly what he had to do when he got there. He would have uncle Chester meet them.

This all would stop and it would all end publicly.

Chapter Sixty-Seven

Karis had refused to supply Inspector Henriquez with a photograph of Erica the last time he called. He must have been crazy if his processing officer neglected to take her photo when he arrested her, then tough if he wants one now to be published on a wanted poster and plastered all over the city. He certainly wouldn't be getting it! When will this nightmare end? She asked herself.

John came and switched on the TV to watch the six o'clock news on Channel 11.The news presenter started by saying that she had an exclusive breaking news account of six very brave young people who had a dramatic story to tell! Karis and John wondered what this was all about and they listened closely.

The presenter started, "This evening we have an exclusive interview with Erica Durr girl arrested for the murder of her father. Viewers are warned that this interview contains disturbing material and video scenes. Erica has an amazing and incredible description of her life on the run in trying to prove her innocence since she was arrested for the murder of her father, Sidney Durr.

She has actual video footage which has been authenticated by Channel 11, of the murder of her father by an individual whose name we cannot as yet divulge. In her possession are files, diaries and transcripts of illegal dealings in gold shipments. These documents identify the names of customs officers in Canada, Miami and right here in Panama City.

Via a video recording, the identity of the killers of *Jane Doe* whose real name is Jasmin Bowman, a Guyanese national, has been revealed during the arson of the immigration office and attempted murder of Michael Burns, also known as Jack of Spades.

This young girl and her friends also have evidence surrounding the murder of Gerardo Abram and finally she has proof that people trafficking is definitely taking place right here in our city and its tentacles stretch from Guyana, to Florida. Sidney Durr and Captain Paul Scott of the Mistral C are also implicated in this dark and murky world of gold smuggling and trading of young girls as prostitutes.

Erica Durr has been helped by three friends, Ethan Avery, Sofia Grant and Carlos Carrillo. These four young people have managed to rescue two young girls from the clutches of the people traffickers in Guyana and those girls are here with us tonight to also share their story."

The news rolled on with every detail showing Carlos' recordings of the Gagnon's admissions of murdering Jasmin and their spreading the petrol on Burns' office. Some scenes of Sidney's murder were shown but not in their entirety for legal reasons.

Karis could hardly move her lips! She looked at John and all that she could do was to run into his arms and shed tears of joy. "Erica, my Erica is innocent! My Erica will be free!" Karis cheered. Teresa, Marie and Emma came in inquiring what was happening and they too joined in the celebration.

The Grants were joined by Chester who informed them of all that had happened. Chester had always known that Susan and Tim worked for the CIA and knew that they had been investigating the Gagnon brothers and McLloyd mining for some time. However those three young people outfoxed them; freed Erica and have brought down a people trafficking ring and exposed illegal gold exports.

Henriquez and Martinez had heard from Channel 11 news prior to the broadcast. They had been provided with copies of everything Erica and Ethan brought in. Henriquez contacted the Guyana police headquarters seeking an arrest warrant for Sergeant Walter Crawford on the grounds of involvement in people trafficking.

Arrest warrants were also issued for Valentina Abram, Jake and Morgan Hawkins on suspicion of kidnapping, theft and murder of Sidney Durr. They however learnt that Valentina had already escaped the clutches of the law and had left Guyana. Elaina Osman and Hanif Osman, the business partner of the deceased Sidney Durr, were also arrested on suspicion of people trafficking, holding girls against their will and illegal gold exports.

Martinez was ordered to place officer Cassandra Myles under arrest on the grounds of suspicion of leaking information to the press and also involvement with her husband Walter Crawford, in people trafficking.

Henriquez took a squad car with three officers and went to the Gagnons residence to place them under arrest for suspicion of murder. The house was empty. They had evaded arrest in Panama City but an international arrest warrant would be sought.

Channel 11 News would ensure that Naveena and Anneeza were housed and that they got the necessary support offered to abused girls.

Chapter Sixty-Eight

Erica 'girl arrested,' had told her story and the ending was filled with emotion of the strength of character, mind and body which developed amongst the four young people bonding them together. Looking out over the calm river from the window of the Channel 11 news station, Erica was now deeply aware that this was a 'tragedy of susceptibility,' for not only her but also for the many young girls who were trafficked and engulfed by deception, especially Jasmin.

Ironically her father's moral sensor which was broken by greed, lust and power, ultimately consumed his life giving him major ownership of this tragedy. However, these immersing events were conquered by profound friendship which developed amongst the four young people.

Soon, the four friends next returned to uncle Chester's for this one last time of being all together. They looked around the sitting room where they had spent many hours in search of answers. They would now miss it. A sense of emotional tranquility pervaded the air. They absorbed it. They sat on the large sofa as uncle Chester reclined in an arm-chair close by. They all looked around the tranquil sitting room. Uncle Chester sat up and smiled at the four.

"Seems awfully quiet in here now." Erica softly remarked and continued. "No more frantic searching, no more papers and diaries!" She wiped her eyes as tears fell from them. Ethan hugged her. She looked around as Uncle Chester leaned forward. His eyes fixed on the three as he spoke to them.

"As you all know, probiotics are bacteria but they help keep our gut healthy so horrendous trouble can bring out good results. I see great loyalty, love and care in you three. Great friendship too!" Uncle Chester stated as he stood and walked over to them. They smiled at him as he leaned over and hugged each one in turn. Sofia stood up and squeezed into her uncle as if to say a big thank you.

"Don't know about you three young people but I am going up to bed, my sell by date is fast approaching, so I need my rest! Good night to you all." Uncle Chester said.

The three laughed as he walked out. They sat in silence. Subsequently after a while, Carlos left the group and went into the cupboard under the stairs. He dragged out a large remaining bag from Sidney's town house. He pulled it into the sitting room, looked at Ethan as they all stared back at him and the bag. With a sly smile across his face he asked Ethan one question.

"*Chief*! *Chief*! What will you do about this bag of *real money*?" Hilarious side-splitting laughter erupted from the four and then they group hugged.

Other Books By This Author

Alexis V

Engulfing Events is a series of three crime fiction novels, written by Alexis V. The series has a multi-cultural setting within South America and the Caribbean, and follows the young characters, Erica Durr, Ethan Miller, Sofia Grant and Carlos Carrillo as they battle through a mine field of unsolicited trouble and dangerous life shaking encounters.

The novels in this trilogy are titled, Girl Arrested release date 2015, Child Taken, 2016 and Fear Undetermined, release date to be announced Each novel although part of a series, is its own standalone story; with a complete climax within the book. You don't need to read the next novel to get to the ending but if you do, you are guaranteed not to be disappointed.

Warm tropical waters, idyllic shores, a paradise in the distance; a Caribbean cruise never to be forgotten. Lurking amidst the calm seas is an evil force; unleashing the never ending nightmare when a child is taken! With forty-eight hours to find her, the gates of agony are thrown wide open. The parents and their friends go through hell on earth to save her! They must fight their way past labyrinths and a host of deadly enemies if they are to rescue the child and hold together the family's enduring love and trust.

Suddenly caught up in deep trouble not of their own making, four young work colleagues find themselves thrown into an intelligent and elaborate operation of an organized plot to bring London to its knees. The trouble which they were in seemed beyond their capabilities, horrifically blood curdling, sinister and death inducing. Being in trouble was just way bigger than any iceberg, as their wits are tested and lives are cold-bloodedly taken. Getting in was easy, but can they get out.

Rebekah Fuller's main encouragement through her limiting teenage years was her friendship with Annabelle Foster, a pretty and popular girl. The two girls meet the boys of each other's dreams but still managed to fall deeply in love, at a time when war is declared and lives are hurled into uncertainty and confusion! The war and Rebekah's mother's excessive tendency to overprotect, sweeps her into a minefield of uncharted pitfalls and dramatic life changes. These dynamics, not only determine Rebekah's future but her passions, her pains, her hopes and dreams. They lead her to several emotional valleys but would she manage to finally reach love's mountain top?

How do you imagine your future? Imagining the future helps us to prepare for problems and be more equipped to solve them but what if your entire future was totally and absolutely within the hands of the State? A State which was based on scoring and your ability for happiness, success and health, rested in those ratings. What would you do? Would you contemplate to leave or to remain? This mini-story is a funny view of things which may possibly come to pass; with hidden truths but powerful meanings!

For many, counterfeit love can masquerade as genuine affection, through manipulation and control. Occurring often during young years, from not wanting to be left out from life's constants and reinforced by great sex. All these fuel a bad bond leading to relationship entrapment. Options for getting out and starting over, appear elusive and emotional walls crumble. Life becomes buried beneath regret and the cycle of hopelessness spins. This short story is a glimpse of the life of a young woman which exposes these relationship issues. Can she find the strength to get out?

A splendid inspirational keepsake, which is an ideal gift for family and friends of any special, loved one. It's filled with heartwarming sentiments, a page with blank lines to insert a personalized recipient's and sender's details. Suitable for a daughter, sister, mother, friend or any woman who has touched the lives of others and has 'passed on' but whose life remains as 'Enduring Memories.'

Is your child a 'runner,' or perhaps one who is autistic with Special Education Needs? Then this book can provide support for helping the child who frequently runs off to understand when it is safe to run and when it is dangerous to do so. The young child and in particular the autistic child, often does not have real awareness of dangers in their environment. This book can provide support to your child in developing safety awareness.

Gordon
Reads
about
Making
Choices

Written by Alexis V.
Illustrated by Peter Vincent

In adolescent years, teenagers can make judgments and decisions on their own but most often in situations where they have time to think. On the other hand, when they have to make quick decisions or in social situations, their choices are often influenced by external elements like the peer group. Read to find out about the different types of choices teenagers face. See if Gordon can resist pressure from others and as a teenager, can you?

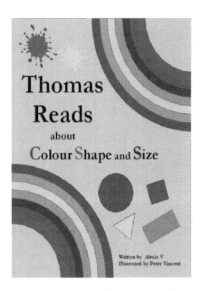

Understanding, colour, shape and size are essentials which children need to know in order to master Reading, Writing, Language and Maths. It is a tool for learning many skills in all subject areas. For autistic children who are mostly visual thinkers and learners, color, shape and size can be used to create learning steps, helping them to pick up words and concepts, and develop basic skills. Ultimately, the goal is to motivate the child to develop better verbal communication skills. Thomas Reads about Colour, Shape and size, can be used to stimulate awareness of these concepts.

Emily
Reads
about
Making
Friends

Written by Alexis V
Illustrated by Peter Vincent

Building friendships can be challenging for any child and especially so for the SEN child who may require additional support as a result of a broad range of needs. These needs may be in regard to emotional and behavioural difficulties, or how the child relates to and behaves with other people. This book is intended to deliberately focus on key social skills to support the child in developing friendships.

Alexis V